PRAISE FOR *ELEVEN DAYS*

'A deeply affecting story about a mother and a son that attests to the debut of an extraordinarily gifted writer . . . Ms. Carpenter makes palpable the immensely complicated emotional arithmetic that binds this mother and son – Sara's cherishing of her only son and her knowledge that she needs to let him find his own way in life; Jason's worries about his mother's worries, clashing up against his passionate embrace of a dangerous profession. In doing so Ms. Carpenter has written a novel that maps – much the way that Jayne Anne Phillips's classic *Machine Dreams* and Bobbie Ann Mason's *In Country* did – the fallout that war has not just on soldiers, who put their lives on the line, but also on their families, who wait anxiously back home.'
Michiko Kakutani, *The New York Times*

'A compelling story made memorable by the strength of its elegant prose.'
Toni Morrison

'Lea Carpenter's *Eleven Days* is an extraordinary accomplishment. Written with an elegant precision, this book is at its core a story about love: between a mother and a son, a son and a father, and a special group of men for each other and the imperfect country they choose to serve. I highly recommend it.'
Kevin Powers, author of *The Yellow Birds*

'What Denis Johnson did for the Vietnam War in *Tree of Smoke*, Lea Carpenter does for Iraq and Afghanistan in her superb *Eleven Days*. At the core of this extraordinary novel is the love of a mother for her child. That's the story of us all, and that's the story that may well break your heart.'
Ben Fountain, author of *Billy Lynn's Long Halftime Walk*

'[An] earnest first novel . . . Carpenter provides a convincing portrait of an exclusive and exclusively male military subculture, and of ~~those formed and deformed by it.~~'

ELEVEN DAYS

Lea Carpenter

www.tworoadsbooks.com

First published in Great Britain in 2013 by Two Roads
An imprint of Hodder & Stoughton
An Hachette UK company

First published in paperback in 2014

1

A CIP catalogue record for this title is available from the British Library

ISBN 978 1 444 77626 3

Printed and bound by Clays Ltd, St Ives plc

Hodder & Stoughton policy is to use papers that are natural,
renewable and recyclable products and made from wood grown in
sustainable forests. The logging and manufacturing processes are
expected to conform to the environmental regulations of the
country of origin.

Hodder & Stoughton Ltd
338 Euston Road
London NW1 3BH

www.hodder.co.uk

For
the one who said,
"only tactical competence, and humility, impresses me."

She looked over his shoulder
For vines and olive trees,
Marble well-governed cities
And ships upon untamed seas,
But there on the shining metal
His hands had put instead
An artificial wilderness
And a sky like lead.

—W. H. Auden,
"The Shield of Achilles"

Contents

Tarawa

The United States Navy SEALs came out of the Teams that served in Vietnam; they in turn came out of the Navy Seabees, the Scouts and Raiders, and the Underwater Demolition Teams used during World War II. The UDTs evolved out of something else: loss of lives. Their unit was born in the wake of the Battle of Tarawa. At Tarawa, for the first time, the Japanese mounted a sophisticated defense against an enemy amphibious landing. In one day, six thousand Americans died or were injured. It was 1943.

Most lives were lost before the Marines reached the beach that day. They drowned. They didn't know how deep the water was; they didn't know where the reefs lay. The moon had skewed the tides. Men stepped from their boats into chest-high waters, and when their gear sank, it took them with it. The coral was sharp, and so close to the surface in places that you could see it catch the sun.

A new force was required where men were as comfortable in water as on land, and the navy's underwater demolition trainees possessed part of the necessary skill set. These were combat swimmers, reconnaissance experts, with a kit of suits, knives, life preservers, and a facemask. On D-day they secured the French beaches.

In 1962 President Kennedy announced a new defense initiative: a focus on "Special Forces," men who would fight in unorthodox condi-

tions against an unorthodox enemy. These were not kids trained for trenches. These were warriors ready for the military equivalent of grand master chess games—only ones where you pushed pawn to queen in the dark. They were one spoke on the Special Operations Forces wheel, but the Teams soon proved unique. Their ability to make critical decisions quickly, in complex situations, marked them apart. A SEAL's best weapon, like a scholar's, is his mind.

ONE

SPOONS

In the bedroom, Sara finds her running shoes. She has not worn
them in a while; there never seemed to be time, although she is no
longer sure what she fills her days with, aside from waiting. The
neighbors bring their new soups, and she pretends to have new
tastes for them, but when they leave, she empties them down the
shiny, stainless drains.

She pulls on an old Academy shirt and starts out the front door.
Where they live now, the driveway is long, almost half a mile, and
she knows a good route for today. If she crosses the neighboring
farm's yard, she can catch a path at the lower end of their garden.
With that path she can come to their pond, the one she once
fished in, and gain access to the main road. The main road leads to
a wood, and out the other side of the wood is the highway. This is
where she can turn back. Yard, to path below pond, to main road,
to highway. If she hits the highway out of breath, she is sure she
can hitch a ride. She is a celebrity of sorts now. Everyone wants
to help.

She long ago adopted the habit of wearing a hat when she
runs. When she puts the hat on, she looks down at laces her son
left for her when he was last home. They're bright red. "Running

is fun, Mommy," he'd said. "Don't take it so seriously." He still calls her Mommy even though he is a man now. He is twenty-seven. He has been missing for nine days.

*

As a child he'd played with spoons, not guns, even though they had some of those around the house, too. His father had bought him a Boss sixteen-gauge, one made between the wars, as a baby present. "He has to learn not to be afraid to hold one," his father had said. But the spoons had him. He liked to line them up on the floor. For his third birthday, a godparent gave him a large tin box of multicolored plastic spoons, and soon the phrase "box of spoons" became a proxy for all delights, as in (while watching football) "that last pass was better than a box of spoons"; or (on Christmas morning) "twinkly lights are my favorite thing ever, except for a box of spoons." On his fifth birthday his father sent him a small silver spoon. It was engraved with the date and this phrase: YOU WERE NOT BORN WITH THIS.

He grew up quickly. He was so creative. Leaving spoons aside at last, and reluctantly, for paintbrushes, he was easily the first choice for class pet of every art teacher. Art and writing: these were his early passions. And that pleased her; it somehow reinforced her sense of herself. It reinforced that she had not ever been owned by anyone—not a government, not a military, not a man. It also reinforced her dreams for what she wanted her son to be. She wanted him to be not only different from his father but also free from the demons that had come with what his father did, or at least from what she knew of what he did. She didn't want a son who grew up to be familiar with words like *Kalashnikov*, *katusha*, or *jezail*—unless he learned them from a Kipling poem.

But anyone who met him today would say, *Soldier. Fighter.* They would want him on their team. As a mother she was willing to engage in pride over fear and to admit the possibility that his sacrifice was hers, too. His sacrifice was something she had been able to give her country.

Sara felt she had failed in so many other areas of her life, including a chance at an elite education, but she could always say her son is a member of a very special group. If his father had been alive, he would have smiled at the irony. He had claimed to distrust the military, despite his obsession with its history. He was a famously great shot but kept to birds and maintained he'd never trained at a range. He mocked things he did not understand, and the military seemed to have been one of those things. He knew more than enough about it to be clear on his views, but still not quite enough. He didn't understand the difference between the power of an idea and the power to put an idea into action, but his son did. Even from a very young age, their son had a sense of respect for action over talk, and a sense of respect for the things he did not know. His father had opinions; he had questions. And the father's guns remained in the house, but they were no longer of interest to the boy as he grew. Since Jason had signed up, Sara never went dove shooting anymore. An old arsenal sat at rest, except the pistol she kept by her bed.

She has not run more than a quarter mile before her knee begins to ache. Sometimes when she runs, she will reach the point where she feels she cannot go on, but then she thinks about her son, the runs he's endured. Multimile runs, on the beach, at night, wet. "Transportation" runs of two miles to a meal, carrying once or twice his body weight in gear. She approaches the path at the base of the yard and she stops for minute. She notices the sky has darkened; it's about to pour.

*

She had met his father when she was still trying to be an artist at Georgetown. A summer job listing at Langley looked interesting, and she was broke, and the art jobs didn't pay the bills. She was asked in her interview if she knew how to work a coffee pot, and she said yes. She was asked to name the secretaries of defense and state and by some miracle, she knew those. She was asked if she scared easily, and she said no. She got the job. She made coffee, sometimes up to twelve pots a day, and carried it to the "boys on the floor." She learned a lot by osmosis but mainly she kept track of her hours and left as early as she could.

One day for whatever reason she earned an invitation to a conference in Charlottesville, at the University of Virginia. ("We'll need coffee there, too," said her boss, with a wink, as way of explanation.) She would have to work overtime, but she would be meeting interesting people. So she went. And at the other end of the conference room there was a man.

She was just standing there, by her coffee pot. He looked at her tag—SARA—and sang the first line from the Fleetwood Mac song by the same name: *Wait a minute baby/Stay with me awhile*. She didn't know the song well but he told her it was very good and suggested she buy the album. Then he clarified the connection by pointing up the song's spelling of "Sara, no 'h,' just like yours." And he said, "Sara without the 'h' is much less *biblical*." He was thirty years older. She would only find that fact appalling much later, when she was old enough to know people thirty years her junior. But by that time she was resolved not to think too deeply about things.

When she asked what he did for a living he said, "Writer," then smiled. There were a lot of "writers" in the intelligence industry, at least according to her nonscientific survey. "Writer" seemed to be the then-contemporary analog to America's Vietnam-era "military advisers." As far as she could tell, the government was madly sending writers all over the place at that time, with varying levels of success. But this one actually looked like a writer. And he talked like one, too. It was 1983. His name was David.

She might have known he was lying when he told her what he did, or what he felt about her, but the lies, which would deepen in complexity along with their relationship, were part of his great game. They were part of what she had chosen to accept when she elected to keep their baby. She was sure that the genes she was incubating had potential to be more—more than a college drop-out carrying coffee for smart chauvinists. And more, too, than a midlevel CIA analyst posing as a journalist. Maybe this child could even be something heroic. *Heroic* to her at that time meant someone who helped people or created things. A surgeon. Or a scientist. She would even accept an architect, too.

Part of the blissful ignorance of not yet having had a first child is the belief that you might just be able to influence the course of their lives. Influence them to greatness. And away from danger. Jason came in May, a little Taurus. May 1984. He was small, but he was perfect.

*

The path is becoming slippery with rain; at least she has a hat. Last year the neighbors invited her to help them enlarge their garden. Perhaps they felt sorry for her. She had said yes, and she had planted all the "green things." The neighbor took a picture of her covered in dirt and said, "Sara, you look good in brown." The picture found a place alongside all the other pictures in the house of young men wearing brown—in deserts, on beaches, and under tarps. Planting had been an exercise in humility and precision since she had never really done it before. The neighbors were forgiving, and they invited her to come daily and monitor her progress. She had not gone in some time.

She can see the young lettuces starting to poke through now. And the green beans, and the broccoli. She slows to a walk and stops to check the radishes. Radishes need rain. *The zucchinis grow so fast*, she thinks. Like a child. If you do not watch them, they disappear into something else before your eyes. A novice can overgrow a zucchini to the size of a watermelon through benign neglect. The meat inside remains edible, but tough. It takes a very sharp knife to slice.

*

Jason was eight when his father died. She had been torn about whether to tell him because at that point they had not seen his father in over two years. Some part of her knew that not telling him would only increase her son's curiosity later. And it did. Eventually, friends of his father's felt it was their role—their duty—to tell the boy about things his father had done. "He helped make this country safer," one of them said, sitting on his porch in Virginia. It disgusted her because she was certain it was a lie. David had done what pleased David, and David had gone where he had the most fun. But then, why ruin a fantasy for a child? It was David, after all, who had given her boy to her.

May 2001 was the birthday when Jason's Washington godfather brought him the photograph: a picture of David standing on an old tank, in a desert (or backed by sand dunes), holding a tiny teddy bear. Sara never knew he had stood on any tank, ever, and her last memory of that bear was that Jason had lost it years ago, at camp. She never knew David had ever been anywhere near a desert. He always said he was c lling from somewhere glamorous and urban, like Paris, and those calls always made her angry because she'd only been to France once (with him). Yet here was hard evidence: the father of her child had carried his son's teddy bear around the world with him. Maybe he had carried it to remind himself of who he was working to protect. Maybe he simply carried it to seduce young girls. She would grant him the former, but suspected the latter was more likely.

Being born out of wedlock might not seem the most auspicious start, but the first hours of Jason's life were perfect. Everyone was present at the hospital that day: one senator, two ambassadors, three surgeons (they knew a lot of people at the hospital), and all four future godfathers—a diplomat, a journalist, a congressional aide, and a law professor. It was a suitably male crew for a baby boy. For those hours at least, they felt like a family. David held the baby and beamed. Sara later thanked him for giving her her own private liberal media elite. She hadn't been consulted on the selection of godparents, but she loved them, every one. She was a kid; what did she know. They would each in their own way help raise the boy, one of them, in particular, over time. None of them believed in God, but no one seemed to mind, or cared to address that irony.

Then he left. He promised to send money, and to write letters, and to come and visit. There was no diamond ring, no allusion to any future, no remorse, and no romance. No one ever even clarified what word would be used to describe his relationship with Jason although "Daddy" felt only slightly less libelous than "Uncle." Having limited family and few close friends (it went with the job, apparently), it was easy to say "The child was an accident." Or, "a happy product of a lazy one-night stand." But people around the office knew there had been, at least briefly, love involved. They joked that the boy was named after Jason and the Argonauts, given his father's self-celebrated faux-pacifism. David never hid his reverence for "brass," especially when walking the E-ring with generals. But in truth the boy was named after her father, whom she had also lost too early.

There was a lot of talk, and a lot of speculation, and a lot of work. She couldn't sustain her office life and an illusion of ambition when all she wanted was to be home, but the reputation earned working from home in that town was rough. So when Jason turned four—not long after discovering his first set of spoons—she decided to leave. She would take him far away from people who felt church on Sunday mornings was a conflict with *Meet the Press.* She would take him to live in America.

Pennsylvania didn't seem that different from Virginia to a child. But the people he met there were very different. His classmates, no longer the sons and daughters of diplomats who knew the names of senators because they'd dined in their homes, were mostly Republicans. They played ice hockey. They would go on to be investment bankers or corporate lawyers or (in the cases of the really wealthy ones) organic farmers and hops brewers. Kids in this new place were kids: they talked about sports and sugared cereals and apple picking. They didn't study Mandarin or think of "Justice" as a place, with an address. Things felt, for a while, very quiet. And though the local mothers murmured about who the new girl was, Sara didn't care. They said she'd lost her husband in a foreign war. Or they said she'd never been married because she was a Communist—or was it *commune*-ist? But in general people were kind. They were not competitive or ambitious enough to be too nosy or too critical—at least not at first.

*

The "main road" is what the two-lane is called around here, and the relief on her knees as she hits the asphalt after running on the wet grass is visceral. Feeling very little pain, she decides to just keep running since she has nothing to go home to but the endless waiting, and even the best books or worst television no longer provide distraction. Sometimes, when Jason was in his first weeks of training, she would run twice a day on this road. It made her feel more connected to what he was going through. But her runs always ended with rest, and dreams. Where did his runs end?

She reaches that point where her breathing evens, and when she knows she can go for a good long while. Her heart beats very slowly, like an athlete's. It had always given her doctors the impression she was calm; it now gives that illusion to everyone else.

*

Sara told her son that his father died of a heart attack. He was traveling for work. And that work, according to him, was so important that he had had to choose it over being a more traditional dad. She always told Jason that his father worked for an embassy in Europe, because that was her understanding. First it had been France, then Spain; in the last years of his life, it was Sweden. But thinking back to a time before cell phones and e-mail, God only knows where he was and what he did. She was so mired in the process of caring for a little child and, when he slept, patching together work, that over time she didn't even ask anymore where David was or what he was doing. She had no illusion he cared for her or would one day be coming home and sitting at a table for meals with the two of them. She would hear rumors from friends about where he was but people didn't ask anymore if she minded. More often they wanted to know how she minded being alone. Didn't she want to marry?

She assumed David did well as the size of the checks he sent began to rise. This meant she could send Jason to good schools, so she forgave the fact that she had no idea what kind of work generated them. She forgave the fact that they came with no letter, no return address. She knew who had sent them. And almost always he would call soon after. "Did you get the cash?" The calls felt cold and transactional, like a drug deal. She quickly stopped caring. She was rational and pragmatic. *Romance is vastly overrated*, she thought.

Jason was a senior in high school when she dropped him off that day in early September ten years ago. As she did on most days, she dropped him off and then returned home to take a nap. She wasn't sleeping well, and the insomnia had worsened as the anniversary—December—of David's death approached. Usually she didn't fall asleep; she just lay in bed, stared at the ceiling, took deep breaths and then made herself get up. When she was ready, she would sit down at her computer and do her work: editing interminably dull research papers written by former colleagues of David's. They all had books, and in the nearer term they had articles, white papers, and always possibly revolutionary essays to be submitted to prize-winning policy journals. They all had editors, too. At first they began giving her work because they felt sorry for her, but then when they saw she was good they would ask her again and again, until the relationship became a dependency, enough of one that they were willing to pay very well for her input. She had a healthy sense of humor about the fact that the content of much of what she worked on was foreign to her; she just tracked the value of the lines by their rhythm and let the politics stand "on author."

It was easy to forget about everything else once she was lost in her work, even as she was filled with mild self-loathing each time she sat down to it. It seemed so odd that she had ended up here, in the "middle of nowhere," poring over details in documents that only a very few people would ever read, and in which most people would fail to see any relevance. But then she would remember she was the mother of an extraordinary boy and she would think, *That's enough*.

Her real job was simply biding her time until school let out. This was perhaps the one reason she had not let Jason have a car. She knew these were the last few months she would have with him. They were already consumed with college applications, and in nine months he would move out. Then there would be marriage, she was sure of it. Jason wanted a "whole" family. When he left, her real work would be taken away. Or, at least, shifted. Being with him was all she had known her entire adult life: she'd become a mother when she was not much older than he was now. Two years older, to be exact.

*

But that September day was different. By nine o'clock, her phone was ringing off the hook. At first, seeing the 202 area code and assuming it was one of her Washington friends calling ("What are you doing with yourself these days?" Or "Have you had time to work on the piece?"), she didn't answer. But then the numbers changed: 202 became 917 and she saw it was Jason's cell, which he almost never used. He was meant to be in math class now. She knew that because he had moaned and groaned about it all the way through egg and cheese sandwiches that morning.

"What's the use of math?"

She tried to argue its practicality.

"Mommy, math never saved anyone's life."

"It might save yours if it gets you into Harvard," she said. Harvard was not out of his reach.

She picked up the phone. Her son was crying. She had not heard him cry in a long time. He possessed a remarkable, almost inhuman gift for tolerating pain, something she'd always attributed to losing a father—not once but twice: as an infant, and then again as a very young boy. To lose the father you never even really had in the first place was a unique tragedy, she knew; it promised a long tail of processing and forgiveness. Yet Jason was stoic. Physical pain didn't affect him at all. The day he'd dislocated his shoulder on the football field he didn't shed a tear. He was the quarterback. He had never been injured in six seasons of play. But that day she was there, and she saw him go down. When he stood up, his arm hung slant from the socket. While they waited for the EMT, the coach said to her, "Miss, I've seen three-hundred-pound linemen weep when this happens. Your boy is tough."

She knew that. This was a kid whose father, while brilliant and very funny, was no model in the morals—or the courage—department. His father played tennis and chess. Jason liked contact. He was an excellent experiment for scientists studying nature versus nurture, or tiger mothers keen to divine the special sauce for making great men, because the template was there was no template. There were genes. She'd done nothing but love him unconditionally. She had loved him and treated him with respect. She had tried to discipline him, but he disciplined himself. Sometimes at night she'd hear him running sprints around the house.

But that September day when he called, he was shaken. He was begging her to come to school and collect him. So she did, and in the car on the radio she heard the news. When they got home, they sat in front of the television, liked two stoned Deadheads post-show. Realizing it was almost nine o'clock, Sara went to make dinner.

"Forget Harvard," Jason said. He was standing in the doorway to the kitchen.

They ate in silence until Sara said, "What do mean, 'Forget Harvard'?"

"I'm not going there," he said. "I'm going to apply to the Naval Academy."

And she looked at her little philosopher with his steaming-hot shepherd's pie, and she knew the argument was over.

"I know what I want," he said.

This phrase took her breath away. Sara had never said those words. *He's still in shock*, she remembers thinking. We all are. This will pass.

*

There are not many cars out, and she keeps heading to a traffic light she has designated as her turnaround point. If she makes it to the light, she will have gone five miles, and so ten by the time she is home. She plans to slow her pace, putting off the return. She knows the house will be clean. She has never had help and it is strange to have it now. Someone from the town sent—and paid for—two housecleaners. They were invisible and meticulous; she rarely saw them but she knew they were there. There was always mess, because her home had become a fort, and a retreat. It had become a base for all those who felt called to protect her.

After years of nights alone, there were so many others around all the time now. They were all good people. She has become close with the local cops; she has their numbers, and they all want to help. One of them offered to move in, too, but she thinks that is overkill. No one is out to hurt her. People only want her story. At the traffic light she stops, and bends over, and takes some very deep breaths.

*

Her increasing interest in all things military ran parallel to her son's becoming an officer. With Jason at the Naval Academy, she got back to D.C.—and Virginia—regularly. She would meet friends for lunch. They were all amused to see how she had changed. She was only thirty-seven, so to many of them she was still a girl.

"You've traded Athens for Sparta," teased her old boss from Langley, the only boss she'd ever had, the one who had got her to the conference where everything had started. Or ended, depending upon your point of view.

"Yes, I guess I have," she said. She was proud of her son. She thought about that trade and thought she was fine with it. Sparta suddenly struck her as mission-driven, and relevant, Athens as lazy. But that wasn't really what was changing in her. What was mission-driven and relevant was what had always been: her love for her boy. Had he decided to join the circus, she might have developed an obsession with elephants.

Elephants would have been easier. There was a new generation of soldiers and sailors born that September day. Sara had not lost a son on 9/11; she lost him later to something she could not provide at home.

*

Rather than slow down she decides to speed up her pace. *What if I could make it home in half the time it took me to make it out here?* she thinks. *What if I could increase my time by ten percent on each run? At what point will my body simply say, Stop.* She runs so fast that, coming to the two-lane she almost trips over a branch thrown down by the storm—one too skinny to see in the dusk but still thick enough to break your leg. The near-miss is exhilarating. She feels like she has been given another chance. She can see the garden up ahead. The tomato vines are bent with rain.

*

The call came late on May 2, the first day of what should have been the last ten days of Jason's fifth tour. First, last, fourth, fifth: everything in military life involved numbers—or letters. This rigorous precision was not just for art; it was necessary for saving lives. Soon she got good at math, at placing events in time precisely, like a criminal witness. She had not known where he was; he had not been able to tell her throughout this deployment. She had given up reading newspapers, although old friends who knew Jason reached out regularly with a question or a view. *Yemen? Libya? It must be the Maghreb.* She simply wanted to know he was safe.

Since it is spring, people at the market talk about yesterday's tennis or last week's lacrosse games; they discuss plans for the upcoming antiques show or their newly cleaned infinity pools. People rarely mention the war because most of them care very little about it. Those who know her and know she has a son serving don't ask either; they are not sure what to say. Sara hasn't met any local veterans although she has heard that there is a retired Army Ranger around. When she thinks of her son, she still thinks of her baby, lining up spoons. She hopes he has enough socks. "Socks" was the request she found most often in a book that was a collection of letters written home by soldiers during World War II. Jason had given it to her.

She'd spent so many years educating him, but now he educated her. *Phronesis* is a word she never knew before she read about it in a memoir written by a former Team guy, a memoir she never would have noticed or even known about at another time in her life. *Phronesis* is a quality. "The most interesting people are the people we don't know," said the father of another Academy boy at graduation. He had leaned over and whispered this to Sara as they sat there in the thick heat, watching their sons, all in white. She had only just met him and thought his comment was a compliment, perhaps a pass, but when she thought about it later she realized he was talking about all the kids that day, the kids who would leave and fight foreign wars for little pay and less power. And she thought: *The bravest people are the people we do not know.*

Phronesis was a word that cropped up once, and then increasingly often, in the e-mails she would receive periodically from her son. She never knew where he was when he was writing them, but his heart and his character were the same as they had always been, despite what had gone on in the course of his days. He was not writing about politics or about war zones. Mostly he was writing about what was on his mind that day, and more and more he was preoccupied with the question of whether to come home. Or, how to come home. Any shrink would have loved that. A father and son, both living the better part of their lives in undisclosed locations.

Phronesis, according to Aristotle, is wisdom learned from action that allows you to make choices about what to do in a given situation. It stands in opposition to *sophia*, or wisdom gained from books. *Phronesis* was less for scholars than for soldiers. And what Sara learned over time was that each division of the military had its own, even if slight, variation on the larger code and culture of the overall enterprise. The Teams had very strict code. Part of it was from their training. Part of it is soldered in the fight. Her son had elected to join the military when there was a major fight on.

"We don't lose our men, ma'am," she was assured, when they—a chaplain, and a casualty assistance calls officer—arrived at the house that May morning, the morning following the phone call, to talk to her in person. On the phone she had only been asked if she would be at home. They had not told her anything more. On the phone, she had imagined a brigade. In person, there were two of them: an older man, maybe in his mid-fifties, in uniform, and a younger man who didn't look much older than her son. He was an officer home on leave. He had heard the news of Jason being missing and had asked that he be the one allowed to come, to be there when she heard. He lived three thousand miles away from where he stood now and had been spending his short time at home with the girl he planned to marry, but he had taken a plane and then driven a car across the country to be there to tell Sara this news. He knew her son. He had trained with him at Coronado and at Otay Lakes, and he had lived with him briefly at Virginia Beach. His name was Sam. She had met him before, but she had forgotten him. He looked older. He was missing an eye. When she saw that, she remembered his story.

The two men asked her to sit down, and then she was told: her son had been missing for two days. They said that they had a general idea of where he was, but that they could not tell her any more than that. They told her that Jason had been part of a very important mission, one she might even read about in the papers, but they could not tell her what that was, either—or where it was.

Sara didn't sense any drama from the word *mission* because it was what her son did every day—and every night. Missions were routine. That was the job. The older man told Sara her son would come home. *Dead or alive; is that implied?* she thought at the time.

As she listened to them talk, her mind drifted back to that night at the same kitchen table they were sitting around now. "Not Harvard" had been about belief; after that, there had been no turning back. She had been so proud throughout those next years, through all the Academy games and then, later, the early, tense selections for "Mini BUD/S," followed by her son's increasingly odds-defying failures to fail. She resolved to remain proud now. And strong. She was not ready for this. She could feel herself starting to faint. It's okay, she thought; one of these guys will catch me. I know how the protocol works.

Later that same day there was another knock on the door. And then another one. First, it was the local Catholic priest. He wanted to pray with her. Then it was the retired Ranger. He looked like he could really break some glass, and she took his number. He said he would come back every day and that she didn't have to worry. Then a man in a beautiful suit. He was a former Middle East–based CIA station chief who had traveled from his retirement in northern Maine and who insisted he would stay as long as she needed, down the road, at the little inn. This was all through word of mouth, as far as she could tell. Neighbors flooded her porch with offerings: sweets and alcohol and honey-baked ham. Someone sent a cook to help organize the kitchen and make dinners. A new refrigerator was installed, a gift from a local store. One of the state's senators arrived and promised to protect her from the press. She thought that was pretty funny. He said the governor would like to come and what time would be convenient for her? She had not even brushed her hair.

Like most people living through such a moment, she did not hear most of what was said or remember who had said it. She knew that things like sleeping and eating were necessary but remembered to do them only when prodded. People fell into various active roles and informally but carefully kept watch over her and the scope creep of her chaos. *Come on in. Yes, please. What beautiful peonies.* She suddenly did not want to be alone.

She was happy to have Sam in her son's room. His left eye was the most sensational blue. Ocean blue. And in the place of his right eye was a glass orb, with the NSW Trident inked onto it. She wanted to look at it closely but knew asking that would sound strange. She knew what the Trident was. Like most Team moms and wives, she had read what she could find of the existing literature and history. And she had heard about the glass-eye Tridents, but she had never seen one up close. It was the contrast with the boy's other eye that made it uniquely upsetting. And yet it was beautiful.

The Trident is made up of four elements: an anchor, a trident, a pistol, and an eagle. When her son had asked her for her interpretation of it, she'd said, "Well, the trident's for Neptune." She paused and said, "And the pistol's for strength?" Jason gave her a little essay on the Trident's meaning (the kind of thing she loved), which she had saved in a drawer somewhere. The part she always remembered was the part about the eagle. Something along the lines of "the eagle keeps his head down, because humility is the true sign of a warrior." When the guys are awarded their Tridents, at the end of their qualification training, their diplomas carry not only their own names but also the names of men killed in action. This tradition was not subtle, but it was powerful.

*

When Jason was seven, Sara left him overnight for only the second time. An old friend was marrying another old friend, in Washington. In her toast, the young bride mentioned Naval Special Warfare training. She had seen a documentary about the base in Coronado that her husband had ordered from the Military Channel. Watching what those young men did, she said, made her think that perhaps they were preparing for the real fight of their lives: marriage. Everyone laughed. The groom worked on the Hill, and the only way he was likely to get close to the barrel of a gun was a weekend skeet shoot. He had an idea of his work as deeply civic and virtuous, and he liked to spend late nights watching reenactments of Civil War battles. He always told his wife and friends that he wished he'd gone into the military, but that given the chance at Stanford, well, there had not been any contest. He would marry this girl, they would raise a family, and he would make his mark in some more socially and politically less flammable way. He would write laws and work hard to try and pass them.

The bride was beautiful. Sara envied her dress. Sara envied the whole experience and ritual, one she knew now for certain she would never have. As the bride's toast went on, the room quieted down. She soon unintentionally stunned the clinking glasses to silence. She was describing an exercise—what they called an "evolution"—known as drown-proofing. In drown-proofing (the bride read this from a printed page), a boy's hands and feet are tied. He is also blindfolded. Like this, he jumps into a pool. He has to bob, and he has to swim fifty meters under water, without emerging for air. This is meant as much to test the will as it is to test physical stamina. And it is meant to test fear, because the fear that results from anticipation of failure is enough to keep a boy from ever reaching the edge of the pool. The bride had been trying to say something about commitment, and about romance, but all anyone could talk about the entire rest of the night was those boys, bobbing in the water, blindfolded.

Driving north the next morning, Sara remembered thinking about the toast. How noble to enter into something so you can save the lives of others; no one she knew did that. What was she doing that was remotely noble? She'd woken feeling guilty about the sandy-haired seven-year-old at home with a sitter. When she got back, it was dark. She sat on the end of his bed for a long time while he slept. She looked at him and she thought, *You are the product of a very poor decision, but you are the most important thing in my life*. She thought, *I could easily swim fifty meters underwater for you*.

*

She checks her watch. She has been gone for nearly two hours. The last stop at the garden must have been longer than she realized. It is time to go home. It is almost all uphill through the neighbor's yard, and it looks different now. It is wet and dark. Does anyone even live there anymore? When was the last time she had seen those neighbors? Were they the ones who brought the blueberry pies? She can't remember. The ground evens out. She can see her favorite tree now in her own yard, a tree that once held a swing and that later served as poor protective cover for a target board. This is the lawn where she learned to shoot the little guns. As she reaches the top of the driveway, she can see a new car out front. It is not a police car, but it has government plates. There are two men standing by it. One of them is in uniform. They have come to bring her news.

ATHENS FOR SPARTA

Jason jumps in feet first. As his heels hit the water, he fills his lungs with air one last time. He knows this test well. He read about it before he practiced for it, and he has practiced for it many times before now performing it in front of his peers. Not all the men will pass this test. He knows that the most important thing is to stay calm and not to panic. Panic is the assurance of failure.

If he can maintain his mental equilibrium, the rest is just water games, at least here. This is not a battle. This is a beautiful pool, near a beautiful beach, in one of America's most idyllic coastal communities. Dinner will be served later, and it will be good. And then he will have a bed to sleep in, a book to read, and rest. Sleep never seemed like a luxury when he was little, but he understands well the price of its absence now.

When he'd searched for information about drown-proofing online, back home, Jason found a chat room where one aspiring operator described how he had trained for drown-proofing by wrestling his brother underwater until one of them passed out. Jason thought that was ridiculous. But then, something about that post stayed in his mind as emblematic of the outlook of so many who wanted to succeed here. Whether or not they had prepared in unwise or sophisticated ways, all of them had prepared. On its own, each element of the training might appear absurd, like a lone tennis player tasked to stand and volley cross-court for forty hours, without a racquet. But for the serious athlete, practice demands breaking down the diverse parts of the body—and of the equipment. Basic Underwater Demolition/SEAL training is what practice looks like when the game is special operations warfare.

Drown-proofing had earned its celebrity within and beyond the community because its simplicity was emblematic of the fact that an operator's best weapon is himself. In drown-proofing, there is no gear, no guns, and no camouflage. With your hands and feet tied, you not only swim underwater but also have to balance, bob, and stay afloat.

Jason sneaks in reading when he can, mainly at bedtime. Books had always been his escape growing up as an only child, alone much of the time, a car ride away from any friend. Books were the excuse not to come downstairs when his mother needed him, when he didn't feel like being needed. And books were his rebellion against the fact that he felt she'd taken him away from what might have been a more exciting place and life, and perhaps she'd also taken him away from his father. What little he has known of David he has known from books: books on topics he knows his father loved, or books written by friends and colleagues of his father's.

Having exhausted those categories, Jason started reading stories he imagined his father might like, or stories his godfathers would tell him had been meaningful to David. Sometimes his godfathers would lend him things that David had lent to them; within their little group, they had an active system of exchange and borrow. You could tell a lot about a man from his library, perhaps even more than from the story he told about himself. Libraries don't lie in quite the same way. David's library seemed to be, like those of most people, aspirational as much as it was honest: it held the things he wanted to have read. But it was also romantic. Arthurian legend was a particular passion.

When Jason read things he thought might be like the man to whom he owed so much, he'd underline a passage. He did know that David loved to travel, and he wanted to be a traveler, too. He knew that David did work he loved, and he hoped to find work he loved, too. And he knew David didn't need anyone, or at least that was what his mother always said, and he longed not to need anyone either. Most of all, he longed to be far away from the familiar, far away from the kids who teased him about the fact that he had no dad.

Now he reads poetry because if your reading is in ten-to-fifteen-minute intervals, eventually anything longer starts to feel like a waste, or a chore. Poems performed in the right amount of time, and then they left him something to think about. High ROI. He picks up the same poem or collection of poems again and again and again, until they are stuck in his mind. He likes war poems. He has memorized most of Wilfred Owen. He likes Wallace Stevens, too. He likes the poem "Sunday Morning." It is part of a collection he stole from his journalist godfather's library, because he had seen that the book was signed and dated by David and that the date was, by coincidence, Jason's birthday. It had been sent from overseas.

Apparently it was one of the last things anyone received from him. After April, David had stopped calling. After May, he stopped writing. In December, he was dead. David had circled lines from the poem's first stanza:

She dreams a little, and she feels the dark
Encroachment of that old catastrophe,
As a calm darkens among water-lights.
The pungent oranges and bright, green wings
Seem things in some procession of the dead,
Winding across wide water, without sound.
The day is like wide water, without sound,
Stilled for the passing of her dreaming feet
Over the seas, to silent Palestine,
Dominion of the blood and sepulchre.

Sepulchre was underlined, and a definition for it was written in the margin: "burial vault, tomb."

He knows his mother thinks the navy was the death knell of any academic ambition. The thought wasn't her fault. She grew up in the seventies; her parents were lapsed hippies, the kind who went to Woodstock too late, in their thirties, and didn't take drugs. They adopted their era's popular politics—anti-Nixon, pro-Kennedy, LBJ-agnostic—and raised their daughter for the first ten years of her life on a modified commune. They were against war, but their experience of war was an image in a newspaper. And when their parents died, they had no trouble absorbing the houses and cars—and ideas—that went with inheritance. Passionate without the education behind their passions to make them actionable, they sent Sara into the world a kind of rabid anti-romantic. As soon as she was old enough, she ran away, separating herself from them to the extent that she could. She wanted something normal. She wanted order. She took an internship working for the government. She surrounded herself with people who had too much education and discrete wills to practical action.

Sara's fears about the downside of her son forgoing Cambridge and convention were mainly fears about adverse psychological effects, not safety. Fears for his safety would come later. While he trained, she was mainly afraid of his drifting onto just another kind of commune, one that would set him apart from the majority of his peers and would certainly result in what finance professors call "high opportunity cost." What would he do after? Would Wall Street or neurosurgery residencies still be available? What were the merits of learning to parachute into the ocean and shoot rocket launchers? She worried that there was an element of play in this that was, well, play qua play. And in some very deep place that she would never admit to him, she worried that the games would be so much fun that they would not permit him to reenter the less rarefied air of real life.

That will to orbit Earth was in his DNA. Starting military training was not the sign she had hoped for. This was not an ordinary boy, interested in ordinary things. Jason felt her fears came from her love, and her ignorance. She was his mother, so he forgave her. She was all he had. He knew that she felt he was all she had, too.

*

There aren't many poets in the mix at Coronado, and there aren't many men who talk to their mothers as often as he does. Or maybe there are, but they don't let on. Some have wives, or girlfriends. Some have children. Family life crowds out intellectual pleasures, to some extent. Yet if Jason is sneaking sonnets, no one knows what else was being read at night, after hours. Epictetus? *The New Republic*? His experience with these guys so far is that they're all pretty relaxed, at least on the surface, and yet they're all inordinately driven. Imagine surfers who hide the *summas* on their degrees.

Leadership is a word used religiously here; and it is about success in action but also about a will to learn. There is a small shelf of books for borrowing at the base. The titles include classics like *Profiles in Courage* and *The Best and the Brightest*. Histories, mainly political or military-based, are stacked up alongside and on top of single volumes left behind by former classes: Clancy, Sledge, Couch, Le Carré, Sun Tzu. Some are signed and dated on the inside; others have annotations that mirror the only-just-post-adolescent enthusiasms of their readers, like "not fucking possible" and "beast." When he describes the books one night to his mother, she says, "It sounds like you need a librarian." Two days later a large box of books arrives with a note from her: "For that shelf." Suddenly the aspiring sailors had Shakespeare. The plays went largely untouched, even *Titus*, but they provided room for broad mockery of the recipient.

BUD/S was about cultivating trust and about learning to attend to detail. The mission of the instructors was not to break their students but to identify and support the best among them. The program had three parts: First Phase, also known as "Two Weeks and a Long Day," was two weeks of rigorous conditioning plus ocean and boat training, followed by Hell Week, where sleep deprivation and disorientation were added to the mix. It is a mystery to physicians and military historians why some succeed and others do not, but often the first boy will drop out within days, and Hell Week can cut what remains of any given class in half. As always, everything is about the team: trust in the team, development of the team, not tipping the delicate ecology of the team. "Being an individual is not the same thing as being a leader," one of their instructors said. He spat out the word "in-di-vi-joo-*el*" as if it were an expletive.

*

Jason soon starts thinking he might choose to spend the rest of his life with most of the men he has met here so far over most of the men he has met at home or in school the last twenty-one years. The men who had moved in and out of Sara's life, who wrote articles about ideas and who positioned and repositioned themselves for increasingly powerful civilian jobs, seemed less intimidating to him now. Was he growing up? Or was he changing. The anger he held against so many of those men was not complicated: he was protecting her. Even after thirteen years, he believed that his father would return. He would return, and they would be a family. And while she would never say as much, he felt that Sara believed this, too, as she carefully deflected each suitor's increasingly serious invitations (dinner, a trip, marriage) by stating that she wasn't over David, and that David was Jason's father. After years of that, they finally left her alone, Penelope unraveling her looms. As far as her son knew, she had not had one real romance in almost ten years, but the admirers remained, lurking around the house like stray cats. She lived a very spare life, and his leaving home had been very difficult but he knew it was time, and he knew leaving would help strengthen her, too.

Training hard with a group brings out emotion. Jason has always prided himself on not showing too much, but cool becomes elusive when you're tired, cold, and wet. He doesn't love running, although he's not bad at it. Sometimes the instructors drive alongside the guys during nighttime runs. If you walk to the beach you can see them, lit by the car's lights. One night the jeep rolls up and when the window rolls down, Jason can hear someone inside reciting the St. Crispin's Day speech from *Henry V.* "We happy few," etc. It's a message: *You have support, and you will get through this.*

He is not yet sure whom he can trust, although slowly the personalities of his classmates emerge. They are all fiercely independent. They have all been overachievers. Many come from families who understand and value the sacrifices that go along with this training; they understand and value it as necessary—or at least, not abnormal. Most of the men arrive in Coronado quite confident that they will succeed, especially those who are back for the second or third time. Each class is never entirely new; a small percentage is always made up of guys who were "rolled back" from previous classes due to injury. One night Jason asks one of those guys, back for his third—and final—try, "How do you do it all over again?"

And the guy thinks about it and says, "Amnesia?" And then, after a long pause, "I just know it's what I want."

"Can you still make it if you're not sure what you want?"

"Well, that's the first time I've ever heard that question."

Expectations management is only second to pain management in the process of making it through each day. And then, a distant third, comes anger management. Pain management allows you to move through the moment; expectations management allows you to move through the day; and anger management allows you to move through being denied not only any privacy but any acknowledgment of being you. When an instructor tips your drawers upside down during room inspection, then fails you for having clothes spilled on the floor? That is a test of the extent to which you can control your anger, and your desire for praise. A rigged room inspection might break a boy who could run the beach in three-minute miles, but it might tell a teacher something about that boy's character that no O-course can.

The quiet nights now give him time to think through his accumulated emotions and all those years in which he'd tried not to express them. He doesn't like to spend too much time thinking about them; it's one reason he's chosen a far less cerebral path than so many of his self-appointed mentors in Washington. They still casually question his choice, not to him but to Sara and to one another. He knows and he doesn't care. Do they question it because they worry it is a waste of time, that it is not going to gain him the kind of access they have? They might question it because for many in their generation a choice to join the navy meant something explicitly different.

Jason will be making decisions that affect people's lives at an age when the ones who judge him most harshly were working as interns at newspapers or as junior legislative aides on the Hill. What kinds of decisions are they making now? Then again, whatever choice one makes when one is young is easy to romanticize. He knows that. There is nothing romantic about the experience he is having, but it was one thing: it was better than all the options. Of this he was certain. He tells his mother one night on the phone, "It's pretty intense. You feel a little sick, so they push you harder. Then once they break you, you're really bonded."

"Now that does sound like love," Sara said, and laughed.

*

His classmates came from all over. That year, in addition to Jason, there were two sets of twins, a BUD/S first. One set was blond, one set brunette. They were the four tallest guys in the class, just over six feet, and heavier than the others. Their boat crew is quickly christened "The Knicks" for its NBA-esque height average. Most of the guys arrived here in shape; they'd played ball, or wrestled, or captained local water polo teams. They'd raised cattle on family ranches. They'd had preternaturally physical brothers, or brothers already in the SOF community. In most cases, you might not notice them on the street. You wouldn't pick them out of a lineup and say, *That's the one who can kill me with his bare hands*. The average shape of a Naval Special Warfare operator, in this way, was its own covert operation. They looked less like Patroclus than like European soccer stars: lean, compact. They were diplomatic—at least the ones who would make it far in the game. Only in NSW do enlisted men and officers train together; there was not a lot of room for attitude when the guy who lacks your academic pedigree is the guy who leaves you begging for breath at the water's edge, or six minutes behind him on a timed run. Yet there was never a clear-cut formula: it was not having been all-American plus tall. It was not your education plus your accent. It was not prior service in an overseas war, even one in which you had proven your valor.

They were all ambitious, but they learned how to measure and play it, like gifted political rookies. The guy who liked to brag about his Oxford boxing, and his altruistic aspirations, didn't make it until midnight the first day of Hell Week. When asked about it later, he'd said simply that he could not stand the noise. He said that the noise of the gunshots during "breakout," the traditional start of the week, had driven him momentarily mad and that he knew then that he was not cut out for that kind of a fight. If pressed, he would go on to say that in fact the very nature of fighting was "inhuman" and in some way "banal"; that the trainee treatment in Coronado was too close to "torture" for his taste. He would tell a newspaper that the NSW culture lacked the nobility of a kind of education he'd thought "would make him a true warrior." He was ridiculous, but sophisticated in the story he told himself, the same story he would tell others for the rest of his life when they asked, at dinner parties, about the time he almost joined the Teams.

This culture was not about how you prepared before you came here, or where you thought the course would take you later on—or at least, it was not only about that. It was about remembering that after this hour, right now, there will be another hour, and it will be harder. After this day, right now, there will be another day. And it will be harder. And after this night's sleep, you will wake up and start all over again. And it is *your choice*, so feel grateful that you have been given the privilege to participate. While Jason had no real idea what he had signed up for, in some small place inside himself he felt sure he could do it. But when he arrived and looked around at the other guys, he realized: *They all think they can do it, too.* All of them arrived carrying pasts that had driven them to this particular point. Jason's past was this: having grown up without a man in his life, he was now determined to pass the world's hardest test for becoming one.

*

When a boy elects to quit, there is also a process. He can approach an instructor and ask to DOR, or Drop On Request. The instructor will often make some attempt to help him change his mind. If he is certain, he knows where to go: there is a bell hanging at the edge of the Grinder, the main courtyard by their rooms, and this is the bell used to "ring out" your DOR. You ring the bell three times, and remove your helmet. The helmets are placed in a line so that all the others can see who has dropped and when. Most say, after ringing the bell, that they regret it. What waits on the other side of that bell—warmth, rest, home—is powerful, especially when you're processing those thoughts under duress. There would be times in training history when ringing the bell would not be necessary to drop out, considered too dramatic, but in the end a new master chief always brought the bell back, feeling that the public nature of the act made it less likely, and so lowered their attrition rates.

One day one of the twins decides to DOR. At six foot five, he is standing on the beach and begging the instructor to let him quit. He had been at the Academy with Jason. They'd played football together. Of all the people Jason knew, this was the one Jason thought would be chairman of the Joint Chiefs one day.

"Don't do this," Jason says. The instructor is shouting something else, something slightly less generous.

The boy's brother is there and he says the same thing Jason is saying: "Don't do it."

And then the older (by three minutes) twin grabs his younger brother, picks him up, and holds him hard until he stops shaking.

"I'm all right," the younger twin says, finally. The rest of the class is half a mile down the beach, and they'll have to catch up. The older twin says to Jason, "Don't you wish you had that on video?" And Jason thinks, *Not as much as I wish I had a brother.*

When Jason's class arrived at Annapolis, in the summer of 2002, they were all filled with purpose. The first class coming in after 9/11, most of them knew they would elect to serve, and most thought they'd perhaps spend the better part of their lives in the military. No writer then would compare them to the Greatest Generation, but the parallels were there: they would enter this war by choice, and they would not question it, and they would feel proud of their decision. They would graduate into a time when the global map was shifting, and their country needed them.

In his last week before graduation, Jason's mother came to take him and a few friends out for dinner. She'd been in Washington for a meeting, and even as she would be returning in a week, she made the drive. She'd picked up his godfather in Georgetown, the one who'd sent the box of spoons all those years ago—he was now chief of staff for the Senate Judiciary Committee. Over dessert, Jason mentioned that he had been given the chance to try for the Teams. His godfather put down his scotch.

"You have got to be kidding me. Why would you want to do *that*? You're talented, Jase. I'll hire you. Or I will find someone to hire you. Do you want to go to Congress? What about the State Department? Do you know how long that training is? It's like a medical residency. And you can fail! You can fail anytime. It's like a medical residency with no insurance of becoming a doctor! It's not for kids like you. If you come work in my office now, before you know it you'll be participating in drafting policy."

His godfather had worked in politics for as long as Jason could remember. He clearly thought "drafting policy" was a sexy sell. He'd started out as a Senate page, progressed swiftly to speechwriter, then evolved into a gifted statistician, an accidental policy wonk who rapidly won favors by keeping his head down and his ideas free and apolitical, posing as a scholar among the power- and pleasure-seekers. Everyone thought he would win a Nobel Prize one day—"not a Peace Prize," he would say, bashful, when pushed on the tease. He was only a few years older than Sara and someone once told Jason that he was also, possibly, a "lost" son of David's, his mother having been notoriously promiscuous, and David's type. He rarely talked about where he was from, his family, his roots. He talked about the pressing questions of the present, like housing starts and interest rates; and he talked about his dreams for the country's future. He was an idealist. He had been to Princeton, Harvard, and Yale (English, business, law: the late twentieth century's most glittery trifecta). Yet he had the heart—and soul, and superficial cynicism—of a salesman. He knew how to talk in a way that was neither grand nor rhetorical; he knew how to argue and how to charm. He felt proper education was incompatible with military service—or rather, that the former allowed you to bypass the latter and still retain a sense of mission and meaning. He felt that if you had a brain and could train it, you could do anything—an *anything* underscored by an unspoken, quietly implied *non-life-threatening*.

Jason knew all this. It had come up before. This was Jason's favorite godfather, a man in his eyes almost infinitely infallible, and a man always watchful of ones he loved. Yet Jason felt sorry for him. He felt that for all his degrees, he had no model for an exception to his elegant rules. His friends had never really lived through a war and had certainly never served in one. His friends believed in diplomacy and tradecraft. They believed in ideas. They believed in progress measured in cups of tea sipped by men who'd never held guns. They were the soon-to-be smartest guys in the room in the smartest room in the world. And they believed that the smartest guys in the room were always right.

Sara cut off an argument by clinking her glass and making a toast. She ended by saying she'd never known what love of country meant until she'd observed her son, and seen him develop his own instinct for it. She described the time four years earlier when she'd given him extra money to buy something special at the market, something to boost his spirits. "I recommended champagne," she said, "or steaks. But my son came home with a flag." She toasted his godfather, too (" 'age cannot wither you, nor custom stale your infinite variety' "—words that reminded everyone of their ongoing casual, platonic flirtation), and recalled the spoons of her son's youth.

The very next day Sara again sat her son down and pressed him on whether he was sure about his choices. She asked if he would not consider waiting a year or two, maybe taking a master's degree or working at home, just doing something to engage him in another, less stressful environment, to pique potential other interests, to have some fun. She wanted him to understand the implications of doing something that seemed, well, so narrow. She expressed her Libran preference for options and for keeping roads open. She felt that the navy was the opposite of that, and that he had done so much "in service" already by spending those four years at the Academy. She saw things so differently. He barely said anything. And because he wanted to please her, he said he would take a day and think about it. And he did.

He didn't really know, even then, what it meant to belong to a culture of warriors or to be affiliated with "special" operations, but he knew he wanted more of a challenge, and the chance to try for the Teams was the best challenge he could get. It was because he felt confident that the military was one place he could excel. He felt sure that it might be the place where he might make an impact and that was something he desperately wanted to do. His skills were physical. But still, he thought about it for a day.

And then, just like that, his mind was made up. And though his mother always said that he had never been indecisive—he had been. But he would never let it show. That was another reason the military's culture suited him: its ethos of invisibility matched his. Somewhere he had developed a deep belief that a man was someone who acted, not someone who spoke, and that honor was about discretion and progress. Honor wasn't about discussing a political decision you hadn't been a part of over vodka tonics. He was not yet nineteen when he began to form these ideas. They were aspirational, and they were naïve. But as he held on to them they deepened, and soon the ideas began to form him.

Jason looks at the long stretch of swimming pool and thinks, *You and I are going to be close friends.* It was ten times the size of even the biggest pools he'd seen as a kid. It is the first morning of the first week in California.

"Flaubert wrote *Madame Bovary* while swimming laps," Jason says. As soon as he says it he wishes he hadn't, but the joke was one frequently repeated in his house, meant to underscore the artist's dislike of exercise.

"That water's fucking cold," says Sam, to another boy in his class. He'd dipped a toe in.

"It's not as cold as the ocean."

"Admirable optimism."

"Survival."

It is the first week, otherwise called INDOC, for Indoctrination Course. INDOC was the crucial first step, five weeks in which, among other things, the guys get to know one another—and get to know the water: the pool, and the surf. It's about about getting acquainted with the cold, with being wet, and with a culture of self-preservation and endurance. BUD/S is the base camp of an aspiring operator's Everest, and it is here that they begin to learn the language, draw the boundaries, and fall even more for the lure of what could lie ahead if they are allowed to progress.

In just days, Jason loses several pounds. He is not quite sure why. He is almost certain that the opposite should have happened. Even with all this running and rolling and pushing and lifting, his muscle mass should be increasing, and so should his base weight. Still, when he looks in the mirror, he can see his ribs. He is covered in sand, but he can still see his bones poking through.

Calories: the concept of counting them is ridiculous, something for silly girls on diets, not for warriors. But calories provide key data points, and calories give you what you needed to survive. Survival means making it successfully from one evolution to the next without dropping out. *The only easy day was yesterday.* This is one of many mantras they will learn and then internalize. *There is no second place in a gunfight* is another one. That one is easy to tease about in the early days of training; it will be only about eighteen months from now when their proximity to the reality of those words will make them much more serious. "Attention to detail, men. Attention to detail is what is going to get you through this. Attention to detail and commitment to team."

The instructors yell variations of the same seemingly simple ideas and words over and over, until they become oddly foreign, and then newly familiar as particular to this time and place. *Team. Detail. Drop. Push. Hoo-yah.* Master Chief Jones is the instructors' instructor, and he is very precise in how he talked to his class. Jason thinks that in another life and another time, the master chief and his mother would have made a great match. He can see them fighting about language and politics—about everything, really.

But he can also see them caring deeply about the simple things. Jones, not unlike Sara, despised pretension.

Detail and *Team* are two of Jones's favorite words, and they describe the larger concept: little things matter, and the fabric holding together the little things is the fabric of the Team. When a Team doesn't coalesce, the entire Team is blamed. There is no room—yet—for entrepreneurial thinking. And there is no room for assholes. Jones drills things into them. For him, training was an almost philosophical experience.

Once the focus of their training moves to the pool, Jason earns a nickname: Priest. Jones starts to call him that because he's so quiet and because he paces the hallways at night while reading ("prepping the sermons"), but also because all the instructors tease him saying that he must have a direct line to God from the pool. His ability to stay underwater without breathing for so long, and with such ease, was something they had not seen before. The others guys notice this gift and how lightly he wears it. "What do you say in your prayers," shouts the master chief. "Do you pray we don't find your third lung?"

*

When he was a baby, Jason and his mother lived in a tiny one-bedroom apartment. There was no bathtub. Sara would bathe him in an old plastic crate she'd emptied of books, set on the floor of the shower stall. He was swimming at two. "My little fish," she'd tell friends as they watched, horrified, as she pushed him out into the pool. "Don't worry. He can do it." By six he was swimming lengths underwater, for fun.

*

He isn't writing novels but sometimes, when he is underwater, when he is swimming as opposed to performing a task, Jason lets his mind wander. He thinks about the moments that have led to this one, and he questions his decision. He will never admit it, but sometimes he does question things. These concentrated thoughts allow him to forget the physical pain. He has made mistakes. On the obstacle course, in the second week, he had slipped and fallen, badly. His ankle had swelled up like a softball, but because he had heard of guys who kept running on broken legs to stay in training, he tried not to let it show. He had always had a system for managing discomfort, and until this point in his life it had worked well: he let his mind wander. He thought about his father. He would imagine meeting him in some exotic place—maybe near the Indian Ocean, maybe in the Middle East, maybe in "Mecca," a word he'd first heard on the answering machine in one of David's runic messages. These waking dreams acted like anesthesia. And he needs them now: for the first time in his life, Jason is experiencing true, sharp physical pain.

*

That last day that last summer at home before he'd left for San Diego, his mother had sat on his bed while he packed and begged him to reconsider his future. Again. She had said, "Don't make me beg." And then she said, "And I want you to know that if you get hurt, you have to tell someone. You cannot hide it anymore." He understood. The irony of which they were both aware that day was the fact that Jason's sense of determination, the same thing that gave rise to his pride, had to have come from somewhere. It had to have come from someone, and it could only have come from her. At least that was what Jason was thinking. Sara was thinking about the fact that her life was a case study in purposelessness. And here was her son, potential future four-star admiral.

If he survives. That was the subtext of her fears. And very soon she would learn that every choice and every moment and every thing in the military, and in the lives of family members who waited back home for their fathers and mothers and brothers and sisters and sons and daughters and lovers, was infused with the same fear. The threat of imminent, physical danger, something she'd only read about in books, was now going to be a central part of her life. But he wanted it. He was clear-headed and that clarity would serve him well.

Sara's height belied her strength. She was five foot six to her son's five foot eleven. He'd surpassed her in fifth grade. When he'd started at Annapolis, she'd taken up running, a form of exercise she'd long mocked as a "transportation sport." She had been born to dreamers, fallen in love with a dreamer, and then given birth to a dreamer, but she was furiously practical. She saved ribbons. She clipped coupons. She didn't dye her hair. Everything about her appearance was natural, another aberration for twenty-first-century postfeminists, everything right up to yet excluding the bright streak of white in her otherwise true brunette hair. It was a birthmark. David used to say, "No, it's my illuminated landing strip, so I can find you from thirty thousand feet at night, when necessary."

She didn't care what people thought about her, which made her a revolutionary in small-town life—or at least that was how Jason saw her. She was well known among his friends primarily for being beautiful, cool—and young. She was careful and consistent in her denial of traditional female rituals, adamant about being the girl who would never wear makeup to the movies or profess to care about her clothes. But most other women considered Sara less a threat than a tragedy, a spouseless loner in a socially networked world. She preferred reading to shopping. She loved ideas and grew into a woman who helped edit the ideas of others.

The night before his last day back east, before she would drive him to the airport, and perhaps in some gesture toward the symbols of commencements, Sara wore a white sundress while helping him prepare. Jason knew it was her very best one. She had her hair down that day, too, tied with a white ribbon, a style she rarely chose as she knew it made her look even more like a girl, even less like a mother, perhaps. He was twenty-one and she was forty. As he had moved around his room, finalizing his packing, she must have tucked the tiny wrapped box, his graduation present, under his pillow. It was a simple gold locket, with a St. Christopher on the outside and, on the inside, a picture of the American flag he had brought home from the market that day, the one that now hung outside their house. When he found it he walked down the hall to her bedroom to thank her.

"I can't believe how corny this is and how much I love it," he'd said.

"I'm allowed to be corny now." There were tears streaming down her face.

*

There were very few whose fathers had not been present at Academy graduation. And there were very few whose ideas of their fathers did not factor into their aspirations to be operators. And the father of all the other fathers is the master chief. It's the master chief who leads the men on their drills and on the long beach runs. Master Chief Jones is tough. He's witty. He has been in the Teams for thirty years. He tells the men stories from other wars, even as he never talks about his own service. He leads the hardest runs during the third week, the Long Day. Have you ever tried running after three nights of no sleep? It's a bit like kickboxing in honey.

It is dark. It is three in the morning. It is the fourth night of Hell Week, so by process of deduction, it's Wednesday. The men are very wet, cold, sandy, and tired. The Hell started on Sunday, with the "breakout." The thinking behind the breakout is that most battles begin in chaos. Chaos can be accurately simulated. Breakout—and Hell Week, more broadly—attempt to simulate the conditions of battle. These five days and five nights take the stress of extreme physical conditioning, then tack on sleep deprivation and the element of surprise.

Breakout begins with the men being told to wait in one large room. They are told they can talk and read and eat and relax, but they've heard the stories. They know exactly how breakout works: by creating chaos—and fear. When the first shots are fired, some are relieved; they've been ready. Others are broken. Suddenly they are in the closest thing they've been in to a live fight. And even knowing it's a simulation, and that adequate safety precautions are taken, some of the bravest-seeming among them will ring out within the first hour. The shock is too much. By Wednesday, those who remain think they will make it one more night. They put one foot in front of the other and rely on muscle memory. They are ready for relief. The Master Chief's songs are a form of relief.

They all know them by heart by now, because he has been singing them since day one—on the beach, on the Grinder, while checking their rooms. He likes to sing. And he likes you to sing, too. Sing softly, and you will drop and push them out. Sing too softly, and you gain the privilege of running once more into the water, and it's like ice. Then you can drop for a hundred more push-ups, in the process of which sand gets in your nose, your mouth, your eyes. The illusion that sand might lodge in your lungs and slow you on runs—or choke you—is powerful. Once you have that image in your mind it is tough to erase.

As the master chief sings, he will periodically slow his pace, or even run in place, allowing him to observe his men. A month ago, this class started with one hundred sixty trainees. Now they were thirty. He can see how red their eyes are. He can sense how close each one of them might be to the edge of breaking. They have been running in and out of the water on this one night for close to four hours. Running is like breathing here. Run to the O course. Run to eat. Run to rest, briefly. Run to gain the privilege of another, longer run.

Most of them are unaware of what hour or even what day it is. Still, somewhere underneath the exhaustion, the pain of spliced tendons and stress fractures and stomach muscles stretched to unholy lengths, there is a sense of release. This is what the singing does. The song goes like this:

> I've seen the bright lights of Memphis,
> And the Commodore Hotel,
> And underneath a streetlamp,
> I met a Southern Belle.
> Well, she took me to the river
> Where she cast her spell
> And in that Southern moonlight
> She sang her song so well
> "If you'll be my Dixie Chicken

I'll be your Tennessee lamb
And we can walk together
Down in Dixieland.
Down in Dixieland."

After Hell Week, the class size shrinks again, to nineteen. After Hell Week, they will have nine weeks of dive training and three weeks of hydrographic reconnaissance work. After that, their class size will stand at seventeen, one guy having injured himself during drown-proofing, another having failed pool competency, the one test Jason never tells his mother about, although she could have found out about it online if she'd wanted. Then the men leave the pool and learn land warfare. In this third and final chapter things become increasingly what might be called fun. The ones who remain will most likely complete the course. The tests they have endured up until this point have been largely psychological. The way their bodies have changed attested to the physical rigors they've endured.

Men about to end BUD/S are like steeplechase jockeys days before a race, only imagine jockeys who have not yet seen a horse, who are unable to distinguish a foal from a thoroughbred. They will have time to train, to learn more about what it means to fight and about which tools they will use. They will learn more about themselves, too. Self-knowledge makes the real warrior, and self-knowledge coupled with tactical skill allows a guy to say he is an operator. Throughout those early weeks, almost everyone was thinking the same thing: *Why did I make it, and why did he fail?* They will have years ahead to talk about it, but over time it will become clear.

On the last night, the few guys left gather at the master chief's house; he's invited them for beers, but most take Cokes. Master

Chief sits at his piano. It is a beautiful instrument, an ebony Steinway grand, a gift from someone at the Department of Defense, or so the story goes. He can really play. The rumor went around that he'd turned down Juilliard for the chance to make the Teams. Another rumor went that he'd been court-martialed after inviting Bobby Seale to speak on counterinsurgency at Quantico, in the 1970s. He played music familiar to most of them, Brahms, Beethoven, and Mozart; he knew the canon. But he knew Bob Dylan, too. He took requests when the class had had a good day. When Jason landed his boat crew on the rocks in a nasty rainstorm, he requested "Queen Jane, Approximately," a song Sara loved.

This night, their last night, he plays the song that has become theirs, a song that would serve for the rest of their lives as a reminder of what they'd been through these last six months. Phrases from it would stand as code in later years when they would meet classmates in unexpected places, allowing them to recognize one another. Only this night Jones sang a slightly different version, with lyrics they hadn't heard before. The guys sing along with the chorus once they get a handle on the words. It goes like this:

> *I've seen the bright lights of Beijing*
> *And the Chairman Mao Hotel*
> *And underneath the streetlamp*
> *I met an Asian Belle*
> *Well she took me to the River*
> *Where she cast her spell*
> *And in that Chinese moonlight*
> *She sang her song so well:*
> *"If you'll free my Dixie Mission*

I'll free your Tokyo lamb;
And we can sleep together
Down in old Ya'nan"

Dixie Mission, more formally called the United States Army Observation Group, was an Allied outpost in China during World War II. Jones tells them the story: how the "missionaries" were actually CBI Theatre experts sent there to observe and report. They were the first post-OSS team to go into China, and the rumor was that their name came from the presence of so many southerners in their midst. Critics keen to flame the fires of Communist fears demonized the Mission's men; they claimed the real mission was Red sympathy. But when the young envoys' reputations were shredded and they were individually stripped of roles at State and elsewhere, they took their case all the way to the Supreme Court to prove their innocence and won.

It was a story of uninformed fears, panic, and blame, of how intelligence collection and things in the category of "classified" are inherently controversial. It was also, Jones tells them, a story of wartime intelligence operations in their infancy. That story continued, in some ways, with Vietnam's Studies and Observations Group, or SOG, America's first joint unconventional force. The first frogmen were there then, and they were meant to be warriors, but they were also trained as witnesses and as interpreters—not of speech but of actions. They were trained to see things, remember them, and report them back home. Time on target ("at the objective," as they say) was preceded by time spent studying the opposition. Everything they did then entered the collective memory banks of mission histories, histories later locked up in places with very few keys.

*

Jason's class has begun the work, but they are not yet warriors. They have proven their ability to do certain things and to withstand others, but they have not yet experienced the hardest parts of the climb. They have not yet been forced to choose whether to take a life. They have not yet been confronted with the delicate task of lying to a loved one in order to protect her. They have not yet held a colleague's broken body in their arms. "The Strand is only a beginning," Jones said that last night, referring to San Diego's Silver Strand State Beach. This was their beach. Its name came from the silver-shelled oysters that washed up on the sand in scores. "The world is yours," Jones said, flipping one, like a coin, in the air.

CLOSE QUARTERS COMBAT

Sara stands and waits. She considers the fact that she's never been dressed properly for any occasion in her life, and here she is, about to receive news of her son, and she's soaking wet from sweat and rain, her hair in the wrecked ponytail that has become her signature.

When Jason was born, he came one month early. She had arrived at the hospital dressed not unlike how she's dressed now, a variation on Standard Issue Third Trimester. Learning that "it was time," she'd meekly left a message on David's office line and only half-expected him to show. But he was there, at the critical moment, and characteristically wry about the sex appeal of scrubs. It was a cesarean. ("A little Caesar!" David bellowed in the OR, much to the distress of the doctor, who didn't approve of the grave situation being mocked.) It was a cesarean, and then her baby boy was on her chest, breathing like a tiny puppy, waiting to be fed.

As she walks closer to the house the men just stand waiting, perhaps out of a sense of respect or perhaps in shock at the manner of her appearance. She can hear music coming from the house—Sam's music. Almost immediately after arriving to stay, he'd put his CDs in her kitchen, and while she never knows what album is about to be played, she was always pleasantly surprised. She likes reggae, and he knows it very well. He grew up in California, not far from Coronado; he loves to surf and spends hours talking about waves and wave patterns, about wind and the thermodynamics of kite boarding. She doesn't really care deeply about any of these things, but having him, and his music and his stories, helps. She remembers it is time to sleep, because he sleeps. She is cued to eat by his careful preparation of meals. And though there is no need for cooking given the amount of food brought as gifts, he can really cook. He cooks guy food: steaks and potatoes and fish pies. And she welcomes it, because these are foods she rarely eats on her own, foods that are not served in fancy D.C. restaurants, so they remind her of nothing.

One of the men puts his hand out and says, "Ma'am, good afternoon. I'm Captain Smith, and this is Master Chief Jones." She can feel her eyes flooding with tears, so she bites her lip.

"Ma'am," the chief says, and he reaches out a hand and holds— gently—on to her forearm, an awkward but powerful gesture. "We still don't know where your son is." Sara can't help the tears on her face. She doesn't care anymore. She is simply trying to keep breathing.

"We are here to see how you are," says the captain. She guesses he's about her age. Younger, perhaps. He has a lot of ribbons on his chest.

"I'm all right," Sara says.

"We want to help," says Smith.

"Thank you," she says.

Jones does not say anything. He looks like he could eat a small child for breakfast. She remembers his name. And possibly having met him. Was it Coronado? He's older, definitely older. He has the start of a beard and very cold eyes. Or maybe he's just tired. She is quite sure her eyes might be assessed as cold at this time.

"Please come in," she says. "And please excuse me a moment."

The men move into the kitchen. She can hear them talking with Sam. She walks back through the foyer to the stairs of the house—old, broken pre-Colonial wood steps she has promised herself to repair since moving there, but whose charm over time became so much a part of the house that she has left them. She looks at the envelope on the landing table, the letter Sam handed her the night he arrived, after convincing her to let him stay over. The letter was formally addressed to her in her full name. But inside the outer envelope, she knew, having opened it last night, is another envelope, and on this one is written one word in her son's handwriting: "Mommy." She was not ready for that. So she placed the letter on the small desk on the landing, right outside her bedroom, next to the phone forever blinking with too many messages.

She goes to the shower and undresses. She stands for a moment wondering what the rule is now, whether these men will expect a meal. Or worse: expect her to sit with them and talk. Who are they anyway? Do they really know her son? She showers, and after she showers, she puts on a pretty dress, something she knows that her son would like, something he would be proud to see her wear when doing the right thing for these men who are, in any event, only here to do something kind for her, something that is right, while being sad and uncomfortable. She finds them in the kitchen, stooped awkwardly on her little lacquer stools; they are laughing when she enters—so they stop.

"Please," she says. "I love having people in the house, and I want you to feel at home. I know that Jason is fine, and I know it is only a matter of time before he is here again, standing in this kitchen and doing exactly what you are doing. Please, will you stay for supper?"

But they demur, and after several glasses each of iced tea, they are on their way. She walks them to the car, and Jones makes an awkward motion to give her a hug. He takes off his sunglasses, and she can see he is emotional; maybe this is why he said so little at first. "Your boy is extraordinary," he says.

"Yes, I know that."

"Excuse me for saying this, but I simply didn't expect you to be so young. You look—you look about twenty-five years old."

"I'm older than that," she says, and can't help a smile. Seeing someone so powerful disarmed charms her.

"We will find him," the captain says. "We will find him."

"I know," she says. "I have a birthday cake for him."

The men drive away. Now here she is in the house at her least favorite part of the day, with an afternoon of hours to fill and that letter on the landing. She doesn't want to read and she doesn't want to sleep and she doesn't want to talk to anyone who is going to say anything sentimental or maudlin. So she goes and finds Sam. He is in the kitchen, cooking. She gets a glass of water and lingers, waiting for him to say something, but he doesn't, so she starts.

"What is he like?" she asks.

"What is who like?" he says.

"My son. What is he like? What is he like to work with?"

And she sits down at the little "eating square," as Jason had called it, the one someone who clearly didn't know her, or her taste, had given her—with the matching stools. And she listens.

"To work with? He's an artist."

"Artist?"

"He's talented. Quiet, talented. He taught me a lot."

"Taught?"

"He taught me about how to dial it down."

"Dial what down."

"Temperament. Emotion. Stress. One of my first memories of him is standing by the side of the pool, in California, that first week. He was referencing some obscure book."

"Do you remember what it was?"

"I don't. But what was cool was that he did it in a way that was not about proving anything; he wasn't arrogant."

"No, but he used to love to read," she says.

"He was quiet."

"He's shy," Sara says.

"Shy?"

"Reserved. The book talk: that's a default setting. He gets that from—"

"Default setting?"

"Yeah. Our default settings are rarely our best selves."

"I think my default setting then was fear."

"The training was tough."

"Yes. Everyone was terrified. Even the guys too proud—or possibly, too stupid—to show it."

"Or maybe just too young."

"Having to hide a broken ankle teaches you something about yourself," Sam says.

Sara has an instinct to say something along the lines of *you can go you don't have to stay*, but instead she just keeps listening. And Sam says, "You sent the books."

"It sounded like the pickings were slim."

"Well, everybody took note of the fact that you sent them to all of us."

"Thirty-seven plays is a lot for any one person."

"Those books are still in the little library at the Naval Special Warfare Center."

"I remember sending th m. I remember—"

"Shakespeare."

"Yeah, Shakespeare. And a few other things." She notices how careful he is with the food. He never asked if he could use the kitchen; he just saw that no one was cooking, and he moved to fill the void.

"He was into thinking and talking about thinking. And helping."

"Helping?"

"Yeah. He always helped the other guys."

"Kind of sounds like a group of guys who don't need that much help."

"Not true," Sam says. "Guys get tired. You're pushed. One guy was really struggling. It's due to Jason that he made it to the Teams. On the runs, he would fall behind, and Jason would drop back and run behind him. He would push him—literally push him forward so he could make it. That struck everyone."

"He's good at that. Helping."

"And in the water he was like a fish."

"He loves the water," Sara says.

"The guys used to joke that maybe he had a third lung. And he always said these crazy things."

"Like what crazy," she says.

"Like 'follow knowledge like a sinking star, beyond the utmost realm of human thought.' "

"Tennyson," she says.

At that moment, one of the local cops patroling the property pops his head in the small screen door off the kitchen.

"Hey Sara, we have a little crowd out here building up again," he says. "I think the local reporters saw that government car and wanted to know—"

"We don't have any news," says Sara.

"I'll just keep 'em out at the end of the driveway, okay? They're noisy, but don't worry about it. Guys from the papers, mainly. They shake their pencils, but they don't like it when they think I might use this," he says, tapping his handgun, smiling.

"Thank you," she says. She had seen him remove it and load it the night he had arrived at the house.

And then Sara says, "Alfred, Lord Tennyson. He wrote a poem called 'Ulysses,' and that's a line from that poem. Jason's father used to quote it, too. 'Little remains: but every hour is saved from that eternal silence, something more, a bringer of new things; and vile it were for some three suns to store and hoard myself, and this gray spirit yearning in desire—to follow knowledge like a sinking star, beyond the utmost bound of human thought.' The poem is about a warrior in repose. It's about Ulysses, back from the *Odyssey*. He misses the war."

"What does he miss?"

"Have you read the *Iliad*?"

"I have."

"That's what he misses," she says. And then, "Jason worshipped his father. And his father loved poems."

"We eventually impressed upon him the importance of training his poetry skills on more popular artists."

"Like?"

"Like Eminem." Sam is laughing.

"Eminem?"

"Yeah. It got him into trouble once. We were in the Kill House. Will you eat pesto?"

"Sure," she says. "What's a Kill House?"

"He believed the world could be a better place. He was honest."

"I might call that idealism, not honesty."

"Sorry, two separate thoughts: he believed the world could be a better place. And I believed he was honest. All the guys did. And that meant something."

They sit for a while. Sara doesn't know what to do with herself. She looks out the window, past Sam's shoulders. She can see movement at the end of the drive through the trees and the rain, like a poorly lit silent film. *Signifying nothing*, she thinks.

"The Kill House is where we learn how to clear rooms. Close quarters combat."

"I remember close quarters combat."

"Jason used to call it 'The Royal U.S. Navy Performs *Swan Lake*.' "

Hearing her son talked about in this way only reminded her how little she had seen of him through these past nine years, and how desperately she misses him. Sam keeps talking. "He was—"

"Can you say 'is' please?"

"Yes, of course. I'm just thinking back to Coronado. It feels like a long time ago. Like we were just kids. It all felt so serious. I remember saying to my mother, 'I'm not going to USC. I'm joining the navy.' "

"After nine eleven."

"Yeah."

"What did she say?"

"She thought for sixteen years I'd be a surf rat."

"So she was happy."

"She was happy. She saw it as a calling. She's—she's very religious. She felt that this was my calling."

"Did you see it that way?"

"Well, they beat that out of you pretty quickly. Pretense. Any idea that—"

"Nobility?"

"Nobility," Sam says, laughing. "Nobility doesn't place a gun in the fight." And then he says, "On my last leave, I went to the Imperial War Museum in London. I'd never been there."

"I should go," says Sara.

"They have a diorama in one room of the World War I trenches. You could see, you know, the 'front line,' and you could see all these tiny little toy soldiers stuck in the trenches. And then you could walk through a real life-size trench they had constructed. When you're in the trench, they have noises playing, like shots ringing out, people screaming. And they've got little scenes re-created, guys in anterooms within the trenches doing things like smoking a pipe or writing a letter or sleeping—like little luxury suites set up within the eye of the storm of war. Within that eye, people are still living and talking and laughing. And I remember thinking, well, of course they can do this in trench warfare because it's all so . . . orderly. I couldn't get over how neat—and how brutal—that trench system was. And then I got back to the base, and Jason was there with, of course, his total history of trench warfare on call, at his fingertips—'abridged for you, dude,' he would have said. He said the difference between waiting in the trenches and doing what we do is the difference between begging for a bullet and learning how to precision fire. Defense versus offense. He said the statistics for quick death were in our favor, even if the enemy was less prone to play by the rules."

"Quick death?"

"I'm not sure whether he stayed up all night online, reading about all these things, or whether he learned about them before he arrived, but he knew so much about so much. We should have called him Encyclopedia."

"What did you call him?" asks Sara.

"We called him Priest."

"Priest?"

Sara smiles at the irony: here was a boy with a lapsed Jewish father and an agnostic mother who grows up to be called Priest. David really would have loved that.

"I think I'll go rest for a while," she says.

"Do you mind the music?"

"I love it. Please don't ever turn it off." And she wanted to add, *And please don't leave me*, but she didn't.

*

Upstairs, she goes to the window in the little office space between her room and Jason's. Looking out, she can see the crowd gathered at the end of the driveway. *I should sell lemonade*, she thinks darkly. *Who are all these people*. But she knows many of them are good people, people who only want to help her, or who want to help her to tell the story of her son. There are two news trucks now, and she can see the blond jailbait on-air reporter circling one of them, adjusting her collar and licking her lips. Perhaps she's the award-winning war correspondent, just back from Iraq, Sara thinks. She decides that the girl has had a life far more interesting than her own: she has traveled, she has seen the world, she has met with heads of state and warlords, and she has her own show on in prime time, viewed by millions. She's an "unqualified" success, and she will wait awhile before having children because she can. She can have it all. Sara wonders, briefly, what that woman would think of a woman like her, but she already knows the answer.

She lies down on her bed, then gets up and walks back into the office. In her desk, she's kept file folders of e-mails from Jason, printed out and carefully arranged according to date. Sometimes when she printed them, she would think, *They'll want these for his biography*, and other times she'd simply think it would be fun to share them with him when he gets home. She'd never sat down to reread them but she's sure when she does, she'll see a stark chart of his evolution in thinking about himself, and about the military, and about the war. She fusses through a few early sets, and then pulls out one marked "SQT," her own title for a series of mails that arrived throughout that first tranche of training after Jason left Coronado. Close quarters combat was one thing he would study during that time, but it was also something he would return to even after assignment to a Team. It would become, she imagined, what he would spend much of his time doing abroad—although once he went abroad (*abroad* is not the word he would have used), the letters became less and less about what he was doing and more and more about what he remembered of being at home. Or, about history. Once he was in the Teams, he never wrote anything too close to his own situation, and she knew that was for a reason.

The first letter starts out like they all do: "Dear M."

Dear M.,

How are you? Is the house quiet now? Do you prefer it like that? I know the answer.

So Otay Lakes: that's where we are. Jump school used to be at Ft. Benning, where Buddy Glass recovered from pleurisy. Did you remember that? Buddy was in the army; I bet he got a better bed.

We are here for a kind of recovery, too; recovery from real training. (That's a joke.) We're here for Tactical Air Operations. It's a bit of the best bits and the worst bits about any holiday: a little restful; a little dull; lots of long stretches of waiting broken by moments of discovery.

The moments of discovery come in the air, mostly. Jumping out of a plane is not nearly as terrifying an experience as I imagined it might be. I'd never really thought about heights until that wide-open aircraft door, nothing to halt my fall but sky. We never lived anywhere higher than the second floor, did we. I realized, looking down—rather than up—at the clouds, that I had spent almost my entire life at low altitude.

Once you jump, you really can imagine, for the briefest moment, that that isolation, calm, and sense of freedom can last forever. At the very start of the jump, things move fast. Then once your chute opens they move v e r y s l o w l y. It's peaceful. It's exhilarating. Then before you know it, it's landing time, and there's the ground rushing up beneath your feet. Fast. And you know you'll be all right because you have to be all right. And then you are grateful when you are. Very grateful.

Air's a major source of transportation for us. You once told me that when you look at words on a page, you only notice when they're not working. So with chutes. Of course, certain death being the outcome of malfunction in this case is a factor that focuses a guy's mind.

The chutes are beautiful. Sometimes you might open your chute, look around, and see tens of other chutes opening, too, one by one. Pop. Pop. Pop. Pop. I think of them like ice cream cones—colored ice cream cones in the air. Here is a picture.

What else: yes, I am eating enough. And yes, they let us sleep more now. And no, I am not getting into any trouble. Yet.

Love,

Jason

She had printed out the picture attached to the e-mail: the ice cream cones. He must have taken it from the ground, after landing, and it was truly beautiful. It was strange that something where a group of young men were risking their lives could look so elegant, so effortlessly coordinated. She thinks about the luxury suites in the trenches. She pulls out the next letter.

Dear M.,

Remember that little baby turtle? I kept him in that dish. And then he escaped. He had a lot of courage to climb out of that dish, didn't he—and out of our house. They call it "turtle-backing" when we swim on the surface. Turtle backing helps conserve energy, which perhaps explains our little prisoner's strength for his solo expedition back to the pond.

Conservation is key. In the water, with your weapons—you're always conserving something. I know you like stories of swimming or soaring through the air, but the learning of what we do on the ground has felt less a curve than a hockey stick: quick panic and first failure followed by a steady upward trajectory. Some things require less physical endurance but more mental precision. Most of the guys here are not entirely new to guns.

Whatever happened to the guns in the basement in Virginia? If there is anything left in our basement now, I promise I can identify each piece. I could also put a price tag on each piece. Who knows: you might have a very valuable collection. More valuable than melons.

I can now use the following: an M4 rifle, and Mk46 machine gun; an Mk48 machine gun; an AK-47; a hand grenade; a Carl Gustaf rocket; a LAAW; a Claymore mine. ("LAAW" stands for Light Anti Armor Weapon, by the way.) Before this the only weapon I had any skill with was my electric toothbrush.

I've been thinking about Dad a lot. I wish I had had the

chance to talk with him again. There are so many questions I was never able to ask.

I know he had his reasons for leaving. I can remember certain things he said. I remember him saying: where your skills intersect with your interests is where you should try and spend the majority of your time, or the man who finds the work he loves, the gods have smiled on him, or carpe diem. I think my skills intersect with my interests in the navy. I know you probably don't want to hear that. It's true. You can tell my godfather. Please tell him I bet they don't teach land warfare to legislative aides.

How is that garden? I know the neighbors invite you over every night, and I know you never go. You should go.

Love,

Jason

She had called his godfather after receiving that letter and gone insane about the weapons.

He was laughing on the other end of the line.

"He's enjoying himself."

"He's not meant to be *enjoying* himself!"

"Sara."

"It sounds dangerous."

"Sara."

"It sounds unsupervised."

"*Sara.*"

"Rocket?"

"What did you expect, Sara? That he'd be baking apple pies? War requires weapons, and someone has to shoot them. This is what war means. Remember: Naval Special *War*fare?"

"I thought—"

"But don't worry: the training's all a bunch of simulations. He's at no risk."

"None?"

"None. You think they want to soak up that liability? They just shake them up and scare them."

"No risk?"

"Risk comes later."

"That's comforting."

"I was the one who tried to talk him out of it." And there was a long pause on the line, and she could hear him wishing he hadn't just said that.

"I don't think I can handle this," she said, eventually.

"It gets easier," he said gently. "And statistically, I can assure you that he will be fine."

"Statistically. And emotionally?"

"That's why I'm waiting to have children until I no longer feel anything."

She had gone and methodically looked up each one of those guns online. The only one she'd ever heard of before was the AK-47, and that was from some movie about the Soviets in Afghanistan. Google gave up the facts: Kalashnikov was twenty-seven when he designed the AK; he attributed its simplicity to ideas he'd learned reading Russian novels. And he said, she read, "to make something simple is a thousand times harder than to make something complicated." When she looked at the pictures of it, she imagined her son holding one. She had to let go of that thought. It was too foreign.

Most of the letters were not about guns or weapons. Only when she prodded him with questions would he answer with an ordnance lesson. She looks through the letters for the one about close quarters training. She wants to see whether there was ever any reference to a Kill House. She is sure there wasn't; she would have remembered that phrase. But her interest is piqued from Sam's mentioning it. She wants to imagine what it looks like, and she wants to believe that the skills her son learned training in that house are the same skills keeping him alive now, wherever he is. She wants to learn that the nature of his training was so specific—and so rigorous—that it will see him through this, whatever "this" is. He loved history.

Dear M.,

I had an e-mail from my history professor at the Naval Academy. He sends me articles, things he thinks I might not otherwise see. He always believed in me. He always listened. He understood why I wanted to do this; he didn't think it was weak or wrong or easy. Or romantic. He never pushed us into it, but he understood. He was a pilot; did you know that? He was the first one who told us that the way people would fight now would be very different from the way they fought in past wars.

He was right. What we are learning now is that so much of warfare is fought at close quarters, and the essence of fighting in close quarters is restraint. Restraint, intelligence, conservation. This emphasis changes the calculus of war. Think about 1916: in forty-eight hours, something like four thousand men were wounded. Four thousand men. And by the end of the Battle of the Somme there were another half million casualties. One of the guys here showed me a book where the authors excerpt memoirs written by the medics who helped the wounded in the Great War. The medics all said the same thing: the young men they encountered on their rounds possessed a remarkable self-lessness. And many of them, mortally wounded, would say to the medics, "Hey, help the next guy." Or they would say, "My friend over there needs water." Most of those soldiers were younger than I am now.

There was an acceptance of suffering as necessary. People didn't know anything else. Technology didn't promise a "surgical" solution. Planes didn't go down without pilots in them.

"Teamwork" is the word I hear again and again here. We're not heading into the Somme, and we know it. But that's one thing that binds past wars to present ones: everything is about the Team. The aim of fighting now is to restrict casualties. We are being taught how to enter rooms in foreign places, and the most important thing is making sure that anyone in those rooms who is not armed is not hurt.

I'm trying to say something about the difference between a battlefield and a room. And I'm trying to say that a lot has changed, but some things stay the same.

Love,

Jase

"Think about 1916": that was very David. Ever so gently professorial. Who said things like that. He wants her to feel like she's there. He wants her to know he's learning something. And he never complains. She tries not to complain, but she does feel alone, even with Sam in the house. She thinks about this while sifting through the other letters, and then she sees it, right there on the page, and she realizes that she had either completely forgotten about it or—is it possible—printed out this letter without ever having reading it.

Dear M.,

Not much news. More close quarters work. In this phase of the training we use a real house—it's meant to mimic a real house, but it's been built for us to train for real-life situations. We use Sims—the Simunitions. The pistols and rifles we use have been re-chambered and re-barreled: they fire, basically, paint pellets.

The exercises make me think about the paintball games at home. Remember those highly orchestrated all-day "wars" we played in the woods out back of the farm in Chadds Ford? Do you remember how scared I was about them right after we moved there? Those kids were fierce. And they took it so seriously. I remember it was such a big deal—who would play with whom, who got what color, who had the best-quality pellets, who had the most of whatever. I remember everybody sitting around discussing their "guns" and their "victories" and their "victims." We were in sixth grade.

I remember that it was a real point of pride to come to school on Monday mornings after the games with some paint on your shirt. It was always the same guys who showed up with a little bit of paint. Just a little bit. They couldn't resist. Like they didn't have another shirt. Or a washing machine. Those paint pellets actually really hurt when they hit you. Just for a minute they really hurt, like a shot at the doctor's office.

So here I am, about to begin the next phase of what probably seems to you like a never-ending training process. It *is* a bit like a medical residency, although there is less blood, more physical contact. And there is probably about as much information to be processed and memorized. But I can read a map, and I can staunch a wound, and I can hit a target from three times as far away as I could have done before. I know what you're thinking: is any of this worth anything?

You'd appreciate the language. For almost every word you can think of in civilian life, there is a military analog, another word, a slang term or nickname or code. Or acronym.

I never thought about certain things before. I never thought about how I stand, how I allocate my weight and how stable—or unstable—that makes me. I never thought about how best to brace myself against a blow. I never thought about how best to make contact with another person, especially if that person is threatening me. And I never thought about what they call our Inner Warrior. The Inner Warrior might not be the most unique name (I know: unique doesn't need a modifier), but the concept is connected to so many things that you talked to me about through the years.

The Inner Warrior is kind of like the Editor inside us. It is the voice you hear that tells you not just what to do but what not to do, too. The Inner Warrior is always at his desk, checking errors of commission v. omission, etc. We talk a lot about variable force skill, which is exactly what it sounds like: you have to be able to do everything, and then you have to have the ability to refrain from doing anything. That last skill is often the most powerful of all.

For example: if I was entering a room and there was a man there that I knew to be a threat, but there was also a woman standing next to him, what would I do. And what if that woman is holding the hand of a small child. Well, I would handle that situation differently than if I entered a room and there were three men there, military age men (MAMs). I would handle that situation differently, perhaps, depending on the ages of those men, depending on what they were holding in their hands, and depending on what time of day it was, and depending how we were configured for backup assistance.

Each choice—or option—has to be mapped out in your mind so clearly that executing any one of them is like picking ties off a rack to match your shirt. You select on instinct, not emotion: my shirt is blue, so I need the red tie. White shirt, blue tie. And those instincts come from learning the rules, then practicing them. What it means is: internalizing the available patterns of behavior removes—or slims—the margins of error. There should be no margin of error, even as the existence of a margin of error is inherent in making a choice.

Warfare is not like "shoot-'em-ups," as Dad would say.

There is a precision to all of our actions. Having the guns and knowing what to do with them is a little like having access to a new language. And there are lots of challenging environments where saying less is more. Restraint might not be the first thing next to Godliness, but it's close. Restraint is part of the ethos.

Love,

J

"Shoot-'em-ups" was another Davidism, one that had trickled down into Sara's vocabulary and so—she was only mildly shocked to see—into her son's. David had used it to describe unlinked, diverse things, to describe anything violent—a bloody movie, a bloody battle, a fight between lovers. He would have appreciated life in the presence of these new technologies that allowed you to lie in bed and watch a real war at the same time as you watched a war movie at the same time as you navigated a fight with a lover in texts. He had always claimed to prefer staying home, as most people who rarely stay home tend to do, and she could imagine him managing multiple small screens at once to maximum effect. Life was so quiet before all the technology, and in the months after Jason was born they shared a special stretch of downtime. David was not traveling and almost every night he would come over, even if he didn't stay. They would watch films in between feedings.

David loved the movies. One of their first dates, in steaming hot D.C. that summer they met, was at the multiplex. She remembered wondering if the ticket taker thought David was her father, and then feeling that she really didn't care. He made her laugh. And even in the years after she came to be angry with him for leaving her, he could still make her laugh. He would have loved these letters from his son; he would have seen himself in them.

One irony of Jason being gone was that, unlike other mothers who perhaps saw their sons more often, these letters were a look into the soul of a boy becoming a man. She knew each time she saw him throughout those years of training he would be changed slightly, yet forever. The letters prepared her. He was slipping away.

There is another picture, loose in the box. It is a close-up of a boy's shoulder, and on it are tattooed these lines:

> *But after the fires and the wrath*
> *But after searching and pain,*
> *His mercy opens us a path*
> *To live with ourselves again.*

When she saw it for the first time, she could not believe he had a tattoo. But then she saw by the bit of hair in the frame that it was not her son's shoulder. The hair was too dark. And the shoulder wasn't shaped the same way. Her son had strong shoulders. She finds the letter accompanying it.

Dear M.,

This is a picture of a tattoo one of the guys here has. He's a good friend of mine. I asked him what the words meant, and he said they were from a poem. Do you know it? I think the poem is about learning to process and live with the scars of war. I love "His mercy opens us a path."

I do think God watches over us and over what we do. I do think that there is something else besides just us out there. Don't you think that there has to be? Aside from stars. It's curious to some of the guys I've met that we don't go to church. Even on Christmas.

We talk about family. A few guys here are closer to their

grandfathers than they are to their fathers. Some of the guys have grandfathers who fought in World War II; they told stories that inspired their grandsons to serve. One guy's grandfather was in Vietnam; his father's not much older than you are. Doing the math now, I was thinking it's possible that Dad's father was in WWII.

I have a new pistol. When I am home next, I am going to set up a little target in the backyard and show you how to use it.

Love,

Jason

This letter was the first time her son had asked about David's past or his family. But the truth was she didn't know. She had never met David's parents. David was so much a "grown-up" in her eyes when they met that that part of a more normal courtship ritual hadn't been assumed, nor had its absence been questioned. They didn't talk about their parents. They didn't talk about where they grew up or where they went to school or who they'd dated. David didn't care about her past, and perhaps she was too intimidated to ask about his. He was secretive. As far as she knew, his life began at Yale. Before that, there was nothing but a wide, blank slate. He liked it that way.

They were more interested in the present. They would argue about what was in the paper on any one day, or what someone had said in the hallway at work. David liked to intelligently undermine others' attempts at Meaning, in case someone started to take life too seriously. He mocked friends who posed questions not unlike the ones she now saw in the letters from their son. He mocked anyone who wanted something more or, worse, who believed that there actually was more than what lay right in front of you. And while she was with him, she'd absorbed some of this, even if it never quite fit her. But it was only when she read Jason's letters that it occurred to her that underneath his shell, David had probably been someone who had also raised the same kinds of questions, who had tried to *follow knowledge like a sinking star,* who had believed in something greater than himself.

What do you say to a boy about the fact that you barely knew the man who was his father. She had written back something brief and general, something like "your father loved you and he would be so proud of you." Which was true. And it was also true that David had done things for her that no one before or since had done. She always knew that other men would step in to assist with the things fathers traditionally did. But most of David's friends were so much older, with lives that seemed much larger than hers. As Jason grew up, she placed herself outside the center of David's life story. She didn't have the perspective then to see his side of things. David would have placed her in the center.

If David were alive and around, he'd be summoning up some classical reference, then immediately undercutting the references with a joke. He loved mythology. He used to tell Sara stories from D'Aulaires or Edith Hamilton on their dates. She was impressed, even when she learned later that he had reread the stories right before picking her up. "Proper planning prevents poor performance," he would say when caught out. One of the myths she loved best and begged David to tell and retell was the story of Thetis and Achilles. Thetis, the glamorous sea nymph, held her son by his ankle and dipped him in the River of Immortality. How could she not have thought about the fact that the place where she held him the tightest would be the place left uniquely vulnerable? David would argue that the myth is about the fact that behind all great warriors there is a great woman. But Sara felt the story was a parable of motherhood. We must love them, and then let them go. She wishes she'd had a chance to dip her son in that river. She would not have been as careless as Thetis.

*

Sara hears Van Morrison's "Sweet Thing" downstairs and realizes it must be getting on in the afternoon. She had promised Sam she would come to the table tonight and eat a proper meal. She wonders what might take her mind off things because she has been unable to focus on anything for more than ten minutes these last days. The nights are worse because she can't sleep, and she has read too many newspapers and too many books not to imagine where her son is and what might be happening to him. One thing she cannot imagine: that a faraway war, one to which she has felt connected in an extremely peripheral way but connected to nonetheless—is now one in which she has become a well-known name, a headline, a new nexus for fresh analysis.

She goes to the window. The trucks remain. The cops corral them. She can see a young girl who lives in the town coming up the driveway with some packages, escorted by another cop. She thinks that she is more likely coming to see Sam. Maybe they will cook dinner together, allowing her to remain upstairs without seeming rude. Maybe he'll throw over his fiancée, fall in love here, and get married, in her garden. Maybe they will ask Sara to speak at the wedding, and she will give a talk about glass eyes and glass hearts—the former impenetrable, the latter quick to shatter. Maybe they will have a child who will be born into a world of newly smart wars, where there are no longer even weapons, just rows of video screens where we touch and swipe the places we want to destroy, or make circles around the places we want to protect. The individual operator will be less necessary, but the concept of service will remain.

She looks at the box of letters and remembers one about a series of congressional hearings following 9/11, and thinks she will take it out and fold it up and send it to Jason's godfather. She knows that others miss Jason almost as much as she does, and she knows his godfather feels uniquely at fault—that somehow he was the one who was meant, and failed, to steer her son away from this path. But no one could have steered him away. Still, she'll look at the letters and send them to the different people who have been meaningful in her son's life. This will give them something personal. And she doesn't want them anymore. They're reminders of a different time, when there was more hope on all sides. Looking for that one letter, she finds another one she had entirely forgotten about.

Dear M.,

Did you know how President Kennedy supported the idea of America having dedicated "special" operators? Kennedy commissioned the first two Teams; these were the guys who went into Vietnam. After Cuba, the president realized that one thing we needed was a force fit for unconventional warfare.

The president knew keeping kill ratios in one's favor was the way you won wars then; statistics were the tool for communicating how a fight was faring. Were there fewer bombs, more bodies? No, there were lots of bombs, lots of bodies. And now we have "smarter bombs," fewer bodies. It's a better equation. Did Dad ever talk about the war, his war? Vietnam. Did he ever mention the Teams. The guys in that war had it rough. And then they came home, and they had it even rougher.

After the Second World War, our men came home on boats.

Those crossings allowed the soldiers time to connect to others who had fought. They had time to talk about what they had been through, where they had been, what they had seen. I bet they sat on those boats and they told stories. And then they came home, and most of them didn't say a thing. Maybe it was that time talking with one another that meant they didn't need to talk as much when they came home. Or maybe they had a code, like we do. They were coming home heroes. They were coming home to a time when America felt a lot of pride. But I bet they saw some things they weren't proud of.

After Vietnam, we airlifted our guys out; they came home on planes. A few hours, and they went from a jungle to a Dairy Queen. They didn't have the chance to talk. They didn't have a chance to share their stories. Maybe we have not looked closely enough at the importance of how you exit a war, at the importance—the risk—of keeping civilian life's rituals in such close proximity to the realities of war.

What happens after our wars? I think about you saying that the three months after having the baby is the "fourth trimester." Maybe something comes after the end of a war that's like that: a fourth trimester. You said the fourth trimester is the hardest. You said, once you give birth, the baby has a mind of his own.

Love,

Jason

He is so naïve, she thinks—with a great deal of love. And envy. She wonders if her own mind ever worked that way, with that clarity, and she thinks that what's really ironic is the contrast between what he's doing and what he's thinking. The letters grew shorter. She was embarrassed to be relieved when she saw a shorter letter, but she was. It meant fewer questions. And that meant fewer things for which she lacked answers.

Dear M.,

The guys are passing around these memos. They were submitted to the *Congressional Record* during hearings over "enhanced interrogation techniques"—after 9/11. They were written by judge advocates general serving overseas. Have you read them? Have you heard about them? They're amazing. What's amazing is that the JAGs are the ones defending the existing rules. It's the JAGs who are saying, "Give our guys wise boundaries." What they are defending is the preservation of a culture. They argue that to change the military culture is to place that culture at risk, and that it's the culture that holds the diverse communities in the military together. The culture, and the history. They are saying, If you change the culture, you risk breaking down the entire system. Remember my letter about the use of wise restraint? Rules are comforting; it's not a fine officer's instinct to break rules. We're highly trained to hew to rule.

(I know what you're thinking: you're thinking that I should go to law school when I get out of here.)

Speaking of future and alternative career paths, I got a package from the Hill. Typically, it came by FedEx even though there's no rush on my side. There was no letter, just a box of tiny little cards, like business cards, but thicker. I knew who they were from given the return address. Instead of my name, they have this quote:

The soldier above all other people prays for peace, for they must suffer and bear the deepest wounds and scars of war.

It's General MacArthur. I couldn't tell if his sending me this was a sign of support, or a reminder. I couldn't tell if he intends for me to distribute them, or maybe he means for me to paste them on the base doors?

Whatever he means, you can tell him: I pray for peace. I include a lot in my prayers these days, but peace is right up there at the top of the list. We all do. We pray for peace, and we pray for the preservation of our culture. Just like everybody else, we're into survival.

Your parents would find it funny: their grandson goes to war only to learn to pray for peace. Consistency, rule, restraint, peace. Peace is a word that has always meant the same thing, hasn't it? Like rules, definitions that don't change have something comforting about them. Consistency helps a culture hold. Culture seems like a soft idea, but culture can change a kill ratio. Culture can save a life. This is one of the things I've learned, and believe.

Love,

J.

She would find those JAG memos, and she would read all of them, and her son was right. They all say more or less the same thing: *Don't adjust the means to suit an end. Don't place our tradition at risk.* Through her son, she had begun to see another side to military culture. She had begun to understand. *The most interesting people are the people you don't know. The eagle bows his head.*

*

David had died in December 1992. She had found out only minutes before leaving the house to pick Jason up from school. She was already running late. She was abrupt when she answered the phone—*"Yes?"*

It was a death too close to Christmas. Still, in the car, when the local public station reported news of "an American dead in the embassy" in Jeddah, Sara turned it up, not off. A few people she'd never heard of said things she wouldn't remember about David and his career. In time, David's friends would all have their say, too, one in an op-ed in a major newspaper. She would clip it and save it for Jason because the author, a federal judge, had written about what she'd always believed was David's actual talent: telling stories. In that, he'd been gifted and relentless and generous. He would spend hours talking into the night with peers or protégés, deadlines be damned, rest shelved as an unnecessary indulgence. And somehow he made ideas neither novel nor unique to him sound necessary, relevant, and new. He believed the world could be made a better place by conversation and argument—and wit. That was his religion, or had been.

She remembered spending hours considering Jeddah on a map in an atlas in her office. It's in Saudi Arabia, a coastal city on the Red Sea. It gets its name from the Arabic word for "grand-mother," after the idea that Eve's tomb is there. *Eve: of course he died somewhere called after Eve*, Sara had thought. She had rung a former assistant of his, with whom she'd once been close, and the assistant had said, "Sara, he loved it there. Jeddah is considered the Gate to the Holy City, the gate to Mecca. He died in the right place. He died doing what he loved." But what did he love? She felt shock and anger: shock that he was gone, and anger that there was so much she didn't know. She fought hard not to remember the last time she saw him, as she knew the most crucial thing now was to keep calm. She had to protect their son.

As she drove to collect Jason, the snow was falling, and she was thinking that in three years she would be thirty. When he got into the car, she decided not to tell him anything until she was clear on how to talk about it, on exactly which words to use. And she knew he would try not to cry; already at such a young age his resistance to pain in all forms had become a recurring quirk. When they got home, he went up to his room, and she had called his godfather, in a panic. "Help me, please." He offered to drive out and take Jason for a walk and talk to him, which he did. On Christmas Eve when she tucked her son into bed, he had said, "Mommy, do you think Daddy decided to die right before Christmas so we would never forget him?"

And she had said, "Yes, definitely. That's just like your daddy."

There was no formal memorial service. David wouldn't have wanted one. But a few of his closest friends gathered other friends at a house near the Mall, and Sara went, and took Jason. There were lots of beautiful women, women she'd never met, and several of them seemed mildly drunk and very upset. Sara asked Jason's godfather, "Are these all the lovers?"

And he had said, "At Brecht's funeral, there were many mistresses, but everyone knew who the great love was."

"How?"

"She was the only one who wasn't crying."

"Thank you," said Sara, as if his anointment meant anything. And then she left, because she wanted to get her son to bed, but also because she felt alone and strange in that room, filled with its walking validations of how little she had known the man who was the father of her child. Still, she missed him. Her anger for his having left was only ever in inverse proportion to her wishing he had stayed.

Apparently David hadn't been taking care of himself, which was not surprising. Within six months of the memorial drinks party, as she thought of it, she was sent a very large check in the mail along with several boxes of David's books and a few smaller odds and ends—lighters, broken early-era cell phones, a belt buckle. David didn't smoke, and he didn't wear belts. The phones' SIM cards had been removed or damaged. Said another way, these were not his prized possessions. If he had any possessions at all, she was not sure where those went. But David didn't care about things; he cared about people, ideas, and information. Once they went away together for a week when she was pregnant. He had met her at the airport with a briefcase. "Hey," he'd said, responding to her raised eyebrow and her two suitcases. "I travel light." Sara refused to be the widow taking up the pose of mourning. It had been too long. It was not her place. Those women at the party probably shared more intimate interactions with him than she had. But could any one of them say that he had been her first love?

Still, she saved the condolence letters. No one in the government wrote (they preferred to call), but many friends did. Many of them told stories of being with David in places she never realized he'd been to but places that they clearly assumed she knew about, as if David had been keeping their romance alive in theory to others all these years, long after he'd left it in practice. One of the letters was from a Saudi prince. When she mentioned that to a friend, a journalist, her friend had said, "Oh, there are hundreds of those. You don't need to save it." But she did, because it was the most beautiful.

Most of the condolence letters were more about the writer than the subject; most were dashed off with cold formality or uncomfortably excessive in their assumption of knowledge about the experience of loss. Or their knowledge about the one who was lost. David had admirers and detractors, but he had many more people who claimed to have known him well than actually did. Unlike Sara, he enjoyed elevating webs of acquaintance into relationships where words like *love* and *miss* were casually applied.

The prince's letter was informal, almost rambling. It was handwritten. It opened with a bit about the history of Saudi Arabia and the importance of Jeddah in particular. It talked about David as a man standing somewhere "close to" the center of that historical importance, because the importance hinged on a friendship with America, another country not un-new in the world, and another country at pains to define itself in a hostile world. "The importance hinges on faith, too," the prince wrote, and that struck Sara as odd, as David was many things but "faith" and "faithful" were not the first words that came to mind. The letter described David's "good work" as fitting into a larger framework—a "tradition"—of diplomatic "visionaries," and the fact that his death would remain a symbol for all those who knew him because of where he was when he died, and because he had chosen to give so much of his life to a place so few Americans understood. Sara didn't love these sentiments because they were true or familiar; she loved them because they were so thoughtfully put. She loved the letter for its writing, like she'd love a well-constructed short story.

But clearly the prince had known David. In the letter he said he knew about Jason, too. He said that David had spoken of his only son often, and with pride, and that he had talked even more about the boy's mother, who had been "a great love and also like a daughter" to David. There was no awkwardness or apology around this framing, and Sara was not offended. She can imagine how two men of that generation might situate and assess the kind of affair she and David had had. She wished that the reality of how he left had not belied the angelic man described in this letter. She wished she had known that man. Maybe this was a part of him and maybe he had other reasons for disappearing. It's possible—no, probable—that this prince knew David better than she ever had. He wrote (with sly self-aware irony) about David's strong heart.

*

She checks her watch. It is almost five o'clock.

Maybe a walk to the garden and back would feel good. She can cut around the porch to avoid being seen from the driveway—maybe that will calm her down before dinner, which, by the smell, she can tell is some variation on pasta with ham and peas. She loves this dish. He is making it because he knows it is her favorite. Or maybe because the young girl is still there and she likes it, too.

Her little white clapboard farmhouse was built around 1910. The land it sits on is largely under easement, thanks to visionary conservationists from another era. From her house, Sara can see only two others and just glimpses of their barns through trees. They are also quite small in foundation, made exclusively of stone and wood and glass. In the winter, under snow, you wouldn't know it was 2011 here. You wouldn't even guess the centuries had changed. And she likes that. Most of the time, inside her house, there was no cell signal.

At the edge of the woods there was a small series of flat stones—graves, she was sure, but she did not know for whom. Jason used to guess, and when he was little he imagined they were for animals. Now she thinks, *Maybe they're for unknown soldiers*. After David died, Jason started calling the woods the "Holiday Grave" because of the combination of evergreens and those stones. Looking at them now, she thinks maybe they were just an accident of nature. Why couldn't nature have arranged stones like that? Nature did all sorts of unexpected things, and maybe the stones were there to buck desire for meaning, not the opposite.

The woods are so quiet. These are the woods where she ran with her son, once he was old enough. They would make up stories on their jogs, stories about secret missions they were tasked with, including specific trees they were meant to tag and identify, special flowers they were meant to collect and bring home for "research." Jason's imagination outpaced hers by a mile; he was always dreaming up clever new solutions for fallen branches, new plans for scorched earth where a fox or a deer had torn through what had once been a sprout of a daisy. He was so precise. Everything had its place. She was sure this served him well in his training. It may have been a pose, but he was skilled at pretending to listen, pretending to do what he was told. He was told he had to go on this last mission. She was hoping he would be home for Easter, but then he was called back. "An opportunity" is what he had said. She had taken deep breaths and realized that her role now was to say, "I understand. And I am proud of you."

He had sent her an e-mail that night from his place in Virginia Beach, where he stopped, as he put it wryly, to "get some clean shirts." She knew the purpose of the e-mail: to tell her that he might not write for a while. And he would spell that out, although not much of his correspondence spelled out anything more. He never said things like "I can't tell you where I am going," or "I can't tell you what I am doing." All that went without saying. Those things were like the Nicene Creed of Team families; you just knew them by heart, and they became a part of the fabric of your days. *I don't know where my son is, and I have no idea what he is doing* is not standard-issue mother-think. But in her case it was not a big deal. Then again, it was not ever *not* a big deal. You placed your trust in the people leading the battle. You placed your trust in the admirals and the West Wing, and you took deep breaths. Once he deployed, there were no more letters. An e-mail would come occasionally, but more often he would reach out by phone. There were no more questions, no more history lessons. There were no more photographs or specific descriptions of friends. There were no more names.

This was typical:

Dear M.,

Here I am, ready to go. House is clean. You'd be proud. It is so hot here now. I wouldn't mind a run in those cool woods, checking up on our rabbits and squirrels, making sure those deer are minding their place. The guys here can never believe it when I tell them we live among so many deer and that I have never shot one. I told them about the albino. They think I made him up.

Love,

J.

Those runs through the woods had bonded them. They were something that a boy would have done with a father. And she had always ended them in exhaustion, whereas Jason always ended them exhilarated.

Her phone rings. She picks it up.

"Yes?"

"Sara, we have him."

"What?"

"Sara, they have Jason. He is alive. You need to get on a train to Washington. Pack enough for one night or two, and bring your things, and I will take care of the rest. I will pick you up at Union Station, and we will fly the rest of the way together. Okay? You need to get on a flight or train as soon as possible. Can you do that? Is there someone there to help you? Is there someone there to drive you?"

"Is he all right?"

"I don't know any details. But he is alive. You have to come now. I am not sure how long they can keep this quiet, and I want to get you out before this leaks."

"I'm coming."

She turns and runs back to the house. She has no idea where she will be going from Washington, whether it will be someplace hot or cold, whether she will need a rain slicker or hiking boots or an arctic parka.

She enters the house and closes the door carefully behind her.

Sam calls out from the kitchen. "Is everything all right?"

"They've found him. Washington. I—"

And this young United States Special Operations Forces warrior, highly trained alongside her son to practice wise restraint in the presence of threat; to place sophisticated miniature explosive devices secretly on the hulls of enemy ships; to drop into oceans from fast-moving stealth helicopters; and to possess casual expertise in a larger weapons cache than she knows to exist (also trained not to question orders, and to believe in his country)—this young man comes out of her kitchen, wearing an apron, with tears in his eyes. The moisture obscures the outline of the Trident.

"I will take you to the train," he says.

"Please," she says, before heading up the stairs. "Please go tell the police to clear the driveway. Tell them—tell them we are going for some air. Tell them we are going to the market."

In the small bag she elects to take, there isn't much room for more than a few things, but before closing the top, she takes the letters she was reading and folds them into the side pocket. Something for the plane, she thinks. She knows she won't be able to read much more than that. She checks her office. She checks the landing. She checks her son's room for anything that he might like to have. *Stop wasting time*, she scolds herself. And she hurries downstairs.

"I'm ready," she says.

He has put on a new shirt and a jacket, and he is ready, too.

The police, miraculously, have already all but cleared the end of the driveway, and the crush she expected to occur there is not what happens at all. For once, for the first time since she watched them as they started to gather there, the day after she had first learned the news, the reporters have put down their microphones and video cameras. They are all standing absolutely still, as her old, beaten-up blue Audi pulls past them. She wonders what the cops told them to get them to heel. Maybe they told them she had an armed escort. Maybe they told them to shut the fuck up. Maybe they told them that she was fragile, and that the sound of clicking cameras might break her in two. *It doesn't matter. My son is coming home.*

GIFTS

Jason and several of his teammates are gathered outside the entrance to the small house, the one they are using to practice room clearance. This is not their first time, or their tenth. They have done this so many times, they could build this house from sand, in their sleep. They know it well, and their bodies have, to some extent, internalized the kinesthetics of the drill. When you train, you walk a house first, no guns, in daylight. Then you walk with guns, unloaded. Then you walk with guns, loaded. Then you run with guns, loaded. Then you run at night—etc. Each step adds an increment of complexity. And this is before you start incorporating accidents and contingencies.

They look like warriors now: they are wearing their full kit—the pants, the vests, the helmets, the boots. Many have beards. And they all have their rifles. The only nod to trend is the Oakleys, ballistic eyewear almost all of the guys who don't opt for goggles use, and which they like for this practice in particular; the lenses are tight, and they have an effect like laying slats of magnifying glass over already perfect eyes. Skiers love them, too. They pop the contours of objects, and in the kill house to be able to see any additional dust or hidden corner exposed is helpful.

The guys all have tiny mikes inside their helmets. They can talk to each other by MBTIR, the intra-team radio, too. Peltor headsets with boom mikes linked to earpieces: these things facilitate coordination, but on an op they'll mainly talk with their hands. This not being a combat zone, new tools also occasionally facilitate antics. Especially today, because this newly formed platoon will think they know well how the next minutes will play out, and also because it happens to be a very cold, rainy day, and they're all keen for distraction. The first time Jason saw the little mikes, he'd made a crack about their being better than what Eminem takes on tour. So that started a running Eminem joke, one that played hard on the fact that Jason was in so many ways wholly un-Eminem-like. The jokes eventually led to playing more Eminem around the base. *The Eminem Show*, the artist's fourth album, was the uncontested favorite. It had been released nine months after 9/11.

Jason isn't sure if the guys actually like the music or if they simply enjoy the irony of the predictability of liking it. They are all smart enough to know this. They don't care. They just like the songs. And the more he listens, the more lyrics he remembers and respects. " 'Where's my snare? I have no snare in my headphones,' " says Jason softly into his mike. They are all standing and waiting. Jason will be the one to kick open the door. " 'A-chick, a-chick, a-chick, a-chick,' " he sings softly. As he moves through the door, he's thinking of the first lines of one song in particular; they go like this:

Have you ever been hated or discriminated against? I have;
I've been protested and demonstrated against, picket signs for my
  wicked crimes.

When he sings it, he changes *rhymes* to *crimes*. He thinks that this makes the lines more applicable to the young guys' situation. They don't think of themselves as criminals, of course; they're not criminals. But even at this stage of their development, the guys are aware that many people think of them like that, that many people don't believe that these wars are the right thing or that the warriors' roles in them are justified. Most people wouldn't know a Team guy from a Ranger or which side we fought on in Vietnam. Most people might concede the merits of World War I or Korea but be unable to identify the details. And most people, in the abstract, prefer butter to guns, but most mostly prefer not to think about it all. Has it always been that way? Does a public's opinion rise and fall like a stock on the occasion of new information and new numbers—of dead, of days fighting, of the change in the price of gas? More likely it fluctuates with something more banal and abstract: the length of their attention span. But the kids who are fighting are not tracking MSNBC polls. They are aware that what they do and the *choice* to do it will never make sense to most people.

*

Room clearance is stressful because there is a lot happening in a very small space, at high speed. Navigating a room is an elegant contrast to being underwater. Underwater, in a wide and completely silent environment, there is the illusion of calm. The stress of those old diving drills seems quaint now, as the men work through their final months of predeployment training. After qualification training, the platoon forms up at a Team (even-numbered Teams on the East Coast, at Virginia Beach; odd-numbered Teams on the West Coast, at Coronado). For the next eighteen months, the new guys will work with "old" guys, learning—and, critically, developing the platoon's standard operating procedures. They are prepared to follow, and most will be ready to lead when given that opportunity. Yet despite over a full year of work, they have not spent one night in a fight.

Keep your teammates close, and your weapon even closer. An operator holds his gun with extreme care and doesn't drop his sights. It sounds simple, but try holding a seven-pound piece of complex machinery straight, at shoulder height, while leaning low over it to maintain your aim. Having to hold the gun like that, ironically, limits your field of vision, but the trade-off is possessing the readiness to fire. When Jason mentioned the words *room clearing* once to his mother on the phone, she heard *room cleaning.* Forever after that she was constantly teasing him about the Defense Department's budgetary allocations for soaps and brooms. Jason told the guys, and they loved it. "Clean-up time!" someone would yell invariably as they headed out to the house. Jokes help cut tension. Room clearing is serious business, and close quarters fighting is a case study in team interplay. You can watch six different sets of guys clear the same room, and the subtle differences belie the leaders—and the flaws.

*

And this moment in their training is serious, too. It is not all physical drills and fully loaded extractions. The men feel a certain pride in having come this far, at having achieved a reasonable level of expertise with things they had never heard of before, and in subjects many of them had never studied, from physics to ballistics to triage to weather. It's school. The classroom time prepares them in the most essential way for the trickiest physical tasks, like leading a sixteen-man team through a warren of rooms in a cave, or dropping a twenty-four-man team from a moving helo into a fortified compound. Getting in is only prelude: then you have to identify the bad guys ("threats"), isolate the other guys ("unknowns"), and emerge unharmed. Anyone unarmed is "unknown," even a female hostage or a child. A hostage might be suffering from Stockholm syndrome, and a six-year-old can press a button. The opposite of being underwater, clearing a room—or a house, or a building—is also the opposite of dropping a precision bomb from a plane onto a place you've never been, to hit a target whose hand you've never shaken. Violence at a distance is an entirely different art and requires different skills.

" 'His gift is his curse,' " says/sings Jason, again into the mike. There must be some technical glitch due to snow. They usually don't have to wait like this, and it's making them antsy. "Just be patient, guys," one of the instructors says. "It's the ice. One of our terrorists slipped on the ice." They all laugh a little until someone shuts them up and says, *It's time.*

Clearing a house means understanding what is in it. It also means removing anything from it, dead or alive, that is dangerous. You want to move as quickly as possible, but too much rush can have an adverse effect. Ten minutes can feel like an hour for the men involved; it is powerful, because you are not aware that your body and your mind are being tapped at their maximum capacity. It's a little like runner's high, plus weapons and threat of death. When done at night, even with the finest new NVGs, an operator's visibility is compromised, adding another layer to the confusion.

This is what war looks like, and we're in it: this goes through some of the men's minds in the last weeks before their first deployment, especially for these men at this time in history, when the kind of fighting they are being trained to do is in unprecedented demand. Jason wonders whether and how that thrill will change once the drills become real. The point of drilling is to eliminate surprise or shock. But all drills can become tiresome. The guys are starting to want to make good on all the training they have done. They are anxious to know where they are going, and what the range of their missions will be.

As Jason moves into the last room in the house, he lets his mind wander—just for a second. He can't help it, he was thinking about something else just before they started, and some echo of that thought just came into his mind when his eye caught something about the light through the window. It looked like a fold of bright fabric, like a dress, but that would mean a girl, and that would be impossible, so did that mean he was dreaming? When was the last time he saw a girl? When was the last time he thought about it? And in that half of a quarter of a second of stray, *click*: a pistol is cocked at his left ear.

"Put the gun down." It is one of their guys pretending to be a hostile. He is wearing a black balaclava with a Steal Your Face embroidered on it. Jason cannot see who he is but he knows they know one another; the voice is familiar. "Whisky Tango Foxtrot, Eminem," he says. "Here's your 'Fuck you for Christmas.'" He laughs. He puts his weapon down, and Jason does the same. The other guy turns to stretch, and when he does, Jason sees a patch he recognizes on the back of the guy's jacket. The patch was made by an NSW platoon in Iraq, and only guys who have served there are merited to wear it. It's a skull wearing a pirate's hat, foregrounded by crossed swords. The skull's eyes are red. *It's a nice counterpart to the Steal Your Face*, Jason thinks. And then he thinks that the Venn diagram of guys who have that particular patch as well as an appreciation of Bob Weir is quite small. It occurs to him that the other guy has much more experience than he does. Even the way he held on to and then lowered his gun, shifting it from hand to hand—that was something Jason has not seen yet. Finesse, ease, confidence: these were things Jason had not yet acquired. These were things that only came from time spent downrange.

"I'm sorry, sir," says Jason. He doesn't know the other guy's rank but knows enough to show deference when he's on the wrong side of the barrel. He also knows he fucked up, and it makes him very angry. He shouldn't have been fooling around. "Situational awareness, JG," the officer says. He says it quietly, leaning in close to Jason's ear. "Situational awareness." And the officer is right. Punishment for this would be physical, and it would be more than a rap on his knuckles.

*

Jason doesn't like to admit when he makes a mistake. It's rare. Things were going well; he had distinguished himself throughout ULT, in particular during land warfare. Tactical bars were raised, and he rose to meet them. His platoon chief rarely isolated anyone for praise, but he'd taken Jason aside and made it clear he was pleased. This made the slip-up in the kill house particularly tough. It wouldn't happen again.

There is so much going on now because the Teams are all on deck for these wars. After 9/11, the Naval Special Warfare org chart underwent the classic institutional revisions begged by shifting circumstances, particularly in the Middle East. What was needed now was a force whose skill set was deeper, whose logistics were leaner. The new demands ran smack into the absence of a draft and into an enemy harder to understand than any predecessor. Deployment cycles shifted to accommodate demand. An aggressive operator could spend more time downrange than in any prior conflict.

Jason knows this. And he tries to keep focused. But sometimes he feels waves of anxiety, and these can bring on waves of doubt or distraction. He will never mention these episodes to anyone and is careful to keep up a calm front of total commitment and total confidence. Feelings are things to be analyzed and discarded before the load-out. Now, only weeks before leaving for war for the first time, controlling his emotions is his primary goal. It is one he will reach.

Ironically, once he is sent into a real house in a real city with real unknowns, he is absolutely calm. Abroad, on the base, there are no more nightmares. By his second deployment, he rarely has the anxiety pangs anymore, and he rarely experiences doubt. By his third, he is in complete control of his emotions—even, he sometimes thinks, while sleeping, as increasingly his dreams are mission-specific and take place underwater. By his fourth, having seen one too many things he is not sure he can ever forget, he will slowly start to relearn how to access his feelings. He knows he'll need them in new ways when back home. The emotional arc of an operator is not unlike that of most civilians: born idealistic, cynicism comes with experience and then develops into a cautious optimism—or acceptance—of the tasks at hand. Controlling emotion when op tempo is high isn't a skill; it is an art.

*

Another young guy, a guy who had joined their BUD/S class near the end, having been rolled back two times prior, was never able to master this art. He had cracked up during the predeployment period, at the end of ULT, and was fired. This is extremely rare. And the effect it had on the others was the opposite of the effect of the bell ringing out for DORs in BUD/S. When someone rang that bell, it soldered the resolve of the ones who stayed. When a person dropped during BUD/S, some of those left behind felt the bell was ringing to applaud their own resistance to it; another bell meant another time that you had not rung it. But for someone sent home at this later stage in the game, almost two years since they had all arrived in Coronado, there was no bell. No one was dropping out now because they were tired or cold or wet—or hungry. "Poor nutrition," said one of the other guys, by way of rumor. "He wasn't eating, apparently. He got dehydrated. You've got to drink. Lack of water is lack of oxygen to the brain." Variations on this became the theme of the One Who Left.

It was true that the young E-5 had stopped eating. At first the others thought he was ill. And then they thought he was engaging in some kind of a hunger strike. This platoon would soon find itself at the epicenter of the international political landscape. And most of them didn't have time to consider the one guy in their midst who was slowly losing himself. His fast went on, and by the time it was time to take action, it was too late. These guys are not callous; most have big hearts. But it never occurred to most of them that someone who had seemed so strong could in fact be slipping away and changing psychological course dramatically. It occurred to Jason; he'd tried to intervene.

The boy was one of the youngest. He had grown up in West

Texas, near Marfa, with a father who mistreated him and a mother, a painter, who left when he was two. He was whip-smart; he'd gone to Austin on full scholarship and studied astrophysics. Stars and poetry were his passions. He'd had four lines from a Kipling poem tattooed on the back of his left shoulder in a bar near Fort Hood. And he was one of the finest guns on the range, the one all the others envied, the one they were all sure would end up acing sniper school with the chance to take the shot at UBL. Jason and he had bonded over books and had spent hours talking about their hopes of becoming wise warriors. They'd obsess over various historical scenarios of the perfect shot—in Team lore, these were legion. The perfect shot followed by the perfect silence: snipers prefer their big kills to go unremarked. Jason hoped they would end up somewhere together, in a position to do some serious damage—which is to say, some serious good.

So when Kipling started slipping, Jason noticed right away. At first he'd chalked it up to nerves. When you see someone daily, sometimes you never notice the most shocking changes, but Jason's watch on his guys was close. He knew about their lives; he knew the names of their sisters and brothers, the makes of their dream cars, the reasons they came to serve. Jason tried to draw them out, source any problems. But in Kipling's case, he'd failed. The night before Kipling left the Teams, Jason had sat in his room with him, as if on watch.

"Do you ever get scared?" Kip asked.

"Nah," said Jason. "Not anymore."

"Really?"

"Nope." Here was the art in high gear: controlling any appearance of emotion was crucial.

"How do you shut it off?"

"Shut what off?" Jason asked.

"How do you shut off your mind?"

"You don't shut it off. You just think about—you just think about what's right in front of you. You concentrate."

"My mind is starting to wander more and more," Kipling said. "I see things."

"Like what kinds of things?"

"I see the house where I grew up. When I was little. I see the windows in the house, and I worry that the windows need repairing. I see the girl I lost my virginity to. I see, like, myself sitting in an office somewhere."

"What do you think that's about?"

"I think I am afraid to go back."

"But, buddy, you're right here." Jason grabbed Kipling's wrist. "We haven't even started yet."

"I know. And I feel like each day I move forward is another day I will be less able to go back."

"Back to what?"

"Right. I don't know back to what. And that's what's driving me silly."

"Yeah, well, I'm not so sure going back is so great. But what can we know? Let's be logical. The only thing that matters is now."

"Suffering—" said Kipling.

" 'Suffering does exist. Suffering arises from attachment to desire. Suffering ceases when attachment to desire ceases. Freedom—' "

" 'Freedom from suffering is possible by practicing the path,' " said Kipling, and laughed. "Not so sure about that bit."

"You taught me," said Jason.

"I did," Kipling said. And then he said, "I'm not free."

"Rome wasn't built in a day," Jason said. "You're *fine*."

"I don't like the dreams."

"Focus on the girl."

"You mean—"

"Focus on the girl, and forget about the window."

"I will try."

They sat for a while. Jason was reading Al Jazeera online, and Kipling was playing solitaire on his phone. And then Kipling said, "I know this sounds crazy, but sometimes I think that child soldiers are not an entirely insane idea. You send young kids to do these things, and they have no idea what they are doing. And they are not leaving children and lovers behind. They have never been in love. They are just fresh enough to face battle without either preconceived notions or hesitations. In fact, they still possess the sense of fantasy to approach it like a game."

"That's fucked up," said Jason. "Children leave behind their mothers."

And then he remembered that Kipling hadn't had a mother. That made the things he said make more sense, even if it did not make them rational or acceptable. Kipling could end up like Kurtz in a cave, Jason thought, if this continued. Something has broken in him. And Jason resolved not to leave him that night; he'd stay up all night if he had to, and he did. They talked more broadly about a few things—the last several American presidents, and which ones they'd liked; the games they'd watched the week before, which they hadn't liked at all; the other guys in the Teams, and which ones they most hoped would be by their side if things ever got complicated. Finally Jason closed his eyes. Maybe if he fell asleep, or pretended to, Kipling would, too. Maybe if he fell asleep, he would wake up, and all this would have been a dream. He didn't want to lose this guy. He didn't know what else to say.

He was almost asleep when Kipling poked him awake. It had been over an hour.

"I'd definitely want you," Kipling said.

"What?" Jason said.

"I'd definitely want you in a fight."

And even though he knew the answer, Jason asked, "Is there anything I can do?"

"Nope," Kipling said.

"You sure?"

"Yup."

"Keep in touch. We can talk about your girls and my absence of girls."

"That sounds good, man."

"Good night," said Jason.

"Good night. And flights of angels sing thee to thy rest."

Three hours later Kipling was gone. Jason arrived at breakfast to find the others were all talking about it. Jason would continue to quiet any talk on the topic as the weeks went on. It didn't look good, someone leaving at that time. The types of guys who would leave should have been well screened out by this point in time. Discovering someone who had been so unhappy was like discovering a bomb had been ticking inside an Academy classroom. Jason understood that dispassion toward Kipling would turn into distrust and then, eventually, disdain. There was nothing he could do about that. There was not a lot of acceptance—yet—of this kind of behavior, even as variations on this behavior would be something the guys would see more of during future deployments and, increasingly, on leaves. Jason would have to watch more closely. Would a closer watch keep them all sane?

Jason did not hear about his friend again for a long time. Then, following his fourth deployment, while home for a brief leave before returning for what would become the mission where he would go missing, he heard something. He heard it casually, sitting in a jeep going from the airport to where he would be renting a new little house in Virginia Beach. The young enlisted guy driving him, a newly minted Team member just starting PRO-DEV, or "professional development," the first six months of three final predeployment training phases, asked Jason if he'd known someone the guys all called Kipling. The kid had done the math and figured out that Jason and Kip would have been the same class. He told Jason he had heard the facts back home (he was also from Texas) when he was first starting to think about trying to sign up for the navy. Special operations stories inevitably traveled local veterans networks like AP feeds, so it wasn't surprising. The story had not deterred him, but he was not sure how much of it was myth.

What he had heard was that Kipling had requested dismissal for medical reasons and that, following an evaluation in which he was pronounced clinically depressed, suicidal, and at serious risk to himself and his peers (an evaluation, Jason realized, that must have taken place before that night they'd stayed up so late), discharge was granted. He had gone back to Texas. Not long after arriving home to no family and no job, he'd attempted suicide and failed. He'd used an M4 rifle. The failure was a fact that didn't sound right to Jason. A highly trained operator failing to shoot himself? Unlikely. But perhaps the attempt was a cry for help. Or perhaps it was the signal to the world outside that he had been sick enough that he had had to leave.

"Did he marry?" Jason asked the young boy that day.

"Yes, sir. He was married not far from Waco. There was a piece about it in the paper. And a picture. He married a really pretty girl, and he teaches at a local public school—a really good school, I know some people there. I know a guy who went there and said it was really tough, really disciplined. I thought about driving over and trying to meet him."

"Was he—was he wearing his uniform in the wedding picture?"

"Yes, sir, I remember that."

"Do you know what subject he teaches?" Jason asked.

"History. I know that because they talked about it in the article. He is very popular. He teaches military history. And he has a blog, too."

All of this made Jason feel slightly sick. The uniform—the blog. But he resolved not to judge. He resolved to visit Kipling once his service was complete. Despite their differences, he'd liked him. And he'd tried, and failed, to fully understand him. He had taken a photograph of his tattoo once and sent it to his mother.

"Sir, what was he like?"

"He was—he was a big thinker," Jason said.

"And sir, why did he leave?"

"I don't know. Could have been the girl."

*

Throughout the Teams, the guy with the magical lungs is increasingly well known, but not for his swimming. And following his first two deployments, he is increasingly well respected as an operator. Jason approaches his work with dispassionate, methodical precision; he loves what he does, and he knows he does it well. As the cycle of deployments begins, most of the missions he's called on to assist with have not even involved water. If he's holding his breath, he's holding it in houses. *So much pool comp, so few pools*, he thinks. His Draeger LAR V, the underwater breathing device that became a fifth limb through certain chapters of training, sits in the corner of a safe on base like a big black bug, unused and acting more as an amortization input for U.S. Defense as a percentage of GDP than as a conduit for better breathing.

Sam became a close friend during that first predeployment period. He would lose an eye during their second tour, out at night in a city that has to be one of the most godforsaken on Earth, a city the guys could never quite believe they'd been stationed in. Jason was there when it happened, and he had held Sam's head in his hands, his heart beating out of his chest—not with fear but with anger. When they'd got home, Sam would opt to have a glass eye with a Trident put in its place. Jason has seen glass eye Tridents before, but Sam's was the first one from his generation—from his class. Sam's other eye looked like he stole it from Paul Newman.

Sam was a water lover, too. He grew up in Hermosa Beach, California, and had basically been born on a short board. He referred to the Navy's IBS (inflatable boat, small) as "Illegal But Surfable." He was almost exactly Jason's height and build, on the smaller side among the guys, and the two of them—both sandy blonds—got teased for being pretty. Their CO once told them that when their Team got its Hollywood movie, they could be one another's stunt doubles—the joke being not that the two of them could be one another's double; the joke being that Team guys don't need doubles. Sam was awarded a medal for his lost eye, and that set him apart from the others. Still, the first thing he had said to Jason when Jason went to visit him in the hospital was "Don't go back without me." He always maintained that before retirement, he would surf the Red Sea and swim the Bosporus. They have both grown up and aged ten years in the last few.

They have other key differences. Jason dreams about big things, and Sam stays firmly focused on the little ones, like his next hot meal or the rhythm of his fingers as he imitates a wave. Jason often wonders how being in the military might fit the broader context of the rest of his life, but Sam thanks God each night for giving him one more day. One more day is one more chance to get back to the breaks at Point Dume.

Sam and Jason run and train together, too. Wherever in the world they end up making their camp, there is always a gym, and the retreat to a workout is a retreat to order, lifting weights being the typical off-duty activity for restless warriors. Lifting weights, and eventually Skype and e-mail, pass the downtime. "I'm giving up e-mail; it's way too ambiguous," says Sam one day, after hearing from a girl he had met and liked on his last leave. " 'All ambiguous behavior is interpreted negatively.' I read that in a book—by a Harvard professor." He looks at Jason when he says this and draws out the word *Harvard* with a long mock–South Boston accent. They laugh. There aren't any Harvard men on their Team this time.

Jason's godfathers all write, in particular the one writing from Washington, and he writes back. They plot the future, in fits and starts, the future always being something rich and bright. His godfather played fast and loose with the rhetoric of possibility, flipping words like *rosy* and *options* and *potential* like cards in a deck he knew how to lay. Sara writes almost daily, too, always ending her e-mails with "no pressure to call" and "you don't need to write back." But he always does. Heading into their second deployment, Jason and Sam make a pact: they will e-mail only their mothers. And then they make another one: that if anything ever happens to either one of them, the other will go and tell the family. "Mine's not really a family," says Jason, shyly. "I mean, it's just my mom. She's all I've got." And Sam says, "That's cool. She'll love my cooking."

Jason changes out the chain on the necklace his mother gave him each time he leaves the U.S. He prefers to loop the small locket through a strip of leather when he's working. Almost always now, he needs to move around unrecognized, and the glints from the chain's gold links could easily catch the light and attract attention, or heat. Often he simply wraps the necklace around his wrist or loops it through his belt. But at night—or on jumps—he always returns the locket to his neck. It's less likely to slip off from there, tucked into his vest, and he likes the idea that there it is closer to his heart.

*

Throughout the first few deployments, Jason's peers have shed illusions, one by one. Once you have seen a man killed at close range, you will never see things quite the same way again. Most of the guys shared the necessary sense of humor about their chosen line of work, about the "sacrifices," and about their views on the fight. Most had things they deeply missed back home—in addition to family. Jason and Sam play a game where one of them says something he misses, and the other has to top it, in degree and wit, until one of them calls *uncle*. Things they miss included: beach volleyball, long baths, girls, southern California girls, seeing the Washington Monument lit up at night, watching Flyers games live, having time to make bacon, having time to make steaks, better steaks, better bacon, Mom. The names and places changed, but the macro themes of things missed didn't: family, food, romance—usually, but not always, in that order. The game could be a drinking game, with the loser tasked to buy. It could also be an effective way to pass time when you're waiting on a Fallujah rooftop for days, staring through a very small sight.

*

When Jason cleans his guns, he thinks about how the wow factor of having them, and knowing how to use them, has gone. His sense of purpose has not dimmed, but by the end of his first two deployments his early romance for his profession has shifted to an old, enduring love, respect, and sense of duty. Like anyone nearing the end of their twenties, he cannot remember when the shift occurred that took him from boy to man, from looking up to everyone else to starting to command respect in his own right. Team seniority is not determined by the strength of your lungs, but it isn't determined only by years either. Jason has now been in charge of guys almost twice his age, guys who have chosen to remain in this life through their late thirties, to cycle in and out of wars on an ongoing basis, indefinitely. These are guys who had spent ten years in this line of work before the average American knew what Al Qaeda was. They are uniquely dedicated. They also represent a choice Jason doesn't want to make.

One night, back home, he is carefully lining up gear on the floor of his little living room. He is missing something and wants to be sure that he has it somewhere, as he has learned he might be called to work on something interesting, something that would require a tool he has not used in a while. He has a flashback to being a very small boy and playing in the pantry of his father's house in Georgetown. It was a brick townhouse, its lawn famously contiguous to the house where Jacqueline Kennedy lived after the president was shot. He remembers David being there but cannot remember anything that he said. He can only remember being on the floor, doing something like what he is doing now, trying to line things up, but failing because the little things kept slipping between bits of the lumpy carpet. What were those things? Were they toy soldiers? His memory of David is hazy. His idea of him is not.

Jason is not sure how he will feel about leaving the Teams, but he has made it clear in his own mind that this is the year he will set down firm plans to go home. He will call up his godfather in Washington when he next gets back to Virginia and say that he is ready for that office job, for researching policy papers or whatever the hell it will be he is allowed to do there in the Russell Senate Office Building, ready to use his body for an hour a day, or maybe two, rather than twenty, ready to stop lying about what he does, ready to start sleeping late, to fall in love. Maybe he'll move out west, and Sam can show him Maui's fabled North Shore. He thinks he could live very simply and maybe not do anything too ambitious—for a little while. Mostly, he simply wants to see what things are like on the outside, because the inside is the only side he has seen since he was a kid, since entering the Academy a young seventeen. How had he first gotten it in his head to go there and then to come here? Was it those toy soldiers on the carpet on P Street?

Sometimes he questions how he'll do without the trappings of this life. Will he miss it? Will he be granted time to tell his stories, even if he's given the slow boat home to civilian life? It is in those moments of questioning that he knows it's time to go; this life can become an addiction.

"Hey, man." Someone is knocking on his door. Or more specifically, someone is knocking on the wooden frame surrounding the screen door he keeps meaning to replace. They knock three times, and he can hear the frame cracking. And then a whistle: Dixie Chicken.

"Just a minute," he calls out, thinking, *shit*, looking at the array of ordnance laid out on the floor—his own guns, the ones he kept at home. "Just a minute." He can slide the doors to the living room shut, and he does. And there in the doorway, like lilacs blooming, is his platoon chief, his wide, tan face pressed right up against and into the screen, threatening to force it to break. He is making a face. The screen is creaking; it's about to burst open. He pulls his face back just before the mesh starts to tear. He's six feet four inches tall.

"Happy you have the place well fortified," he says, and laughs, as Jason turns the lock. "I looked through the window. Your curtains are see-through. May I come in?"

"Of course."

Jason gives him a Coke and takes one, too. He opens the sliding doors and motions for his guest to sit on the sofa. The platoon chief looks at the gear and the guns and smiles.

"All dressed up and no place to go," he says.

"I don't know," says Jason, carefully. "I was missing something so I took everything out to see what's what."

"You got to keep everything in its place. You know that."

"I know. I got lazy. Or I don't know. I don't know what I did with this one fucking thing."

"Excuse your language."

"Excuse my language."

The platoon chief notes a broken mask. "Swimming laps in your spare time?"

"Yeah, it would be nice to have a pool when we go back."

"Well, a desert's preferable to a jungle. Fewer bugs. Better weather."

"True."

"Glass half full."

"I'm thinking about retiring."

"Nah. You say that now, but you love it too much."

Jason finishes his Coke, crumples the can in one hand, and pitches it to land, perfectly, in the tiny trash bin tucked in the corner. His platoon chief takes one long sip very slowly, then puts his can down and announces, "Too much sugar for me." He sits on the floor and pulls his legs into a lotus position. He cracks his shoulders. Jason thinks about where they were only weeks ago, the things he'd seen the chief do. He'd learned a lot from him, and he wanted his respect.

"What do you tell people when they ask you what you do?" Jason asks.

"Do you mean, what would I tell a girl if I met a cute girl?" And his look said, *If I tell you this, you're going to have to tell me about the girl.*

"Sure. What would you tell a girl if she asked you what you do?"

"Are we in a bar?"

"I don't know where you are," Jason says, laughing. "Does it matter?"

"Well, what time is it?"

"Any time."

"Be specific, lieutenant."

"It's zero six hundred hours, and you're—"

"*Okay.*"

"And you're just talking."

"Just talking."

"Just talking."

"At zero six hundred."

"Zero nine hundred!"

"*After breakfast.*"

"Come on."

"What was for breakfast?"

"I'm serious."

And the platoon chief leans forward and says, "I would tell her, 'Honey, I look into rooms.' "

"Rooms?"

"I would say, 'Honey, my job is *room-looking-into.* I look into rooms, and I see what goes on in those rooms. And when I see something not quite right, and sometimes it takes hours—or even days—to catch something not quite right, sometimes it takes weeks or months or years to see something just a little, let's say, *uncomfortable*, then I go into that room. I go into that room at night, without making a sound, and I take out the one thing that made me just a little bit stressed, that thing that wasn't quite right or quite good or quite clean. And no one will ever know that I was there."

"That's what you tell her?"

"That's what I tell her. After breakfast."

"I bet that speech gets them into bed every time."

"You'd be surprised. Girls like a clean room. And I hear you're pretty good at cleaning things up." And then he squints his eyes and says, "And weren't we already *in* bed?"

The chief, the senior enlisted guy in the platoon, had a gift, too; he could make you say things you thought he already knew. In truth, he knew little about Jason. They hadn't exchanged confidences. They hadn't shared stories. But they'd been in enough tough places together that they'd each learned how the other functioned when things didn't go to plan. For this, there was mutual admiration.

"So which one's your favorite?" Jones asks.

"My favorite what?"

"Your favorite weapon. You have something you like to use above sea level?"

"I like . . . my pistol," says Jason. "I don't know. I use what they give me and do what they tell me."

"I don't believe that. You're *en-tre-pre-neu-ri-al*." He draws out the word, teasing; clearly, he heard the word used by someone else to describe Jason, and Jason is not yet sure if it is meant as a compliment.

"I follow orders. That's, in fact, the definition of the opposite of entrepreneurial."

"Thanks for that clarification."

"I only mean—I only mean I'm happy where I am."

"Money gets better if you stick around," his platoon chief says. "Power gets pretty intense. You could run for president one day."

"I wouldn't want to live in that big white house." They laugh.

"No one thought that if we left Vietnam they'd come after us." The platoon chief is looking at a picture on a shelf of David. He's wearing a flak jacket and a camera around his neck. The picture was taken in Nha Trang. Jason had taken it from his mother's house without telling her, when he left for Coronado. In it, David's looking up, shielding his eyes with one hand. Jason always imagined he was looking up at a plane.

"Pardon?" says Jason. He's thinking about the White House. He's thinking about his godfather. He went to the White House when he was little. He shook Reagan's hand.

"No one thought those VCs would have followed us home with weapons of mass destruction."

"No one thought you could take down a commercial airplane with a knife and a box cutter."

"I'm only saying that the price of leaving then was a bit— different. You got in and you counted the nights until you left. Six months until transfer to a desk job? A year? And then you could say, 'I left,' and people understood. Leaving now is different."

"You can't compare—"

"We still haven't got the guys we need to get. There're still too many dirty rooms. Leaving now is like—is like leaving the woods when the deer is dancing right into your sights."

Jason disagrees. "Respectfully, it's never a good time," he says. "The deer's always right there. Or it's the ninth inning. It's always the time where commitment is most crucial."

"You don't hunt." The platoon chief leans back on his elbows, looking over the room. He has never been to visit Jason like this before. He's never stayed this long.

"I get the idea. Only the deer is not just one deer. There are too many deer. I see deer in my sleep at night." And then, after what feels like a while, he adds, "I am my mother's only son."

"Right. You could be the one to take out the world's most wanted criminal, but to her you'll always be the only one responsible for providing the grandkids."

"Something like that," Jason says.

As they talk, the platoon chief picks up one of Jason's knives and flips it open and shut, casually. They talk about their last trip, the increased attention given now to where they are, what they think about the quality of the platoon. They talk about an article that ran recently in a military journal about the Israeli raid on Entebbe, and about that mission's place in the history of terrorist acts and hostage rescues. They talk about the Mossad, and a guy who came through the base recently who is apparently now working with the Sayeret Matkal out of Beirut.

"Entebbe. That was a work of art of an op," the platoon chief says.

"July Fourth."

"Yep. Independence Day. I've heard it's beautiful there."

"Uganda?" says Jason.

"Israel." They laugh. And the platoon chief continues:

"Look, just don't drop out now because you're *tired*, all right? Or because you feel guilty about other . . . responsibilities. You have a gift for this. And God doesn't give a lot of gifts. Men raised by single mothers tend to think really highly of themselves. They also tend to be really vulnerable when pressed to a place where they don't feel protected. I expected you to be lazy. Fancy parents, private schools."

"I sense a 'but' coming?"

"But you're not like that. That's all. That's what's 'but.' "

"My parents weren't fancy," Jason says.

"I am simply saying."

"I'm listening."

"Your mother will be fine. Want me to call her?" And nodding his head in the direction of a framed photograph of Sara on the desk he says, "Please, can I call her?"

"I'm not going anywhere."

"Other jobs aren't going anywhere either. Girls aren't going anywhere. Girls. Fishes in the sea, Priest. And you can swim faster than all the other predators."

"This may be true."

"Glass half full," the platoon chief says again, as he stands to leave.

In October, Jason plans a short leave and a return home. He will
surprise his mother for her birthday. She deserves it, and he needs
it. As he thinks seriously about the next year, and about whether or
not he will move forward with any concrete exit plans, he knows
his first advice should come from Sara. Her birthday is October 3,
so he decides to drive north that morning, to arrive at the house
in the early afternoon in time to catch the magic light off the
porch, the light that almost always hangs around for an Indian
summer in that part of the world. If he had to guess, he would
say that at that hour she would be up in her office, staring at the
screen while dreaming about something other than the words she
was working on. When he asked her once how she could rape and
pillage an article so quickly with so much red ink, she responded,
after objecting to the uses of *rape* and *pillage*, that when reading
something for the first time, she didn't read for "macro ideas";
she simply read for misplaced semicolons. "The grammar line of
battle," she called the first read. "The front line."

Sometimes when a sniper gets a target in his sights, before he
shoots, he still needs to press another button on the barrel, the
one that links a signal home, sometimes even to the White House,
for final approval. It occurs to Jason that his mother's work has a

similar shape to this: while not about life and death, her work is service in support of Other People's Ideas. She is like a shooter, never credited. Yet if he made this observation to her, she would mock it. For all her heart, she takes her work at once deeply seriously and not seriously at all. Upon realizing it is the perfect hour for raspberries, she can walk away from editing an op-ed calling for regime change in sub-Saharan Africa, on deadline. She will drop her red pencils and go gather the new berries from the backyard bush, being careful not to bruise them in case they wreck her recipes. *Focus, restraint; focus, restraint; focus, restraint.* Her mind is not unlike her son's in its nimbleness—and its depth. It is also like his in its inveterate optimism. She spends a lot of time reading about wrongs in the world, but she still gets up most mornings feeling calm and hopeful.

This particular skill speaks to her resilience—of mind, of spirit, of character. It is the gene that makes Jason think he can take or leave his current work. When the time comes, he will commit. Pulling into the driveway, he is thinking that marriage may be even harder for Sara to face than his time in the military. In marriage, there is more chance—and more chaos. *A son is your son until he takes a wife—*

Sara's car is there, with the windows open. *There's that optimism again,* Jason thinks. She doesn't count the clouds. He can tell from the angle at which the truck is parked, and the way the front door is positioned on its hinge: she's home.

He smiles to see the flag, still in the same place, even after he encouraged her to affix it to the house itself rather than leave it poled in the ground by the oak trees. Most houses in the neighborhood have flags now, the locals having separated their politics from their views about the troops. He thinks about the flag sitting on the floor of his bedroom in Virginia Beach, not yet hung, and about the girl who rolled off his bed onto it. "How many stars tall am I?" she'd asked, stretching her arms above her head. "And how many stripes wide?"

He parks his car down the driveway, by the shed that used to be a refuge for old scooters but that as far as he knows now is a palace for rats. Closer to the house, she might hear his engine cut. He enters the house quietly. On a small table in the small foyer, there are the day's newspapers: *New York Times, Washington Post, Financial Times, Wall Street Journal, Wilmington News Journal, Philadelphia Inquirer.* It's Sunday, and he knows she saves the papers to read at night, in bed. He walks up the stairs, very careful to make no noise. He can see that the door to her office—too old and uneven to ever close quite properly—is wide open. "Hey," he says.

She looks up from her desk to see the son she hasn't seen since spring. He is wearing jeans and the cable-knit sweater she gave him years ago that remains her favorite thing to see him in, as he knows. He looks like a kid who wouldn't hurt a fly; there's just something preternaturally gentle about his physical presence. She still sometimes thinks that when he leaves, he's leaving to teach kindergarten in Norfolk, not to save lives in Sana'a or Aqaba. He could pass for a teacher; he could pass for anything. She takes a long look at him before the hug. "You look skinny," she says.

"Don't ever tell a guy he looks skinny, Ma. It's not cool."

"What should I tell him?"

"Tell him he looks—tell him he looks handsome."

"I haven't seen you this handsome since high school."

She holds his face in her hands and takes a deep breath. "Christ," she said. "Why didn't you call?"

"Element of surprise," he says. "And managing expectations. I wasn't sure what my schedule was like. I have to drive back in the morning. Maybe even tonight."

"Well, what do you want to do? Sleep?"

"You know what I'd love to do? Have you run today?"

"Nope," she says. "Let's do that. And then I'll check the icebox. A boy as handsome as you needs a real supper."

"Let me change," he says.

"I'll meet you by the flag."

On his bed is a pile of laundry that was probably placed there the last time he was home—jeans, sweaters, some extra shirts. He chooses one that does not belong to him, but he knows its origin. After David died, Sara had dated someone on the board of the Langley School; things got somewhat serious, and then she'd pulled away. Jason later liked teasing his mother, when she wore it, that she "survived a great relationship and all she got was this lousy T-shirt."

The word *Langley* had meaning for both of them. It still stood as code for the start of Sara's relationship with David, an apt code for something that had been soldered in secrecy. Jason was sure the shirt having been placed on his bed meant his mother was giving it to him. It had never really fit her properly anyhow, and she had lost even more weight since he left home the last time. It was a classic baseball shirt, the kind with bracelet sleeves and a C-shaped hem. It was royal blue and white, with THE LANGLEY SCHOOL LEOPARDS spelled out across the chest.

"That's for you," she said. "It doesn't really fit me anymore."

"You can take my old Academy tops as a trade. As luck would have it"—and he flexes a muscle—"they don't really fit me anymore."

They run slowly and talk. She asks about how things are going, respectfully keeping her questions vague and letting him guide the level of specificity of things. She asks about the leadership of his current platoon and whether he has been able to ask any of the men he looks up to for advice about his future. She knows he always had a rule—"five deployments, maximum"—in his mind when he started, but she also knows that nothing is fixed in life, and that things change; circumstances shift. She's been as ready for her son to say he's staying in the Teams as a freshman who prepares for her breakup with a senior in advance of graduation.

When they arrive at the main road, he looks both ways before crossing and then remembers that the chances of encountering a car, on a Sunday, at this hour, are about the same as the chances of encountering a Playboy bunny in the jungle.

"God, it's so isolated here," he says.

"Haven't you noticed," she says.

"Are you sure—don't you ever think about leaving? What about moving back to D.C.?"

"I don't have the pulse for that anymore."

"I just worry."

"*You* worry?"

"You don't have to worry about me anymore," he says. "You vastly overestimate the risk in what I do, I think. Or maybe you vastly underestimate my level of skill at what I do."

At home, there is a white square box sitting on the front porch. Sara opens it; it's a cake. A beautiful chocolate cake, with a tiny paper American flag affixed to a toothpick stuck into its top. There's a card; Jason takes it and reads it. " 'Happy Birthday, From the CS Office.' What's the CS office?"

"County sheriff."

"How's the county sheriff know it's your birthday?"

"I had a little incident out here a few weeks ago, and they helped me out."

"Incident?"

"Yeah, not a big deal."

"Come on."

"Someone broke into the house. I don't know who it was, and I don't know what they wanted, but—they left. They came and prowled around a bit, and they left."

"Jesus."

"The cops were here right away. The birthday thing came up as the cops were joking about the stars being out that night."

"And?"

"And they were saying that starry nights weren't good for criminals, so clearly this guy was a novice. We were talking about stars, and we started talking about signs. And one of the guys said that a disproportionate number of criminals were Tauruses, to which of course I took objection. Then they thought Taurus was my sign, and then I said, 'No, I'm a Libra.' Et cetera."

"Et cetera? Was he flirting with you?"

"It wasn't a he, it was a they, and I don't know. I don't care. Anyhow, they wanted to reinforce the locks on the house, and I told them, you know, about you."

"What did you tell them?"

"I told them a little bit about what you do. I was trying to imply that I'm well protected."

"But I'm not here anymore."

"But you're—well, I guess you're right. You're not here anymore."

Sara takes the cake out of its box, licking the caught frosting from her fingers. She places it on a plate in the little kitchen. She thinks about what else she can cook that night, in an effort not to think about the fact that her son is leaving within a few hours. In fact, he has already left. The mood has shifted from one of arrival and happiness to one of leaving. It is always like this. And it never gets easier.

"I think I'll just shower," Jason says. And he doesn't move.

"Go on, shower and rest. I will root around for something to make for us that goes with cake."

At dinner, Sara's still careful not to ask any questions that might make him feel pressure. "No pressure," she always said when he was trying to decide whether to come home or not. "No pressure," she always wrote at the end of her letters. She was adamant that she would appreciate the upsides: the fact that he'd elected to surprise her. The fact that he looked well. The fact that he seemed happy. She finds candles in the cupboard and places twenty-seven of them carefully around the little flag. When she places the cake on the table, it takes her son about six seconds to count the candles.

"But it's not *my* birthday."

"But I might not see you on your birthday," she says.

After cake they sit outside. Admiring the stars, Jason says, "Not a great night for criminal activity."

When Jason goes to bed, Sara stays on the porch. She can see some stars; perhaps they waited a bit too late tonight to shine quite as brightly. She remembers attending the Academy Ball in Jason's last year there. A group of kids—eight boys and eight girls—had taken dancing lessons, and that night they put on a show for the parents and guests. As the crowd made a wide circle around them, the pairs performed a classic waltz. The boys wore black tie, and the girls wore white dresses. It was such a simple, old-fashioned image.

Around that same time Sara saw a documentary that someone she knew had worked on as an editor. In it, prominent physicists discuss the existence and history of black holes. One of them, asked to explain how we know that black holes exist, said, "Have you ever been to a debutante ball. Have you ever watched the young men dressed in their black tuxedos, and the girls in their white dresses, and the lights turned low." He went on to say that we know the men are there because the girls are moving. We cannot see the men; they disappear. But the girls continue to hold our eye. "The girls," the physicist put it, "are the ordinary stars. And the boys are the black holes. You can't see a black hole any more than you can see the boy, but the girl going around gives convincing evidence that there must be something there, holding her in orbit."

Sara had looked at those boys that night at Annapolis and thought of them disappearing. There was a war on, and so many of them would join it. *Their absence keeps us in orbit*, she thinks. And she makes a mental note to tell Jason this story in the morning.

But when she wakes up, her son is gone. He left a note on the table, secured by her running shoes, into which he'd threaded new laces:

DON'T WORRY. AND THAT'S AN ORDER. I LOVE YOU.

*

Jason drove through the night. He used to speed a lot, but more recently he often goes under the limit, an ironic gesture of defense against an invisible enemy. He listens to books on tape because radio requires too much effort, and while he's working he never follows new bands anyhow. He likes listening to tapes because he rarely makes time to read these days, and because being forced to listen keeps his mind off other things.

The last book he listened to from start to finish was a gift from Kipling, a collection of poems from the Great War compiled in the late sixties, read by actors who were famous at that time, all of them English and all of them active, public supporters of Americans protesting the war in Vietnam. And yet they had all agreed to donate any proceeds from the tape's sales to veterans. "Do you think it's strange," Jason had asked Kipling, "that this is antiwar art, but the benefits will go to those who fought the war?" And Kipling had said, "It's about the poems." He also told Jason he had bought it on eBay for four dollars, so he doubted much benefit had accrued to the vets.

Should he have told his mother he was leaving? He had tried to sleep, but once in his bed, he started to feel anxious, like he was losing time. The bed didn't quite fit right anymore. Was this place still his home? For how long? The choice quickly became simple: either drive now, or pray yourself to sleep, only to wake up too soon, eat some cereal, hate goodbye, and then take half a day driving. He decided it was better just to go. They had had their time together. She had seen that he was whole and unchanged. He had artfully avoided talking about anything too pressing. And he would be home for Christmas. He would be home to see the snow on the trees.

After Vanessa Redgrave reads Rupert Brooke, Jason ejects the CD. He sets the dial to cheap pop songs for the duration of the drive. The light is starting to come up.

INFIL

If you blink on the drive to the train station, the landscape shifts, from horse country to suburbs. Blink again, and you're in an inner city. In the tall buildings bankers signed contracts and insurance brokers parsed their actuarial tables, minding the arc of loss. Outside the station the men in navy suits walked very fast, but the smokers, forced into exile outside under law, lingered. It was an odd combination of rush and stray.

Sam had driven fast, so fast that Sara was sure they'd be pulled over. He navigated her city's streets with the confidence of a native, although he'd never been there; she had a vague impression he was watching the GPS more than he was watching the road, opting for back streets and quick diversions away from upcoming red lights—driving intelligently, as opposed to simply following the road, which was what most people did, certainly what she did. She looked at his hands. He held his left on the wheel and moved his right back and forth between the gearshift and her keys, twisting them around his finger. She was afraid he might rip them right out of the ignition but didn't want to say so. She didn't want to say anything.

Her keychain was a gold orb, the size of a golf ball. Engraved with a world map, it had two tiny stones, almost imperceptibly tiny diamonds; one marking Mecca, and one marking Rome. It was a gift from David not long before he'd disappeared, one whose meaning she'd never cared to ask after. She simply loved it because it was so unusual, and so precious. Jason had played with it as a child, displacing it from its chain and rolling it along the floor, like a die.

"Eleven eleven," Sara says.

"Eleven eleven?" asks Sam.

"Eleven eleven: that's the number of my train," she says.

"Eleven eleven eleven, like the Armistice," Sam says.

"Right. The side car armistice."

"Side car?"

"The French forced the Germans to sign in the forest, in the railway car. Was it . . . the Fôret Compiègne?"

"Can't say I remember," Sam says, and he laughs.

"Yes, well, it was eleven a.m. *Paris* time, that was the third eleven in 'eleven eleven eleven.' And the French forced the surrender—"

"Not technically a surrender."

"Well, right, but they forced the Germans to sign the agreement in the railcar, in the forest."

"I remember the car, but not the forest."

"Well, the forest was famous. It was a place for Napoleon's formal hunting parties. Napoleon I."

"What's a formal hunting party?"

"You know, linens on the tables and beaters for the birds."

"Better guns," Sam says.

"Yes, better guns."

They pull into the parking lot in the station, and Sara tries to protest, asking Sam to let her out at the curb, and leave her, but he insists on coming inside. He wants to walk her onto the train, be sure she has a seat. They get her ticket, but they still have awhile to wait. He buys her a coffee in the shop, where Mother's Day cards are on sale for half price. They find a place to sit and Sara leans back in the small plastic chair, pulling her knees into her chest for a stretch. She's anxious not to get upset in front of him before she says goodbye. The train is delayed.

"Yes," she says, "formal hunting parties. The kings then even had a position on their staff, something like *le grand veneur*—"

"I failed French."

"Well, it was like chief of hunting. It was basically a cabinet-level position, with better pay."

"Just to run the hunts?"

"Just to run the hunts. And, you know, coordinate the army of staff required to run them well. And the best hunts were in that forest."

"And then they caught the Germans there."

"They didn't catch them. They invited them. To sign."

"Invited—like to a party."

"Yes. But the Germans got their revenge," Sara says.

"How was that?"

"With another party. The *second* armistice at Compiègne. Nineteen forty. Hitler forced the French to return to the same spot. He sat in Foch's chair. That's when they turned over their freedom; after that, the Germans held northern France."

"And the car?"

"Hitler brought it home, showed it off in his garden as a trophy. He had the entire rest of the Armistice site destroyed."

"Wow."

"Yes, he didn't fool around."

"Well, I guess that was his choice. But after the war—"

"After the war the French made a new carriage, returned it to the forest, and rebuilt the site as a kind of shrine."

"Have you been there?"

"No. But I—we had a picture of that railcar in our house at one point, a gift from a German friend. I can't even remember the circumstances, exactly. There was some celebration happening there. We'd been invited—or Jason's father had been invited, and I was given the chance to tag along. But didn't." She looks around the station; she used to take this train once a week. She used to know the porters' names, and they'd save seats for her when she ran late. "You know the Armistice—the first one—went into effect at eleven a.m., but they'd signed it earlier that morning. They must have been up all night."

"Yeah?" Sam says, looping the orb's long chain into a knot, then untying it—with one hand.

"Interesting only insofar as there wasn't much art in the agreement. It was basically a wholesale destruction of the German forces—and economy."

"No wonder they wanted to—"

"Make the French pay."

"Yes."

"The symbolism of it all is . . ."

"Is what?"

"It seems like such a different time."

"There's still a lot of symbolism in diplomacy."

"Railcars?"

"I can't think of the contemporary equivalent of railcars off the top of my head, but I'll give it some thought."

When her train is called, Sara again asks Sam not to escort her to the platform, but again he insists. He has his arm around her, and he wants to walk the length of the train to find a car that looks quiet, a tall order when boarding an Acela (the fast train, the only train with open seats at this time) on the Northeast Corridor at rush hour. They find space in the car closest to the café, and Sam walks onto the train, still holding on to her.

"Please, you'll get stuck here," she says.

"Are you sure you don't want me to come?"

"You don't have a ticket," she says.

And he gives her a look that says, *Not the biggest problem I've ever solved.* "Are you sure you have your ticket?" he asks.

"I have it."

"Passport?"

"Yes."

"And—"

"Sam, I'm more pulled together than I look. Slightly, but still."

"Are you sure?"

"I promise."

"Bring him home."

"I will."

"I'll be here."

"I'll call you."

Sam looks like he has something to say, but he does not move.

"Sam. You okay." She opens her arms for a hug. She wants him to believe that she believes.

"Facebook," he says into her ear.

"What," she says, and laughs.

"The contemporary equivalent of railway cars. Facebook." And just as the conductor moves toward them, Sam slips away and doesn't pause on the platform. He's off down the stairs and disappears.

The train is hot; the air conditioning tends to work sporadically this time of year, so a space of three hot days can make the cars compress with stale air. Sara used to like to walk the length of the train during these trips, moving between cars and catching the change in temperature in the spaces where each connects to each. That change was especially bracing in winter. Afraid she might fall asleep, she moves to the café car to get another coffee. This is where she sees the Marines.

There are five of them. They're large, six feet three at least, to a man. They're drinking beers—Heineken, in bottles. She empties half her coffee cup in the trash and fills the rest with milk. And then she stands by the window and eavesdrops. They are talking about girls and about their plans for their holiday.

"The critical aspect of armistice is that no one surrenders," David had said, after that invitation had arrived in the mail. "Armistice is not surrender. Armistice is simply a cessation of hostilities. From the Latin *arma*, meaning weapons, and *stadium*—stopping. Stopping arms." And he told Sara the story of the couple giving the party, two people who had fallen in love, then fallen out of love, then fallen back in again. He was French and she was German, hence the tiny brass railcars they would hand out as favors, one of which David brought back for Jason, who'd added it to his arsenal. He taught the boy to say "armistice," which sounded like "I miss this" in toddlerese. "Mommy's going to sign my armistice agreement," he'd said to their son, lying on her floor, pushing the toy back and forth.

Sara moves back through the cars and finds her seat, although it doesn't really matter where she sits back down. Everyone else on the train looks highly occupied, phones and laptops plugged into side sockets. She has her phone but no computer, nothing to read, not even a paper. She closes her eyes and considers sleep, but her mind won't comply. Her mind wants to remain on high alert, while her heart wants the entire system to shut down until she can open her eyes and hold her boy.

Out the window, the light changes to the kind of bright dark you can get in late spring and early summer, still light enough to drive around without lights but not quite light enough for reading without assistance. Philadelphia, Baltimore, Washington: having lived in such close proximity to these places, it sometimes amazed her how little she knew them. At the station in D.C., she thought, she would stop and get something to eat. There was never anything edible on airplanes, and she knew they were in for a long flight, perhaps several flights. She would buy something to eat and something to read. She had the same feeling in her stomach she'd had each time she knew Jason was about to come home; the feeling of anticipation and relief that before long she would be laughing with him as they had always done together, and hearing what was new in his life. It was the feeling that coupled the ease of being with family with the comfort of no longer being alone.

He would leave again, but at least for a while he'd be home, and this time she'd be able to take care of him. She thinks if he is injured badly, she can always organize a bedroom on the first floor of the house, off the living room. There is a porch there but she could move out all the furniture and bring his bed downstairs. She could ask someone to install a television for him; he would have a view over the whole yard. It was a very pretty view, a therapeutic view. And if needed, for a while, she could sleep on the couch in the living room, to be near him. She would have to think of a list of new things to cook, things he might not expect but would like. New things, alongside his old favorites: shirred eggs, pepper steaks, BLTs with avocado. Maybe the neighbor would market for her if she sent a list, by e-mail, on the way home. Yes, she would make a list for the neighbor to send, and perhaps new sheets for his bed, and some extra pillows. And ice. They were forever running out of ice and perhaps she should have a new ice machine installed.

These were the things on her mind as the train pulled into the station.

There was a man on the platform holding a sign with her name; he had a cart to expedite the trip. "I can walk," she says, but he insists, and so she sits, like an invalid, in the backseat of the little car while he drives her past the shops and restaurants and through the evening crush. At the entrance, looking up, she sees the godfather standing by his car. He looks concerned until he spots her, then his mouth breaks open into a wide smile. The last time she'd seen him in person was just after Christmas. He'd undergone another breakup and, as was his habit, had come north for Sara's solace and a home-cooked meal. They'd stayed up late talking about life and how odd it was that they had both become such loners, though in different ways. They talked about the musical chairs on the Hill and where he might go next should he leave his current role. They talked about today, and about the future, following the unspoken rule of their bond, which was not to dwell on their strange pasts, the person who bonded them and who—lover to her, mentor to him—had left them both emotionally in the lurch and unmoored.

Of all the godfathers, this was the one who had held on and worked hard to stay involved in Jason's life after David died. He was closest in age to Sara, so it made sense. And absent a family of his own, he could prioritize hers. He would never forget an occasion and would move heaven and earth as needed not to miss a game or even, in the rare case, a doctor's visit. He might well be the reason she'd never married, as he'd fulfilled just enough of the spousal functions. And he filled them with creativity and fun; his default setting was wit. He was handsome but too ambitious to put much stock in something he would consider as superficial as appearance, too consumed with being identified as other things, like wise.

He was always missing a button on his shirt or wearing a stained tie, little wrecks that humanized the maniacal precision he applied to all other aspects of this life. And while he had dipped in and out of a lifelong dalliance with recreational drugs, as drugs waned in popularity he fought harder to control his addictions. Sara periodically offered alternatives ("Have you tried peanut butter? Or bicycling?"), but as any addict knows, substitution is not the solution. Nor, in his case, was prayer. Or abstinence. Failing to kick it was his one flaw, the one thing that kept him away from elected office, and likely the one thing that kept him away from the altar. But it was a flaw that, ironically, he held on to like a great achievement, a flaw he nurtured even as it ran right up against the things he professed to want most in life. Discovered with drugs in the Senate cloakroom once, he'd been told to keep his habits off the Hill.

They had become like siblings. This was a great relief to her, as she'd never had a sibling, and a great novelty to him, the last of seven sons. She felt entirely at ease around him. He was the one person with whom she could make this trip and retain her sanity.

He gave her a long hug and then pulled back and looked at her. Her eyes were red and tired, but her affect was as always: aloof, thoughtful. It was this affect that had always put some people off and drew others in. Those close to her knew: it wasn't aloofness, it was simply shyness.

"Do you have a raincoat," he said.

"Yes," she said, holding it up.

"Sweater?"

"Yes."

"Pulse?" he said, folding his hands around her wrist.

"Yes," she said, and smiled.

"*On y va,*" he said, and opened the door of the car for her to duck inside.

INK

Jason walks into his Team CO's office. The elder officer has a photograph up on the screen of his laptop: a series of fire trucks, ten or twelve of them, parked perpendicularly along a leafy suburban street, their ladders lifted and—hung across and between each pair of facing trucks—an American flag. Looking down the line was like looking into an Escher print; the way the flags were arranged made them seem to go on forever, a neat trick of the eye. The flags that day had been thirty feet by thirty feet each, to give some sense of the scale of the scene.

Jason has seen this picture before. It is from a funeral procession given for an operator KIA in 2005, an operator who risked his life to save the lives of his colleagues (only one of whom would survive), and who went on to receive the Medal of Honor posthumously—the fourth of five MOH recipients from the NSW community, two of whom came from these latest wars, the other three from Vietnam. The medal was created in 1862, when war was more central to the culture's psyche, and not only because it was occurring on our own ground. Six hundred twenty-five thousand lives were lost in Civil War combat when the U.S. population was at 31.4 million. Those dead were 1.988 percent of the population. For the Global War on Terror, to date, that same number stood at 0.002 percent. And it was not standing still. Jason remembers Kipling reading out loud one night, "Due to the nature of its criteria, the Medal of Honor is often awarded posthumously." Its ribbon is blue, like water.

What happened that day in '05, in Kunar Province, is well known within the community; it's another celebrated story of heroism, battle, and courage, of how wars are fought now against enemies who don't always look like threats, in places where you wouldn't want to honeymoon. It's also emblematic of how operators don't leave their men behind. That day was a tragedy that involved a moral lesson. Across Teams, guys would argue and analyze the story of the goat herders and their goats, and how the guys that day—there were only four of them—had to decide whether to slaughter the goats, and the herders, or let them go and risk that they talk and betray the operators' presence to the Taliban. The vote that day came down on the side of conscience. It came down on the side of the herders, who were civilians. You cannot kill civilians.

The herders didn't keep their secret. The result of that vote of conscience and rule was one of the largest losses of life in the Afghanistan campaign and in Special Operations Forces history. A lieutenant and three petty officers: this was the scope of their brigade. Estimates of the enemy contingent that arrived to take them down: around two hundred. All sixteen men on the quick reaction force copter died; rocket-propelled grenade. The one survivor on the ground was taken in by a Pashtun villager. The villager saved his life.

"I was here for the—one of the—memorial services," the CO says. "I know you've seen your share."

"Yes, sir."

"Very moving. Very intense."

"Yes, sir."

"This community went almost three decades without waves of memorials. Are we any better at processing loss now than we were then?"

"I don't know."

"I think about that a lot. Did I ever show you this?"

And explaining that one of the eulogists that day had told the story of King Leonidas of Sparta, and about how the king had selected his troops for their celebrated battle, he pulls a piece of paper from his desk and asks Jason to read it:

Leonidas, the Spartan King, hand-picked and led a force to go on what all knew to be a one-way mission. He selected three hundred men to stand against an invading Persian force of over two million. Most of us know this story. But most of us don't know how Leonidas selected those three hundred men. Should he take the older, seasoned warriors who have lived a full life? Should he take the young lions that felt they were invincible? Should he take the battle-hardened, backbone-proven warrior elites in their prime? Or should he sacrifice his Olympic champions? The force he chose would reflect every demographic of the Spartan Warrior class. Why? Because he selected those who would go based on the strength of the women in their lives. After such great loss, he reasoned, if the women faltered in their commitment, Sparta would fall. The rest of Greece would think it useless to stand against the Persian invaders. The democratic flame that started there would be extinguished.

And as he places the piece of paper back down on the desk, Jason thinks, *This is his version of an artful segue.*

Was that piece of paper waiting for Jason's arrival, and for this meeting? Maybe this had all been prepared as neatly as a mission briefing, because perhaps this was the talk with which the CO would remind Jason why he does what he does. He knows the young officer is at an inflection point in his Team tenure, and he knows he might lose him if he doesn't make the sale for him to stay. The art of any sale is to make it look like your goods are precious. The art of the sale in the military is to reinforce the mythology of valor and justice and history.

From the CO's perspective, he simply wants Jason to know he has a future in the Teams. He wants to know how the young officer is doing. And he wants to gauge his taste for change. Like a father gently grilling a daughter's eligible date, he wants to learn as well as teach. It's not a lecture. It's not an ambush. And it's not quite a confessional. It's an exchange. Jason obliges.

"Are you happy?" his CO asks.

"Yes, sir."

"Are you learning?"

"Yes, sir."

"Happiness plus learning equals growth." And he thinks about that for a minute before asking, "Is that the right math?"

"Well, what doesn't kill us certainly makes us stronger."

"This is true. I know you've been in some tough situations."

"We've been busy."

"Any plans to start a family?"

"One day."

Jason stays confident (as he knows he should) but vague (as he knows he must), by the latter leaving open the option that his attitude will be interpreted as rational but flexible. He hasn't mentioned the set of grad school applications he has stacked on his desk—or the girl asleep in his bed.

The CO talks for a while about when he was Jason's age. He talks about the importance of a stable personal life and about the importance of choosing the right person to share a life with—any life, but "particularly this one." He tells Jason how he made it through BUD/S, how it all came down to a vision of his future. He tells him about the moment he almost quit, during Rock Portage. RP is considered one of the tougher evolutions because it is one of the most frightening. It's the essence of the *S*, for sea; it's docking on rocks at night.

He tells Jason how he remembered that "right at that moment, right up on those rocks, with my life passing before my eyes, all I could think was, well, my father had five daughters, and my brother *has* five daughters, and one day I'll marry and I'll quite likely have daughters. And one day those daughters will bring home boys. And they can bring those boys home either to a father who was almost a Team guy or to a father who *is* a Team guy. And that was it. After that, quitting never crossed my mind."

"Have they brought home any boys yet?" Jason asks. He knows the CO has daughters.

"They have."

"And?"

"And exactly what you think 'and.' What was your moment, lieutenant?"

"My moment?"

"You ever think about quitting?"

"No. I guess I never had that moment."

"Impressive."

"I was probably too cold to think straight. Definitely too cold to think about . . ."

"Think about?"

"Think about . . . goals."

Check.

The CO leans forward.

"And what are your goals?"

"Sir, my only goal is to make it to tomorrow."

"In the Teams?"

Checkmate.

And Jason says, "As of today, yes."

And the CO closes his eyes, opens them, and raises an eyebrow. "Is that a new tattoo?"

"It is," Jason says. Even he concedes it's extreme, and he's not quite sure why he got it, but now it's part of who he is—the quite literally indelible inkings of war. He knows the older guys don't understand. They think his generation is too competitive, too ambitious, too needy for immediate success. The ink's emblematic of that. The ink's a proxy for emotion, maybe. Or a proxy for stars on one's shoulders. It says, *I was there. I was in it.* He'd thought about Kipling when he got it; he'd thought about getting it on his back but had opted for his forearm instead, a decision he's deeply regretting in this moment.

"Also impressive," says the CO.

Jason rolls down his sleeve, a rare moment of self-consciousness. "A bit silly, I guess."

"Sign of the times. Things change."

"When you—"

"When I came through, there were two billets to BUD/S, Jason. *Two.* No Mini-BUD/S, no pretraining courses. Guys worth their weight wanted to be pilots, not frogmen. What they told us about special warfare was that the guys had to take daily breaks for sun tanning. They had to take breaks to tan so they wouldn't burn in the middle of a mission. Sailors sunning themselves on the Strand: that was the rumor about life in the Teams. No one had a clue what this community was capable of."

"Now they have one," Jason says quietly.

"They do," the CO says loudly, and laughs, spinning his chair to consider a map on his wall. The map had tiny pins placed in areas of interest. "We're at the crest of a wave here. You know what the crest of a wave feels like?"

"I can imagine."

"You surf?" And he moves his hand—as Jason had seen Sam do countless times—to fold his fingers in the shape of a wave—the perfect wave. At the end of the fold, his fingers close into a fist.

"I'd like to learn."

"The crest is when you're riding on the top. Obviously. The crest is when you're coming near the peak but with the knowledge that after the peak there comes the challenge of how to ride down the other side. And we've been on the other side. There was a time when Special Operations Forces weren't considered central."

"Sir."

"It was an army world. We were—we were a bit like the relief pitchers. Or some might say, we were a bit like the magic show."

"Magic show?"

"You can't afford a magic show when economics are tight; magic shows are the first things to go. You give your kids cake and ice cream at the party, and not one of them will ask, 'Hey, where's the magician?' Only one day you realize, hey, cake makes me fat. I can learn from a magician. He can do some neat things. Maybe I reallocate my *strategic interests* to ensure we always have a magician on hand."

The choice of metaphor makes Jason smile. The CO keeps talking.

"When I came in, op tempo was low. It was the end of the Cold War. The Greatest Generation saved the world, and then the Vietnam generation almost threw it wide open again. We trusted that Greatest Generation. And they trusted us. Then nobody trusted anybody. Lindsay said that there would be 'a more violent peace.' *General* Lindsay."

"A more violent peace."

"A more violent peace. Sometimes I think we're preaching a more peaceful violence."

"What makes a peace violent?" Jason asks after a while.

"Ah: now there's a 'known unknown.'"

"We're not at peace."

"Well, there's no Terrorism Treaty of Versailles happening anytime or anywhere as far as I can see."

Jason's mind began to wander. His mother had a book on Versailles; she'd been there. The CO kept talking.

"In 1966 the CO of the UDTs was a lieutenant commander. Our CO now is a four-star admiral. We have ten admirals now."

"Yes, sir."

"We need guys like you, Jason."

"That's kind of you to say."

"I know you lost your dad when you were little. And I know you have no siblings."

"That's—"

"And I know your guys love you."

"Thank you."

The CO closes the computer and stands up, so Jason stands up. The CO folds the piece of paper with the eulogy and hands it to him. "Some guy came in here the other day and asked me to bet him on a match-up between one of our platoons and a platoon in Vietnam," he says.

"Not sure I would take that bet." Jason puts the paper in his pocket.

"'There is no bet.' That's what he said. And then he said, 'Your guys would eliminate them before they even got out of the boat.

It's not because you're smarter than they were. Or faster. They were smart and fast and tough, and they grew up a lot less coddled than you. That war was as brutal as these. But you'd still kill every one of them before they got out of their boat for a reason that has absolutely nothing to do with character or strength: you'd kill them before they got out of the boat because you carry better guns.' "

"Technology."

"Progress. *Progress* is the word he used."

"Was he a vet?"

"Progress is the game changer. And politics creates an environment that's either receptive to or destructive of technological change. And geopolitics defines the need for those new technologies. Technology. Politics. Geopolitics. The Global Want Monster."

"Did he say all that?"

"I'm saying it. There is no more room for rogues in the Teams, Jason. We need leaders. You can be a warrior for only so long, and then you'll need weapons fit to serve you well on other fields. Weapons like diplomatic instinct. Political acumen." He taps a finger to his temple.

"Does that mean I have to get a Ph.D.?" Jason asks. They laugh.

"It means you have to make choices to show you understand the challenges. 'Irregular warfare is far more intellectual than a bayonet charge.' "

"T. E. Lawrence."

"I thought you'd like that one."

Jason had ordered *Seven Pillars of Wisdom* off of Amazon months ago, after the CO had recommended it. He learned from Lawrence that knowledge of a people and place are not irrelevant. But he knew that already. Wasn't that why the younger guys were now adding Arabic to their training? But hearts and minds weren't within the classic wheelhouse of Naval Special Warfare. "Learning Arabic is opening a door into an empty room," his troop commander told him, out on his first op. "That's for Special Forces. You won't be needing to talk quite as much as they do." He considered the T. E. Lawrence story quaint, in its way. There is no Arabia now, full stop. Lawrence wrote his Jesus College thesis on Syrian Crusader castles. He approached battle like a philosopher. He approached it like a humanitarian.

As he leaves his CO's office, Jason stops at the door. "Sir?"

And without looking up from his desk, the CO says, "Yes, you might be eligible for screening." *Dam Neck*. "Was that the question?"

"The question is, if a mission isn't worth risking lives, what's the worth of the mission?"

And the meaning of the conversation is understood by both men. As Jason heads into the hall, the CO calls out after him.

"Yes, he was a vet."

And Jason turns, raises the untattooed arm, and gives the other officer a gentle salute.

*

Four deployments, and how many missions? The number of missions depended on a constellation of factors beyond the control of even the savviest four-star. It was weather, for example. In winter, there's less fighting in Afghanistan. It was length of deployment. It was area of operations. It was period of conflict (start versus surge). It was battle space owner. One deployment could include thirty missions or one hundred. And the size and scope of each depended. But all the guys who had been out over these past years had seen enough to lose the view that the world could be converted to good—or to peace—permanently. The world could be policed, perhaps, but the taste for bloodshed was alive and well in places most Americans will never go. Some of the things he has seen he has willfully forgotten. Some of the things he has seen he can never forget.

In Afghanistan, his platoon's sniper lost an ear. Jason was standing about three feet away from him when it happened, and for months that moment would play over and over and over in his mind. They were working an overwatch for a group of Marines. Things had quieted down significantly in this particular part of this town; that could change at any minute but the mood—for the moment—was verging on boredom. Their job was to watch the street.

The guy was younger than Jason, married with three sons. He was quickly becoming one of the finest shooters in the Teams. That had been his dream, apparently, since he was a boy, even though he grew up in a place nowhere near a gun range, in a family that had no guns. The practice fit his temperament. He was precise. He was patient. Jason was certain his veins ran half blood, half ice water because nothing ever shook him. He was capable of waiting for hours or days in order to get the perfect shot, sometimes losing as much as eight or nine pounds simply from the pressure of the watch. Stillness, it turns out, is an athletic experience.

On that day, the two of them had been sent into a house in a city that was much in the news back home, a city Jason hoped his mother never noticed in the papers in connection with the phrase "Special Operations Forces." The job was very basic: the Marines cleared the streets; NSW was there in case of a problem. And they worked well with those guys; they'd come to know them at the base, and there was mutual respect. But the Marines had become careless. Ironically, they'd become careless because of their increased confidence in the sniper's skills and, more broadly, because of their confidence in the fact that they were being covered by guys they knew would never let them down. It was the "pool fence" problem, one with which any mother is familiar: confidence in visible protection elevates the probability of defeat. When two of the soldiers walked into—rather than ran through—the square below where Jason and his sniper sat, shots rang out. By the time the shooter located the origin of the bullets, the originator of those bullets had located him, and Jason felt something graze his plate at almost the exact same second something flew (or at least looked as though it flew) right under the shooter's helmet. The young father lowered his weapon slowly and said, "I think I've been hit." And when he turned to look at Jason, his face was covered in blood.

Jason went to see him in the base hospital afterward. Both his eyes were bandaged. The doctors had told him he would regain full vision in one, but that the other would be chronically compromised and near-blind; it had been compromised due to the wound and the necessary attendant operations. It was the end of his career as a sniper.

"Hey," said Jason.

"Shine a light," said the sniper weakly. It was a reference to a song they both liked. Jason looked at him and felt a wave of nausea. And guilt. The doctors had said it might be wise to walk his friend around the floor, for circulation.

"Up for a walk?"

"Nah, too slow. Let's hike up the Hindu Kush, take a picnic. I think my future holds a lot of fucking picnics."

"What's wrong with fucking picnics?"

The doctors said it was a miracle. They said the shot certainly could have killed him or—a better but still close-to-worst case—left him brain-dead. But the shot had taken out the operator's prized possession, his talent; the silver lining that he would see again was one he would only be willing to accept, over time, as God's grace.

"Do you think . . ." the sniper started, turning his head away.

"Do I think what."

"Nothing."

"Do I think what?" Jason noticed the guy's hands were shaking.

"Forget it."

"*What.*"

And Jason saw something wet spread across the lower edge of the bandage on the side of the good eye.

In Iraq, Jason was involved in clearing a house where a woman was found holding a baby. The woman was seriously injured—not by their guys, but by whom was unclear. Had they not arrived in time, and had she died, what would have happened to that baby? Jason couldn't shake that question from his mind either. When his teammate lifted the baby from the mother's arms, he handed the child to Jason. He could feel his heart rate accelerate; this was not a procedure they'd covered in SERE. He had never held something this small. Was she hungry? Was she well? Would she grow up to remember this? How far back did memory go, and what were the relevant and necessary defense mechanisms countering the horrors? "Don't drop that baby," his platoon OIC said, putting a hand on his shoulder. And when Jason looked up, he saw that the other officer was smiling. "She's the same age as my littlest one," he said. "She's all right. She's all right now." And Jason was relieved that someone else had some experience with this. There was no room in his vest for the infant, so he wrapped her—she was in only the thinnest of robes—in a VS-17 panel. It was bright pink. "Cover her head," said the OIC. "She has to stay warm." And so Jason jerry-rigged a tiny do-rag using a torn piece of tourniquet.

In Africa, sent in to rescue an American held in a house apparently occupied by AQAP cell members, they'd found the hostage barely breathing and lying alongside a group of partially buried bodies in the basement. It was unclear whether the bodies were those of military men or aid workers. It was even unclear whether the bodies were men or women. And it was unclear how they had been killed, and so, time being of the essence, the guys lacked the chance for forensic speculation. It might have been a mini-mass suicide. They were all blindfolded; that is what he would remember. Each body had cloth wrapped around where their eyes would have been; their eyes had been cut out or at least damaged. The cloths were red and hid the blood. Somehow that cloth humanized them. Somehow that cloth said, *These were once my eyes.* But what was the cloth preventing them from seeing?

None of these stories would appear in print, nor would Jason share details of them with anyone. Some of the guys, he knew, talked to their priests about things that they did and saw, but most talked only among themselves. This was not a profession that gave rise to many memoirs. The slim literature—necessarily crippled by the periodic publication of wildly inaccurate analyses—helped perpetuate the myths and the conspiracies, but the central humanness of the community kept the men in line. Back at the beaches, they were real people, with real responsibilities.

These experiences, among others, reinforced for Jason what had become a central trope: nothing is what it seems. What was most amazing about the day they found those bodies was that no one had discussed it. It was a quick op, the pressure was high, they were there to try and find one thing, and once they had found it, it was time to go. They weren't archaeologists. They weren't war correspondents. They were warriors.

They had exfiltrated by MH-6 Little Bird, and when they boarded, the pilot, a Nightstalker, called out, seeing they had the hostage, "Did you guys get me my slice, too?" And no one had said anything. It wasn't until days later that, sitting at a meal, staring into his soup, another guy who had been there said to Jason, "Those bodies were—." And Jason said, "Yes." They were both thinking the same thing, which was that they couldn't stop thinking about them. But they would. Nightmares, for most men, could be willed away with discipline just as well as they could be with therapy. Of course, the outer edge of this ability to forget was numbness, anomie, despair.

Did these contemporary war stories lack the grandeur and arc of their predecessors? Sadr City was not the Somme. That was like comparing *Mad Max* to *Madame Bovary*. But they were alike in this simple fact: men were killing other men across a small space to save the lives of millions of others half a world away. Historians would eventually take their pick of the facts and look at the larger questions, but the first wave of understanding would come from the guys who were there, the guys who could say, *I saw the bodies. I carried the baby. I swallowed the dust.* The first phase of history was simply recollections from the survivors, the ones able to describe the details, like *In the early days of OIF we smashed the windows of the helos out so we could see better* and *The maximum effective range of an M4 with a fourteen-inch barrel is five hundred yards* and *The breacher prepared the slap charge, but we were lucky he brought the sledgehammer as backup when things got complicated.* These were not sentences formed anywhere else in the history of warfare. It was a new language, but they embraced it with characteristic grace.

*

Walking from the CO's office to his own, one he shared with another lieutenant, Jason realizes that one chapter of his training has ended, and a new one—what might be called the political one—has begun. As platoon assistant officer in charge, one aspect of mission planning he oversees now is actions at the objective, or what actually occurs when the guys arrive at their destination. He is skilled in this, as one becomes in anything after practice and after errors. He is increasingly sure of himself across a range of conditions. These skills and this confidence will afford him the chance to play a critical role in an upcoming mission, one for which he will undergo a new kind of training, and one that will require a new level of secrecy and risk.

If his timing works out, he'll be sitting on a beach next summer and in a Contracts classroom in New Haven next fall. He wouldn't trade the things he has learned since leaving Annapolis; they have changed him. Even more than the statistics and rituals of battle, he has learned how to compartmentalize his emotions and his thoughts. There is Work; there is The Rest. He enjoys his considerable skill at separating things—necessary in his current line of work but one that is, he believes, transferable. Over time it has simply become second nature.

Jason feels the reason for the new, intense attention from his colleagues is this: increasingly, SOF missions involve Langley, and Jason knows that some of the guys at Langley today knew David and know Sara. And they know that the child born out of that match is now in the Teams. As he's done well, perhaps he's being tested. Does he possess a political appetite? Will he stay the course? His godfather's in line for a prominent position in the sweet spot where politics and intelligence intersect, and Jason

knows his godfather's dreams for him exceed the county boundaries of Little Creek. His mother, too, has friends and admirers throughout Georgetown and McLean. While she never asks
anything of the scholars and congressmen with whom she works,
their networks are impressive, and she's looped in. For those
overseeing the shots of upcoming operations, they can mention
they know someone whose son serves. It's an effective inroad in an
audience with an admiral, for example. So Jason's name is known
in certain circles.

And he had been told where he is going next. One of the High
Value Individuals that intelligence had been tracking had moved,
and an SOF platoon would follow. Deserts and snowy mountain-
tops were increasingly the American warrior's courts of choice,
or where they were in high demand, but this time Jason would
return to the port town he'd spent the better part of the last two
years in, a place that looks and feels a lot like how he imagines
Hell might look and feel. What the platoon chief wanted to know,
and what his CO wanted to know, was whether he had the stamina to extend his stay in this world. They both know the lure for
extension is increased if the meaning of the work is clarified and
reinforced.

*

Kick down enough doors and most guys start thinking about
other things. Jason knew two officers who reactivated through the
reserves after 9/11, in the interim having taken Harvard MBAs.
In their spare time, they'd calculated the procurement and release
rates of Iraqi prisoners and saw bad math: the number of detain-
ees cycling through holding facilities exceeded the size of the
insurgency itself. The military was placing innocent men in bed,

literally, with criminals, creating an informal recruitment loop. When the guys showed a waterfall chart of these stats to their commander, he asked, "And why is this happening?" "Bad incentive alignment, sir," they said. Later one of them qualified that: "I mean, *fucking* bad incentive alignment."

When Jason asked, "What's incentive alignment?" he got a lecture about the fog of war, and about math, how math made Western Front attrition rates mean something and formed the philosophies of men in Ford C-suites who once ran the world. The lecture ended with an 0–6 saying, "But math can conflate success and activity, you know what I mean?" And while Jason thought about that, the officer said, "Let me put it like this: If history repeats itself a second time, what do you call the thing that follows tragedy and farce?"

TWO

MYRRH

Just before Christmas, Jason decorates a tree in his house at the beach with the girl he has been seeing. He had called his godfather first to clear his choice not to go home for the holiday (being accustomed to the confidence that comes from gaining clearances). His godfather assured him Sara won't be alone.

"She has more invitations at holidays than the first lady, J.," he says, into a speakerphone. Jason can picture his English partners' desk, covered with dark green felt. Sara always called it "the pool table," as it was almost as large. He's had the same series of little things on it since he moved to that office. Jason remembers every one, and closing his eyes he can see where each is set, like a snapshot, another side effect of his training: the Davidoff humidor, the photograph with the last six SECDEFs, the Lucite box with Lincoln's inaugural engraved on it, the Ivy Club ashtray, the cigarettes in a silver julep cup. He also had pictures of Sara and David and Jason. One of them was taken the day Jason was born; he suspected his godfather slipped it in a drawer when his mother dropped by.

"She'll never accept them," Jason says.

"Well, that's her own fault. I can ask her down to D.C.—"

"She won't go."

"She won't go. You're exactly right."

"She won't leave the house. Or doesn't seem to. When I call, she's always there. I don't know what she thinks is going to happen if she leaves."

"Maybe she thinks she'll miss one of your phone calls. Look, she leaves the house. She doesn't tell you everything. She has her life. She's your mother; stop worrying. You know, just as you don't tell her everything, perhaps she doesn't share everything with you. She's strong. Live your life. She checks in with me to check in on you, and I know my script."

" 'He sits at Starbucks on the base drinking lattes'?"

"Something like that, yeah. She doesn't know enough about what you do to be too worried. She doesn't *want* to know."

"She suspects."

"She's suspected too much since before you were born. You have to understand that. And respect it—how she handles it. She elects to think you swim around scoping container ships, or escorting Iraqi diplomats to breakfast meetings. She will believe what she wants to believe, which is how she survived all those years with your dad. She can do it. She's a storyteller at heart. She respects you, and she's been brave through this time. And this time is almost up, right? *Right?*"

"What does 'scoping container ships' mean?" He's teasing.

"It means you've served your country. Time to come back and work for the home team."

"Are you the home team?"

"Happy Christmas. Call me before you head out again."

"Yes, sir."

"And Jesus Christ, don't call me 'sir.' "

"Yes, sir."

"Happy Christmas."

*

The girl is an associate professor of history at the University of Richmond, the daughter of one Team guy and the sister of another one. She's three years his senior. She is quiet and reserved and brilliant and fierce, and she asks nothing of him—at least, "nothing" on a relative basis compared to other girls he's known. She loves to be around his house and around him. They're good at not talking together for long stretches of time, and not much fazes—or impresses—her. She'll break his heart ultimately, because when he finally says goodbye before leaving later that spring, he expects her to ask for something—to ask him to stay, to ask him to commit, to ask him for more emotion. But she won't ask for anything, and the absence of her expectations upsets his sense of how things should be. But the absence of her expectation is a trick she's been trained to perform. Her relative sophistication and his relative optimism ran headlong into one another, like opposable magnetic fields.

They have been together, whatever that means, since his last stretch of time spent in Virginia Beach, almost one year ago, but they met years before that, just after his move back east. She speaks four languages: English, French, Hebrew, and Arabic. But despite such lofty credentials, she's adamantly down to earth. She knows all of Lynyrd Skynyrd's lyrics by heart; "Watergate does not bother me; does your conscience bother you?" was one of her preferred come-ons, in fact the one she'd used on Jason. They can discuss cooking as easily as kill chains because she grew up around guns and gun ranges and gun talk and didn't think gear was "cool"—or frightening. Jason thinks her studied calm comes not from the men in her life but rather from having been raised by a woman married to an officer, as well as having been raised alongside a half-brother who had put his life on the line many times and was highly respected throughout the Teams.

Her brother was at Dam Neck, a member of the Naval Special Warfare Development Group, or DEVGRU, or Six, the one Team whose line on the NSW org chart skipped Coronado and went straight up to JSOC. Her father was a DEVGRU plank owner, a member of the very first Team. So she was connected. And as is true of deep knowledge of any topic passed down through generations (rather than absorbed through headlines), she understood the DNA of Team culture. She knew the risks because she had lived with them, and yet she believed that the fact that her father and her brother were alive was not a trick of statistics or chance. It was how things were meant to be. She expected character in a man, and depth; on these things she would be strict. And even better for the preservation of peace at home, she had the right mix of reverence for and cynicism about what Jason did for a living to keep him interested, while keeping his ego in check. It was a balance that mirrored his mother's, in a way, one that girls learn from growing up in close proximity to power.

Her mother was also a teacher and had taken on her brother when he was a toddler. Married to one warrior and having helped raise another, she was tough. But for her daughter she reserved—and fiercely guarded—"a life of the mind," pushing the young girl away from the bars on Shore Drive during high school, holding up an education, or even an advanced degree, as the way to find a meaning in her life equal to what her brother and father had found, and as worthy of respect in another world as the men's accomplishments were in their own.

She was wary of her daughter's choice of Jason as a beau. She knew too much and had a sense of what lay ahead if it lasted: regrets to dinner parties and skipped sports games, forgotten critical milestones and the unexpected choice between appearing in the ER for a child's broken arm and answering an urgent SIPR alert. If the girl married Jason, and if he went back out west, their children would grow up playing on the O course, just as she had done.

And yet there was no pressure to plan: even at her age, she seemed uninterested in ever settling down. In this, too, she was unlike most of the girls he'd met since high school, most of whom made it easy to feel good while doing very little, most of whom wanted rings by spring or double their tuition back. She had held his interest longer than any predecessor, but he was as capable of coyness as she was and, like cats, it would take them a long time to trade pride for something as dubious as love.

On this night, he's cleaning his gear, and she's completing the tree and talking about Christmas. She has the key degrees to know its history.

"Did you know myrrh is a common resin in the Horn of Africa?" she asks.

"Nope."

"Really? You've never stumbled on a patch of myrrh trees?" She's ribbing. And prying—gently.

"Nope."

"*Really?*"

"Well, seeing as I've never been to that part of the world, I'm not sure where I would've stumbled on a set of—"

"*Patch* of."

"Patch of myrrh trees."

"Well, myrrh is very healing. If you ever stumble upon some, you should snap it up."

"What's it heal?"

"Well, I'm not the medical specialist here, you are. Look it up."

"Broken hearts?"

"Broken *arms*, more likely. Wounds. I think of it as something to be rubbed on an open wound."

"Why would you bring something to rub on an open wound as a gift to a new baby?"

"An excellent question. I have no idea. Maybe that was a metaphor. Well, the Wise Men knew what they were doing. They were scholars. I'd consider the presentation of healing power from a scholar—a rather regal scholar, they were kings, too—I'd consider that an extraordinary gift. Actually, the gathering of myrrh is quite . . . bloody."

"Bloody?"

"Bloody. I'm sure the Wise Men didn't gather it themselves."

"How is it—"

"I think they do something like strangle the myrrh trees until they bleed."

"The trees bleed?"

"They bleed the myrrh gum." She's laughing.

"You are completely insane."

"Look it up!"

"I'm busy."

"As am I. What do you think?"

She's meticulous with the tree, which amuses him. She went out and bought tiny white lights. She went out and bought a hundred—at least—sparkly ornaments: balls, obelisks, sugared fake fruits. She brought a wheel of red satin ribbon, too, that she stayed up half the last night cutting into pieces to bow at the ends of branches. And she even brought an angel for the top—a tiny, golden angel, wearing a white caftan rimmed in gold thread, with a tiny halo made of gold wire set above its head. She had found a toy gun that she's fastened to the angel's hands with string. She had guessed that would make Jason smile, and she's right.

"I love it," he says.

"You deserve it. You're the Jesus child."

"What does *that* mean?"

"The only male son? It's what we used to call my brother, teasing him. The Jesus child is the child on whom excessive and at times undue or unreasonable adoration is showered. The child incapable of error. The child of whom much is expected. The child—"

"I get it."

"Is it you?" she asks, eyeing the accuracy of her twinkly garlands.

"I think you'd have to take that up with my mother."

"Well, I plan to withhold adoration until I know for sure. Adoration *and* expectation."

"Adoration: is that a euphemism?"

For Christmas Eve supper, she cooks turkey and gives a toast. Her family was big on toasts, especially at holidays, when apparently they all felt the need to restate their affections for one another. It made him uncomfortable; he'd been raised to show less. It flashed through his mind, but only briefly, that perhaps he should say something too, even ask her to marry him, seal the deal right now. Instead, he says nothing. They drift upstairs, leaving his kitchen a happy mess. "Wake me if you see Santa," she says sleepily, then closes her eyes. She doesn't need him to tell her how he feels. She knows.

In the middle of the night, he gets up. He wants to check once more that he has everything he needs, a nervous habit he's had since well before now, the classic anticipation of failure that inevitably accompanies a history of unbroken success. He is ready to leave again. In fact, he can't wait to go. "Back to the playground," one of the guys says each time they head out. And the statement was a mix of gallows humor and confession: they all knew they were headed to a broken place—most of them sure it was too broken for them to fix.

The lights of the tree are still on and are enough to see by. He lays out everything to take with him under its branches, and sees she's slipped a few gifts there. He makes a mental note not to forget to write down how he feels at this moment and how grateful he is for her. He wants to be sure that she knows. He doesn't ever want her—or anyone, for that matter—to think of him as a Jesus child. *Christ.*

Pushing the presents aside, he lays down his plate carrier, into which he will fit the following: six ChemLights, readily accessible and used for marking different things—deconfliction points (blue), cleared rooms (green), prisoner marshaling areas inside a house (red); two sets of flex-cuffs; three flashlights; two knives (one Microtech, one Emerson) and one Gerber multitool; an E and E kit with signaling mirror, compass, Clif bar, PowerBar gel, batteries, and a magnesium fire-starter kit; a small Garmin GPS Foretrex 401 for the butt of his rifle and a larger Garmin for backup; his Oakleys, with interchangeable lenses (amber, dark, and clear); a Rapid Rod for punching his bore clear in the event that his rifle gets clogged; a VS-17 panel, just like the one he had used for the baby, bright pink on one side and red on the other, for marking positions in the daytime; his small spiral "write in the rain" notebook, Sharpies, grease pencils, and pens; his medical kit, including gauze, nasal pharyngeal tubes, pressure dressings, quick clot, morphine (removed and regulated when he is not working), and Asherman chest seals; tourniquets, kept separate from the medical kit, attached to the outside of the plate carrier; his Peltor noise-canceling headset, connected to an MBITR for intersquad communications, the same one he'd been wearing when chastised in the kill house. All are encrypted. His cutter wrist coach slips onto his arm; inside of it he'll slide the "baseball cards" prepared by the intel officers. These are used for identification—not of an operator, but of a bad guy.

At the armory on base, he has two H&K 416 rifles; two M4s; a SCAR heavy and a SCAR light; and his Sig Sauer 226, safely enclosed in his SERPA holster. Knight's Armament suppressors can silence all of these. For optics, he uses an EOTech with a detachable magnifier. He has an ATPIAL aiming laser (visible and IR) for his rifles, and a small additional flashlight; these last are all operated by pressure pads. Seatbelts take up too much room on the helos, so the guys each have lanyards linked to their plates for hard-pointing in without belts.

In case, everyone carries their medical kit on the same place on the same leg, so when a man is down, his own kit can be easily located and used on him. The basic kit has not altered in generations even as the technological advancements in armaments have changed the game irrevocably. Case in point, the CO's Vietnam example. The guys who fought in that era were fierce in a different way and, correct: they weren't in it to rise up the ranks at NATO. He had a picture in his room at his mother's of a guy his father knew in Saigon. In the photo, he's in his cammies and has several necklaces looped around his neck hung with various charms. He looks a little like a killer, and a little like Dennis Hopper in *Apocalypse Now*. He also looks almost like a child, and as Jason grew older, he was increasingly struck by how young this man seemed. That was before Jason had ever seen a child hold a gun. And that was before he had ever seen a child killed. "He would have been your godfather, too," Sara had told him, as if he needed one more. But Jason never met him because the soldier never got out of Saigon. He remained classified as MIA. His will to stay and serve a place had outlasted that of his own country.

*

When the time comes to head out on a mission, Jason knows, as always, they will be told: whether the environment they'll be operating in is "nonpermissive"; the timeline of their pre-mission training; the timeline of the mission; who, if anyone, will accompany them/act as backup on the mission; what will constitute the multiple platforms of air support within the Restricted Operations Zone—the pilot, the craft, the coordinates of the helicopter's landing zone. Determining the conditions for the ROZ was important—the platoon's joint terminal attack Controller would work with the pilots on that. Selecting HLZ coordinates was important. Like building a ship, building a mission meant every piece of the puzzle had to fit. And in case, contingencies had to be mapped out for scenarios in which one piece might malfunction.

*

Jason fights a strong will to open the presents and goes back upstairs, but he still cannot sleep. Looking at the girl beside him, he thinks how different they are. He has the constant sense that she could leave him at any moment and never look back. She's not reckless, but she's broken in that one way someone truly conditioned against expectations is broken: she can never be happy. In the morning he oversleeps, and she's made breakfast. She invites him to her parents' house for supper that night, and he accepts.

After dinner, a dinner where her father treated him like he was already family, knuckle bumping and hugging and teasing, they go back to his place and unwrap presents. His from her is a tiny wooden box filled with what appear to be rocks. "It's myrrh," she says. "For my Jesus child. Now you'll know it when you see it." And she points out that on the box's back she's carved his initials, and the date: CHRISTMAS 2010. She carved them herself with his knife. His to her is something she'd requested repeatedly, and he'd finally hunted down: a photograph from his Academy graduation. He is in his whites. He looks many years younger than he looks and feels now. "You used to brush your hair," she observes.

Later, Jason and her brother go out the two of them alone. Her brother is in his late thirties. At six two, he's tall. Yet he's somehow physically quiet and unassuming. Jason is sure that if he met this guy in line at the bank, he might mistake him for one of his mother's eggy friends, the ones who didn't like Maine oceans because they were too cold, the ones who played squash at city clubs. Yet he knew exactly who this was: one of the most highly respected operators in the Teams. There was nothing "eggy" about him. He was a guy who did the right thing, and did it quietly, and did it well. Capable of deep thoughts, he rarely shared them to prove himself. He was just the kind of guy Jason wanted to grow up to be. He was just the kind of guy whose future could explode in myriad provocative directions, if he wanted that. And if he survived.

"Your little sister's strong," Jason says.

"Yeah, we're sending her to anhedonia camp for the summer," he laughs.

"Strong, and smart."

"Yes, the women in our family all like to teach, particularly when the pupils are men. Particularly men who serve in the military."

He tells Jason about his own decision to join the Teams, his own time at the Academy, and then at BUD/S, about his "no bell Hell" and the particularly ruthless pre–Hell Week evolution that ensured it. They talk about the meaning of the Teams. And then the older officer says, "How are you doing on sanity?"

"Sanity?" Jason is not sure what he means.

"How are you doing on keeping it all together. Keeping balanced."

"I think all right."

"It's a skill. It can be honed."

"I think I'm—I'm good on that."

"The transitions didn't used to be like they are now—muddy. When I started out, and I'd deploy? I wouldn't even talk to home. There was no e-mail. No cell phones. It wasn't like I knew what I was missing or what was changing out of my control. The media was different, too. Expectations—the relationship expectations—must have been more like they were in other wars. You leave, you come home, you're a hero, you pick up where you left off. It's different now."

"It is."

"Now everyone knows so much about what everybody else is doing. It can be hard to focus. To *re*focus."

"It can."

"It's important to talk about things when you need to. I mean, not to me. You can talk to my sister. You can talk to anybody you like. But it's not a bad idea to talk about things. To someone you trust."

The older operator explains to Jason how he will have to decide why he does what he does and whether he is willing to stay on or whether he's ready to retire. He confesses that speaking to almost any younger guy, his advice would be, without qualification, to consider staying the course, staying active. The American military system—and the Naval Special Warfare system in particular—is undergoing changes, and that's the best time to be at the center of a system. And yet talking to someone who might one day be not only his brother-in-law but also the father of his nieces and nephews? In this case he might even recommend looking into work on Wall Street.

"Yeah, I've had Goldman Sachs beating down my door," Jason says. They laugh.

"Well, send them over to my door, and I'll kick their ass."

They drink without talking for a while. And then Jason says, "Women have more emotional . . . resilience." He's thinking about the girl not caring that he never made a toast. And he's thinking about his mother.

"Free-surface effect."

"Pardon?"

"Free-surface effect. Did you fail your naval architecture class?"

"Free-surface effect is what places the ship in danger."

"Well, it's the accident of architecture that allows water into her hull. And that accident results in destabilization. But it's only when a ship's destabilized that you can identify her weaknesses."

"Like—"

"A little free-surface effect's good for the soul. And women—women tend to let the water in. They're more psychologically porous."

"I don't envy them that."

"You wouldn't, but they don't envy you your effortless tricks of repression, do they? It's Darwinian, right? They need that—that emotional littoral zone—especially in the presence of children, in the presence of the chaos of motherhood. But before that they need it in processing their emotions. What they manage—it's a different chaos than what we see every day. They need easier access to a wider bank of emotional memories. We need the art of clean, immediate forgetting and of easy access to a shallow pool of information."

"Shallow?"

"Shallow. Well, said another way, *factual*. Tactical. We worship at the altar of the tactical. And they understand the essential requirements of . . . of strategy. You know what I'm saying?"

"Tactics are shallow; strategy's deep?"

"What I'm saying is that what attracts us is what puts us at odds, and that's why we stay in it."

"All part of God's plan?"

"You can look at it that way, sure. It certainly keeps the game interesting."

"Shallow pools competing with wide banks?"

"Shallow pools competing with wide banks." He had been married and had two children, now teenagers. The kids had barely seen their father over the last decade. Jason saw at Christmas dinner how the son, in particular, interacted with his dad, and saw through this example that it was possible: he could continue to live this life and continue to have a life. Jason knew he wanted to be a father, and he knew this guy was a good father. Jason knew he wanted to be a husband, and knew this guy was a good husband. And Jason knew enough to know that that wasn't easy.

When they pull into Jason's driveway, the girl's brother puts the car in park. He turns to Jason and says, "In all seriousness now: two things. Are you listening?"

"Yes, sir."

"First, if you get an opportunity to do something different—to go to a new place, or to work with some new guys, and you think this opportunity will stretch you? Say yes."

"Yes."

"Do you understand what I mean by 'stretch'?"

"I do."

"I don't care what your future plans are. I don't want to know if you have them. What matters is where you've been. You know that. It doesn't matter to me whether you end up waiting tables or running special warfare; what matters now is what you do and where you've been and how you treat your guys. Character. The gear does not make the operator."

"Understood."

"And the second thing. If you break her heart, I have no qualms about killing you."

"Also understood."

And they sit for a minute, Jason feeling almost as if he needs a formal dismissal. The car doors are still locked. "And, wait: there's a third thing. No more fucking tattoos." And with that, the man Jason suspects will one day be his brother-in-law, the godfather to his children, and—perhaps—his Teammate, leans over and gives him a big bear hug just as his mother would have done had she been there. Maybe law school can wait.

*

In bed the night before leaving the base, Jason thinks about what the chief had asked him that fall day and decides he does have a favorite weapon: his Sig Sauer. This is the gun he had practiced shooting (illegally) in the backyard in Pennsylvania for days during his first leave. He was determined to get better. He was determined to perfect his shot. This is also the gun he taught his mother to shoot, much to her amusement. "Mommy, it comes in pink." And, "You hit a target not by aiming but by thinking about aiming." He had just learned that line from an instructor at XE, and he loved it. He remembers when he wrote to her about how he would teach her to use it because he thought it was easy when he first learned to shoot. And because he worried constantly in those days about Sara being home alone, unprotected. The more he saw of the evil people were capable of, the more he felt conflict about the forum in which he was working to protect the people he loved. Was this really the front line? Or was the front line closer to home? And the more he thought, the more he wondered where this work—this service—would lead, whether his godfather hadn't been right all those years ago. But he wouldn't be Hamlet. Or Kipling. There was no room for indecision in his life now.

He wishes he could go and see Sara once more but decides that a phone call before he heads back out is enough. On New Year's Day they talk. He assures her he is not alone and that he did not have to cook the turkey. He apologizes for not coming home this one time but tells her he is sure this next deployment will be the last. They discuss graduate schools (law versus business, Yale versus UVA). They discuss what she's reading (a new *Anna Karenina*, the last president's memoir).

"Uplifting stuff."

"Preferable to the papers."

"Why don't you work in something lighter to the cycle, Ma?"

"What do you suggest? *Goldfinger*? I'm *fine*," she says.

"Fucking Insecure Nervous and Emotional?" he says, and they laugh.

"No, really. I'm good. I'm—busy."

"Did you go by the neighbors'?"

"They came here."

"They came there?"

"Yeah, can you believe it? It was really sweet. You know—you know, I don't think you ever saw it—well, we never did it, but there's a bit of a tradition here or, well, in their family. A Christmas tradition where the women, all the cousins you know, the women and children dress up and visit houses in the area bringing gifts—"

"Like elves?"

"Like elves, but not, you know, dressed like elves. Well, not dressed *entirely* like elves. Each woman provides a different gift for one of the twelve days of Christmas, so each—"

"Twelve gifts for each house?"

"Yes. They're little things, silly little things, like fruitcakes. Fondue pots."

"Homemade fruitcake?"

"Yes, of course it's homemade."

"And what else?"

"They might bring . . . chocolates. Chocolates stamped with Thomas Jefferson—that was one thing. A pack of postcards from the museum: Old Pew. A set of little candles carved at Williamsburg. *Americana*."

"Edible Americana."

"Right. Anyhow, they came here. They've never come before. It was very sweet. Thank God I was dressed and had the fire on. They all came in, made a fuss."

"And did they stay?"

"I asked them to, but no, they didn't stay. They'd arranged all the gifts in a darling little basket; I think they made the basket, too. And left it with—with a Thermos of eggnog."

"Eggnog?"

"Yes, but when I opened it, it was only half full. I think it was theirs and they left it by accident. They sprinkle cinnamon on the eggnog. I'd forgotten that."

"Cinnamon."

"You know people don't know what to say."

"About what?"

"About me. About you. People don't know what to say to a mother whose son's not home for Christmas."

"How about 'Merry Christmas, ma'am.' "

"That's *exactly* what they should have said. I should have helped them."

"Are you sure everything's all right?" He knows, but he wants to hear her say it anyhow.

"Everything's swell. I'm attending two parties tonight alone."

"Where?"

"Blair House and the Naval Observatory, where else?" *And in their lies by lies they flattered be*, she thinks.

"I love you."

"I love you, too. Don't drink and drive. Or—don't drink and handle any sophisticated weaponry."

"What's weaponry?"

He hung up the phone and smiled. She hung up the phone and wept.

HEAVEN

In the backseat of the Town Car, driving to D.C.'s Dulles International Airport, Sara closes her eyes and opens them. She is nowhere near sleep. It is almost eight o'clock at night. The godfather has a FIJI water bottle filled with martinis; she can tell because she sees—and smells—the olives. Like David, he takes three. Unlike David, he takes his drinks without rocks.

She thinks about the Marines on the train. She thinks about her conversation with Jason just after Christmas, and his chastising her for referring to his Teammates as "boys" rather than men. She couldn't help it. She still thought of most of the men she knew as boys, too. What is the definition of a man, anyhow? That he can vote? That he's been in love? She stares out the window. It's raining. Would the flights be delayed?

Sara tells the godfather that she only just learned, in the car tonight on the way to the train station with Sam, that Jason has been in love—*is* in love.

"Did you know that?"

"On the advice of counsel, I respectfully assert my right to remain silent."

"Come *on*."

"He's not ten years old, Sara."

"But who is she? Did he use the word 'love'?"

"On the advice of counsel, I respectfully—"

"Forget it. I'll find out."

They drive. It's raining hard now. And Sara says, "You know, Sam said he was very good at what he did. Jason."

"Of course he was. *Is.*"

"*Is.* Yes. At what he *does.* Sam said he *is* very good at what he *does.* Let's talk like that, okay?"

"Okay."

"How long—"

"Long. I have Ambien. You should sleep."

They drive in silence for a while.

And then the godfather says, "He's *twenty-seven*, Sara."

"And?"

"And you're mad if you think a twenty-seven-year-old's never been in love. Especially your Romeo."

"Romeo?"

"He's a flirt."

"He's not."

"He is. Unavoidable, given the gene pool."

"Well, he's never talked to me about any one girl in particular."

"You know how hard it is for a Team guy to find a girl who will worship him?"

"No."

"About as hard as it is to find a lobbyist on K Street."

"That's ridiculous."

"They call them *warriors*, for chrissake, Sara. The girls pursue them like paparazzi."

"You've got to be kidding me."

It's raining harder now.

"Will the flight be delayed?"

"No."

"But—"

"Trust me. And we're not flying out of Dulles. We're flying out of Andrews."

"Andrews?"

"Sara, just—don't stress the flight plan, okay? I'll explain."

"Can you explain the allure of falling in love with someone who regularly places his life on the line?"

"Um, I think I'd have to say that question falls into the category of If You Don't Understand It Immediately It Cannot Be Explained."

"Well, I guess that makes me an idiot."

"It makes you a hypocrite."

"What are you talking about?"

"Sara, David?"

"David didn't place his life on the line."

"He did."

"You romanticize him. David sat at a desk."

"David placed his life on the line for this country."

"Behind a desk."

"I'm not sure you understand the full extent of what he did."

"If I don't, the fault is not mine."

"He—"

"Let's not revisit that, all right? I've made my peace. Please don't compare what David did to what Jason does now. That's ancient history, anyhow. Let's not have history lessons."

They are passing the Washington Monument. At night, lit, it's breathtaking. She always forgets the sheer beauty of this city, how wide the sky seems with its low architectural lines, how pristine the pieces of the Mall's iconography are. She would take it over Paris.

"Anyhow," the godfather says, "Jason doesn't let it get to his head. Most don't. These guys don't spend too much time worrying about the reasons people obsess over them. Or protest their participation. They do their jobs. They move on. They spend about as much time on fan blogs as they do on *The New York Times* op-ed page."

"My son reads *The New York Times*."

"Yeah, but he doesn't take his cues from their views."

"No, he doesn't take cues from anyone. That's what David gave him: a clinical inability to take cues from anyone other than his conscience."

At Andrews, they turn in to the hangar reserved for private planes. She asks—meekly—why they aren't flying commercial and who is paying for this. He tells her there were no direct flights. She asks where they are going. "Jeddah," he tells her. And the first thing she thinks of is "Christmas," because "Christmas" and "Jeddah" have always been synonymous in her mind. She has never seen the inside of a private plane. It is so clean. "Jeddah, by way of Sigonella. We have to stop to refuel, change crews. You should sleep."

"Sigonella—"

"Italy."

"What is this plane?" she asks, mildly alarmed, looking up at it.

"Boeing Business Jet. It's like a converted 737."

"Right. How much does it cost?"

"Fifty million. New."

"Jesus."

The plane was like a piece of art. *And that's perhaps why it costs as much as a Picasso*, she thinks. He tells her a bit about the person who owns it, a defense contractor who runs training camps for international paramilitary groups. "Former Special Operations Forces guy, actually. Former Team guy."

*

The inside of the plane reminds her of a painting by Andrew Wyeth, one that hangs in a small museum only a few miles from her home. It's the one place she took Jason each year at various holidays—Thanksgiving, Easter. It's dedicated to nineteenth- and twentieth-century American art, and Sara loved the romance and the realism of those periods. Her son loved it because many of the paintings in one of its galleries were of pirates, and pigs.

The painting on her mind now is one of a woman looking out the window of a private jet. She is alone on the plane, and she is wearing a white coat. Her head is turned away, so you cannot tell how old she is; in fact, she might be a girl, not a woman, but would a girl travel alone on a private jet? Would anyone? She is looking out her window and through the clouds, almost as if she were looking down from heaven. And for the first time Sara thinks: *Yeah, because in heaven everyone gets to ride on jets like this.* But in the painting what the woman sees through the window isn't angels; it's a house, a little farmhouse. The painting at first appears to be a realistic portrait: a woman on a plane looks out the window. But if you looked more closely you could see the more fantastic, almost disturbing elements in it: the plane's windows are sized like those of a vast ship, not like the traditionally and necessarily tiny rounds of an aircraft. And the chairs are enormous, as is the table between them. The painting owes as much to *Alice in Wonderland* as it does to *Christina's World*.

And Sara loved it for that mix: the harsh, cold American realism and the sly joy of a fantasy whose meaning was left to the imagination of the beholder. Sara had always looked at it as tragic, that this horrible thing was transporting the woman away from the place that she loved. Her view has not changed. Yes, the girl in the painting has her plane, but she is alone. And so she dreams about the house she sees below.

Sara is embarrassed to be in such luxury but also slightly numb and slightly giddy from stress. There is a private bathroom at the back with monogrammed blue linen towels, and tiny soaps wrapped in pleated blue tissue paper. It's all robin's-egg blue, a color she loves. When she lifts up one of the soaps to use it, she notices that the china dish underneath has a Trident painted on it in gold.

There is a girl dressed in blue who brings Sara a menu that includes filet mignon, smoked salmon, and cheeseburgers. The girl offers her a cocktail. The godfather falls asleep and encourages her to do the same. She has a drink, quickly, and starts on a second one. She cannot sleep—yet. This is her first trip abroad since not long after her son was born. David had insisted they get away, and leaving her little one with a friend, they'd taken off just the two of them for a quick Grand Tour: Rome, Paris, Vienna, Salzburg, London, Munich. And Normandy, so she could see the beaches. David had wanted her to understand what had occurred there. The climate at the time—it was summer—was welcoming. They stayed in an enormous château owned by another Yale classmate of David's, where the owner kept his collection of hot air balloons running and staked to the lawn, ready to rise, his horses tacked up in the barn—just in case. She'd been afraid to go up in a balloon for a ride, and David had teased her for being so hesitant. He'd finally convinced her, and then they'd taken it together, with a guide. They flew close to the beaches and, at David's insistence, right over the American cemetery. "They buried the brothers next to each other," he'd said. "Thirty-eight sets." He'd brought binoculars and stood behind her, holding them up to her eyes. As they'd looked down over the nine thousand plus headstones, he'd said in poor French, to the guide, "The Pacific Theater got no respect." He was trying to make a joke.

It was one of her more magical memories of being with him. Those weeks he had been generous and affectionate, and she even thought that he might propose marriage. He was on his home turf: travel and grandeur; good meals broken up only by learning or interesting introductions. He couldn't trade those addictions for more mundane tasks, like negotiating the logistics of parenting or being nice to dull neighbors. He never did propose. His gift to her was a small set of memories. And a son. He was not capable of giving more than that.

She had thought she'd have a life where she traveled more, at least more than along the northeastern train line. But there was never time. When she was younger, her parents dragged her everywhere. They lived lives unallied with any regimen or convention, and often they'd just decide, "It's Tuesday, it's Istanbul." Travel to her in those years was the essence of stress and dislocation, an experience of missed flights and lost tickets and old arguments. And she hated it. Only later, spending the summer in London before the summer when she met David, would she see the lure of being in a foreign place, and the luxury of learning new things coupled with the luxury of anonymity and rootlessness.

That summer she'd pretended to take classes but spent most afternoons at the National Portrait Gallery, and in the War

Rooms. In the Portrait Gallery she liked to sit on the bench by the Ditchley portrait of Elizabeth I, the one where the Virgin Queen stands astride the globe, the one onto which, in tiny script at the bottom, the artist had written the following phrases:

She gives and does not expect
In giving back, she increases
She can, but does not, take revenge

Yes, she would think. *That's the kind of girl I'm going to grow up to be.* Within a year she'd be pregnant and in love with a man who could never commit and who, moreover, was in no position to support her.

She liked the War Rooms not because she liked war but because she liked stories, and she was always so struck by how an entire government had just, as it were, gone to ground in that time of crisis, arranging dinner parties and strategy sessions several levels below English streets. She loved seeing Churchill's bedside ashtrays overflowing with his fat cigar ash. Those speeches, so central to a nation's psyche, were composed largely by a prime minister while in his bed.

She had always planned to take Jason on trips, but then she never felt she could spend the money or take the time. Later, he never wanted her to spend the money, and he never had the time. She hated herself in some ways for the provincial path she had chosen for him. She had believed it would be more honest, but perhaps if she'd raised him somewhere else, they'd be in London right now, touring the Tate, talking about his work in the City, at a bank, with a desk, pushing important papers and assessing vast estate investments, or the price of engagement rings.

Rather, now she is speeding toward a place where she does not speak the language, and while she knows the names of its various political parties and a bit of its history, she possesses no desire to know more. She wishes the place they were heading toward could be Athens, with Jason waiting in jeans and a map of the Acropolis. Why is her son in Jeddah? What was he doing? What did they do to him, and *who are they*? She is not thinking clearly. She is thinking about her grown man as a little boy and praying as any mother would, in a moment like this, that he is all right. She is remembering the story she used to read to him to help him fall asleep at night—because he struggled with sleep—the one he practically begged for night after night, all the way up until he was in junior high and too proud to beg: *Jason and the Argonauts.* Who *was* Jason, and what was the Golden Fleece? Whatever happened to Jason's select team of highly trained seafaring heroes?

Thinking on it now, the story seems to her more than anything a metaphor for the futility of sending sons out into the world to achieve. Wasn't Jason sent after the fleece straight into sure slaughter? Yes: Jason was sent to recover the fleece by the king, his uncle, the king who had been told that Jason would overthrow his reign and overtake his kingdom. So the king sent the boy on a mission from which he was certain Jason would never return—an Odyssean voyage in reverse, where each chapter brought new trials in the shapes of women or beasts or angry gods and goddesses. Even in the presence of a team of "heroes," Jason's chances were slim. But he embraced them. He was clear that his right to the throne was secure. He had good men. And nothing, not even falling in love or the eventual destruction of that love, would keep him from fulfilling his mission. God, she thinks, it doesn't sound like a bedtime story.

Sara thinks about the boy, Sam, back at her house, now watching over things. What was it about Sam that had seduced her to trust him so completely and so quickly? She was usually slow to trust, critical of new people—reserved, even in the face of goodness. But with Sam she had felt immediately at ease, and it might have had less to do with his knowledge of her son than it did with what she knew he had been through. It was the eye. It was his casual happiness in spite of the truth of his history: this is what made him so appealing. It will be good to cook with Sam and Jason, she thinks. She will tease her son about the all the loves he has not shared with her. She thinks about his wedding, what she might say that night and what she might wear.

"We're taking off," the godfather says. As he slips his cell phone into his breast pocket, she sees he has his shirts monogrammed now.

"I can't do my seatbelt," she says, tearing up a bit.

"Jesus, Sara, you don't have to put on your seatbelt," he says.

"Help me," she says. And he knows she's not talking about the belt. He'll hold her hand as the plane rises, sharply and abruptly, through the rain.

*

When she was almost five months pregnant, she had visited—for the first time—Arlington National Cemetery. She was back at Georgetown, if halfheartedly, and one of her teachers had given the class the assignment of visiting the Washington monument they were "least interested in," with the aim of revising their view. An essay was required. The southerners in the class all chose Lincoln, cheekily; the northerners then piled on with plans for Jefferson. And the foreign students split up the remaining mall icons. Sara was alone in selecting Arlington. Typical. What kind of good American girl wouldn't possess an interest in the war dead?

The day she went, it was snowing. The climb uphill to the Tomb of the Unknown Soldier (formerly Robert E. Lee's plantation, a fact she'd guessed most of the southern schools had skipped in their history books) wasn't easy, and especially not easy in the snow four months pregnant. But the air wasn't too cold, and in the late afternoon everything was quiet and still. Pin-dropping still. When she stopped to ask the guide at the information center the best approach to walking the grounds, the guard had said, "If you walk quickly, you'll make the changing of the guard." So she had skipped the eternal flame and gone straight to the top of the hill, to the vast marble domed structure with its Corinthian columns and its amphitheater. She had sat, breathless, only to be told to stand for the changing of the guard. The ceremony was introduced. On the tomb it says, *Here rests in honored glory an American soldier known but to God.* The whole thing was as close as Sara had ever come to experiencing a formal religious service. But here, God (the object of worship) was never named. Taps was played.

Sara walked around the back of the building and stared out over the amphitheater. Looking up, she saw the words on the inside edge of the white half-dome: *When we assumed the soldier we did not lay aside the citizen.* General George Washington said that. General Washington was awarded a sixth star, posthumously. General of the Armies Pershing had been given six for his work, so someone felt it necessary to afford Washington the same rank. David had taught her that; he'd pointed it out on showing her Pershing's portrait at the Pentagon. When Washington crossed the Delaware, did he dream that one day we'd cross broken-down doorways of private homes to preserve our freedoms?

*

On the plane, finally, she sleeps. When she wakes, Jason's godfather takes her hand in his. "It will be fine," he tells her. "You're such a liar," she says. The table has bits of mirror inlaid across its top; the mirrored bits form a mosaic, but she cannot tell what the image is. She leans closer, trying to see just how horrible she looks. She rarely looked this closely.

"What are you doing?" He laughs.

"Looking at my hair."

"Women are so crazy."

"Well, we're capable of holding two opposing ideas in our minds at once, without going mad."

"Someone said that."

"Yes. It's a sign of intelligence."

"What are your two opposing ideas?"

"That my hair is a mess. And that I wish David were here right now."

"What's oppositional about that?"

"Hair, self-preservation. David, self-destruction."

"Ah."

The godfather stands up, stretches, and goes to talk to the pilot. She can hear murmuring but not what they're saying. She can hear a phone ring.

When he comes back, he sits beside her. "Remember the monks and the river?"

"The monks?"

"Do you remember the monks and the river—the parable."

"Remind me?"

"Two monks. An older monk and a younger monk. They meet a woman, weeping at the river. A beautiful woman."

"Of course."

"And the beautiful woman asks them for help crossing to the other side. And so the elder monk, without hesitation, takes her on his back and swims across. And the woman goes on her way, and the monks go on their way."

"But the younger monk is angry," Sara says.

"You remember."

"The younger monk is angry."

"And so the elder monk says, after some time has passed, 'Why are you so angry?' "

"And the younger monk says, 'Because it is a sin to touch a woman, and you carried that woman on your back across the river, and that is a sin.' "

"And the older monk says—"

" 'But my son, you've been carrying her around ever since.' "

"Correct."

"And I'm carrying David."

"That's one way of putting it."

"Well, I'm not a monk."

"Excellent point."

Out the window, she can see nothing but white. She wonders whether this plane has a hatch that could open, out of which she could parachute in case of emergency.

"Did he ever talk to you about what he did in the war?" She's giving him a look that says, *No more parables, please*.

"What war?"

"Vietnam."

"Right. I always forget about that one."

"Well, he was there." Sara is picking at her nails, an old habit her son has since inherited. "I know," she says, "I know he was—wasn't he doing something for the *Times*?" She says this carefully, without raising her eyes, as if she doesn't really care about the answer, as if she knows nothing more specific.

"Technically, he was there to try and write a story about MAC-V-SOG."

"Technically. Mack the what?"

"MAC-V-SOG. Military Assistance Command, Vietnam. Studies and Observations Group."

"The Agency is so artful with words."

"Yeah, well. The SOG were a black-ops group. Overseen by CIA, yes, but they worked with a lot of the guys over there in that time—Rangers, Team guys."

"Team guys?"

"Yes."

"What did they do?"

"They . . . they cleaned things up."

"Cleaned?"

"Cleaned. Examined. Interrogated. The blast-out area from one B-52 bomber stretched two blocks by a mile. *Two blocks by a mile*. David taught me that."

"And the SOG teams excavated the—?"

"The damage."

"Cleaned, examined, interrogated. Killed?"

"They were soldiers, Sara."

"And David?"

"And David knew a guy—one of his close friends then—was a SOG Team one-zero. They called the Team leaders one-zeros. The guy had been at Yale with him, I think. I'm sure. Well, I think David said he was actually kicked out of Yale—"

"*Technically.*"

"Right, *technically*. But then he ended up over there, in the jungle, in this group. 'In country,' as the guys said. That was how David learned about SOG. That was how he was let in a little bit by those guys."

"A guy got kicked out of Yale and went to run a black-ops group in the jungle?"

"Yeah, guess he preferred Fort Benning to Branford."

"The snows of yesteryear." And the godfather doesn't say anything, so she prompts him, trying another tack. "So he knew some of the guys in the Teams at that time?"

"Yeah. And you know, that was sort of the birth of the modern-day Teams. It all started in Vietnam."

"Right." She remembers the letters.

"SOG recon casualties exceeded one hundred percent."

"That sounds like a lot."

"It's the highest sustained U.S. loss rate since the Civil War. Casualty, and loss."

"Wow."

"And David, you know—he *hated* something that looked illogical."

"He hated mess," Sara corrects him.

"He hated the fact that what he saw over there contradicted what he thought he knew. He hated that we were sending 'the best and brightest' not into the Oval Office but into the jungles, to die. He worshipped those guys—the guys he knew then."

"He never talked to me about any of that."

And the godfather leans forward. "And he worshipped you, too."

"He worshipped a sense of his own place in the world. When I fit into that, I absorbed some of the goodwill."

"No."

"Yes."

When the plane hits turbulence, the pilot comes on the audio and assures them, "Just some light rain, folks. Nothing to worry about."

"Excuse me," Sara says, summoning the stewardess, "is there a shower on this plane?"

"Yes, ma'am, there is." And Sara is shown to the shower, and she puts the water on as hot as she can stand it, and stays there for as long as she can bear. She changes back into her clothes, brushes her teeth—and her hair. She puts her makeup on. When she dims the lights, she thinks she does not look so horrible. She checks the time. Her hair will dry in time for landing. When she gets back to where the godfather is sitting, she takes a deep breath.

"All better now?" he says.

"Yes. Now tell me more about the Mac . . . trucks. Or whatever. Tell me."

He tells her about David's brief time as one of the "whiz kids" at the Pentagon, and he gives her a little history of the cultural changes that took place in the intelligence field between the late 1960s and the early 1990s, cultural changes that didn't brook acceptance—or advancement—of the same types of people as in another era. These changes ultimately led to David's needing to leave. He talked about how the "puzzle pieces" in the Middle East shifted, too, and how the places no one wanted to go then became the places David was increasingly interested in. As the Soviets moved out of Afghanistan and as the United States lost—it thought—the necessity of a strategic presence in that part of the world, David saw how our relationships with the Saudis and the Pakistanis would be newly crucial. He wanted to learn about those cultures. He wanted to learn *from* them. The politics in D.C. became too torturous for him to stay; he knew he lacked the unsullied CV to be in line for DCI ("that's DNI now") and lacked the intellectual or cash assets to become a kingmaker, an ambassador, or a businessman.

"Balance sheets scared him," he says. And then pauses, indicating his analysis is over.

"War-torn cities lowered his pulse; debts to pay made it rise," says Sara.

"That's correct. That's who he was."

"He never talked to me about anything," she says, consciously baiting the hook. "He may have thought I had a brain, but I think once Jason—"

"Yet you stayed."

"I stayed for a while. I would never leave the father of my child. Unless he—unless he was placing us at risk."

"I guess it depends on your definition of risk."

"But he defined it for me, didn't he, by leaving first. By leaving, then dying. He was good at dramatic exits."

"He would love Jason. He would understand him."

"Would he? He would understand how much it costs to train an operator. He would understand the percentage of the annual defense budget allocated to education. He would understand the ratio of blondes to brunettes working at any one time at Foggy Bottom. What would he understand about my son?"

"Sara."

"David always understood the numbers. Facts. He was less skilled at nuance. And emotion."

"He understood and valued sacrifice."

"He never served his country."

"Sara, he did."

"He never served his country like my son has done."

"His son, too."

"David wouldn't recognize Jason if he saw him today. David only cared that our son didn't grow up entitled. He was terrified I would spoil him."

"And you did not."

"I did not."

"I never met a kid with less sense of entitlement. He has a lot of his mother in him in that, that's for sure," he says. "Not a kid anymore. It's his time to get out now."

"He loves it too much."

"You don't—"

"I know my son. He loves it too much to ever leave."

"How much does it cost to train an operator," the godfather says after a pause, after motioning to the stewardess to refill his drink, and bring Sara one, too. She hasn't been counting but however many he's had, he's not getting drunk. He must cut the gin with ginger ale, she thinks.

"Five hundred thousand dollars," she says.

"Really?"

"Yup."

"Expensive."

"One hundred operators. One hundred operators times five hundred thousand: equal to the cost of this plane."

*

She wants to know where her son has been and to what extent the godfather may or may not have been hiding the truth of what he's done from her. She wants to know what he knows about the last ten days, and he tells her what he thinks she can handle.

"Look," he says, "after ten days the military shifts the status of a missing officer from DUSTWUN to MIA."

"DUSTWUN?"

"Duty status whereabouts unknown."

"It's been ten days today."

"It's been ten days today since the mission."

"And what was the mission?"

"The mission—well, what we know about the mission was that the guys went to find someone."

"Find who?"

"It was a high-level—at the highest level—it was a mission overseen by and sanctioned via a JSOC/Langley Team, so it was—"

"But why was Jason on it? I thought those missions—"

"I don't know. I don't know any of the details."

"I thought his Team was—"

"What—"

"I thought his Team was somewhere else. When—"

"I got a call telling me the Team number, and I was able to find out who was on the copter. They had to enlist extra guys for backup. And it's possible that Jason was one of those extra guys."

"Extra?"

"Sara."

"When were you going to tell me this?"

"You were notified the minute we knew anything. The navy notified you as soon as they knew."

"To make something simple is a thousand times harder than to make something complicated. Did you know that?"

"You were notified the minute they knew."

Although she had never imagined this moment, if she had, she certainly would have imagined herself better prepared for it. She wanted to present the face of someone strong. That is what her son would have wanted. That is what she would show him when she saw him.

"Sara, it's very unconventional, this—" And he waves his hand around.

"What?"

"It's very unusual that we're sitting on this plane and that you are being brought to your son. This is not protocol."

"Really? You don't give a fifty-million-dollar plane to every primary next of kin?"

"Sara."

"Then what are we doing here?"

"Someone made arrangements for you, and you will be told all of that, but all I can tell you is that you should appreciate the fact that a lot has been done to try and get you—"

"I appreciate the fact that my son risked his life for something that means nothing."

"It means something to him."

"Really? What does it mean? What does it mean?" She pours half her drink into his glass, which he has already half-emptied.

"He didn't risk his life—he doesn't risk his life for the politics, Sara. He risks his life for his Team."

"Is that what he says?"

"I know that's what he feels."

And he knows that soon enough she'll know everything. For the time being, he is trying to manage his own anxiety about what they will find when they reach their destination. Because he does not know. He misses the little line of coke he used to do to relax in these moments, but has decided that for this trip a ratio of two espressos to each drink will keep him stable until they touch down.

Sara asks him to tell her the story of how he met David, a story she has heard many times. He tells her about his days as a young aide for the chief of staff of the air force. He tells her how David used to stop by their rooms regularly for meetings with one or another of the joint chiefs. "He brought a skateboard with him. He used to board down the ramps there on the weekends, and all the girls in the front offices adored him. He hadn't gotten over-weight yet; he was still smoking." He describes the series of oil portraits of historical joint chiefs lining the long corridor, and the scandal that resulted when David once skated there, too. "He'd hand painted it. He'd painted LITERALLY EYES ONLY in red, across its top."

"He took me my first time," Sara says, softening.

"When was that?"

"I was pregnant. I told him I'd never been inside the Pentagon, and he was appalled. It was as if I'd told him I'd never read the Declaration of Independence. He said, 'Oh, let's fix that immedi-ately.' He'd picked me up at Healy Hall, and we drove over there. And he drove right up to the VIP parking and a guard came out."

"And David charmed him."

"David charmed him, and the guard waved us through."

"Sounds about right."

"And then we had this situation at the second security desk because I didn't want them screening me—"

"God, did they have screeners in those days?"

"They had something, maybe more like a crude metal detector, but I was paranoid about the baby—"

"Right."

"And so the guard was hassling David, and he asked him, you know, 'What is the purpose of her visit?' looking at me. And David sort of laughed, and he looked at me and looked at the guard and said—loudly—I remember how loudly it was, he said—no, he *announced*: 'Orientation!' "

"Orientation?"

"Orientation. 'The purpose of her visit is orientation.' And that was that. They waved us in. And he was really proud to take me around, I think. He was so much more interested in, and reverent about, the history of the place—the military history—than I was."

"So Jason walked the halls of the Pentagon even before he was born."

"He did. God's great plan."

"David's great plan, perhaps."

"I was so in love with him."

"I remember being in the hospital."

"Yeah, Château d'Yquem and ice cream—in the *recovery* room. We were—"

"Reckless?"

"We were young."

"He was proud. He didn't know how to be a father, but he was very proud of you, Sara."

They're offered hot coffee. It's very bitter, but she knows she won't sleep again, and drinking it makes her feel like she's participating in the ritual of being present, so she drinks it and asks for another cup.

*

"Do you think he's ever killed someone?" Sara asks a little later, having given him a grace period to relax and nap.

"David?"

"Jason."

"What would be the appropriate answer to that, Sara?"

He's arranging a small mountain of reading materials poured onto his lap from his Hermès briefcase—a gift from a network news bureau chief: *The Economist, Foreign Affairs, Financial Times, The Washington Post, The Wall Street Journal, Time*. She can see small pink Post-it Notes, probably from his assistant, placed on the top of each, indicating pages or titles of articles to be read. How efficient, she thinks.

"Pink?" He ignores the observation, so she continues. "The appropriate answer would be the truth."

"Well, if you cared to read the papers and perhaps the *history* of what your son's been engaged in, you might find you could learn quite a lot about what he does."

"And when your son's in the Teams, you can tell me how often your wife wants to read the papers. Pardon me, when you have a wife."

"Touché."

"I'm just curious now. I want to know what happened and what they did to him. You know he's so . . . tough, but he's also so gentle, in his heart. I can't see him—I can't see him in those situations."

"That's what makes the most effective warrior."

"What does?"

"Being inconspicuous."

She reaches over and takes a small sip from his (now newly replenished) FIJI bottle.

"Is it murder?"

"Is what murder?"

"Is it murder when you kill someone? Is it called murder?"

"It's not murder when you follow ROE, Rules of—"

"I know what ROE stands for."

"—Engagement. But people die in wars, Sara. And someone is at the other end of the gun every time."

"So you can kill a man when he's armed."

"You can kill a man when he's armed."

"But can you kill a man when he's loading a gun?"

"I'm not sure."

"You're on the Select Committee on Intelligence, and you're not sure."

"I believe that you would not kill someone in the process of loading a gun because, technically, that weapon would at that time be unarmed."

She picks at a hardboiled egg. They've been presented on a wide white china plate, rimmed in blue. Blue was the theme here. The eggs were accompanied by an enormous and shiny tin of caviar and cut crystal square dishes of capers, onions, and lemon. Caviar had been a staple of David's, his sole splurge; he ate it plain, with a spoon. She had not seen it in years; it was contraband. *This one's probably Persian*, she thinks. And then says, "It all just sounds a bit Potter Stewart on pornography, you know what I mean?"

"You remember the USS *Cole*?"

"Yemen. The boys in the boat," she says.

"Yes. You know who oversaw security onboard after?"

"CIA?"

"Naval Special Warfare."

She takes a spoonful of caviar and eats it.

"And you know what those guys were told?"

"No."

"They were told that no shots would be taken, because the act that had occurred was a crime. It was a crime scene."

"So."

"There are rules for crimes and rules for wars."

"You're saying that the way we define the threat has changed."

"I'm saying that we're attempting to define something that itself is changing. This isn't Dresden, Sara. This is not Kuwait, 'ninety-one. I mean, thank God for that. You know how many more sons mothers would have lost in these last wars if we still fought the way we did then? The metrics have changed. The strategies have changed. We're more efficient now. We're more precise. We're good at what we do, and these guys—like Jason— they're good at what they do."

"Jason's been good at everything he's ever done."

"Of course."

"You didn't answer my question."

And as the godfather tries to answer, he realizes that his own current level of clearance leaves him in conflict now, and increasingly, for various reasons. He thinks about the concentric circles of "appropriate" honesty he has come to accept as part of his life and career, the same circles he knows David before him and Jason after him have both been subject to, in diverse ways. Why didn't they all end up in lines of work more amenable to "normal" lives? They weren't classic spooks, but they lived in the margins of a world where innocuous policy conflicted with decisions about when and where to drop bombs, a place where obsessions over the size of a madrassa half a world away trumped concerns about the size of one's own son's classroom. And often, dropping bombs was a more precise art than drafting policy. The response was immediate, as was the grade. And the grade was not clouded by subjectivity or argument. You hit a target, or you missed. And for hits, everyone was pleased. For misses, someone's scalp was served. He saw it every single day: the politicians took ownership of their military's skills when things went well and took discreet pains to distance themselves from them when things did not.

Just weeks earlier he had sat on another private plane, slightly smaller than this one but just as tricked out. His companions, six extremely rich businessmen, had all played a contributing role in national intelligence and had all seen unique success in their various fields. Someone had arranged for a tour of an SOF training camp, one hidden within a highly classified, undisclosed location on the East Coast. The plane's windows were blacked out, per protocol, and once the plane left D.C., the men had all melted immediately into the boys they'd been at prep school, playing war games across New England woods. One claimed to have roomed at Lawrenceville with the current king of Saudi Arabia (or was it a brother to the king?), but the story—later fact-checked by the godfather's EA—proved a stretch. These men were all old enough to possess their own war stories, but none of them had seen combat the likes of which was now being seen by their sons—or grandsons. By simple virtue of their birth dates, they'd missed the century's grand chapters of battle. Some of their fathers had been generals or spies; most of their sons worked well away from lines of fire.

The trip was out of the ordinary—another piece of cool candy that came with the godfather's role now, the sugar fed to bureaucrats and politicians to dull their cynicism, the inevitable by-product of congressional life in the partisan era. Their looped tapes of ambition, achievement, and risk demanded something sweet to cut the stress. You could not know the things you learn and know at his level without feeling a deep paranoia and almost hopelessness about the state of things. If Sara knew more, she might concur. But then no one wanted the mothers to know too much because then they would never let their sons become soldiers or sailors. And so rather than say anything else, he simply explains to her that there is very little she can understand, that she must trust that the operators know what they are doing.

"Operators."

"Yes, operators."

"I don't like that word."

"Well, Sara, that's what they're called. It's a term of honor."

"They're so young."

"They're exactly the same ages as the guys who've fought in wars for generations. For centuries."

"The Marines on the train looked like high school kids." Her voice breaks on the word *high*.

"They probably were." He takes her hand.

"But—"

"No, but think about how young you were when you took on big responsibilities."

"Motherhood is not a war."

"Would you die for your child?"

"Of course."

"War is the ability to die for another person without hesitation. War is the belief in the value of another person's life above belief in the value of your own. We send them to war at that time in their lives for specific reasons. They graduate to situation rooms at other times in their lives for other reasons."

He is surprised by her passion on these subjects, and teases her that she should have stayed in Washington. Her enthusiasm is fueled by exhaustion and excitement. She cannot wait to see her son. She wants to know what he was doing. She wants to know more details. The godfather says he knows very little, but that the informal "civilian QRF" that came together to secure this plane and her presence on it was powerful and impressed even him. He tells her the person who arranged for her to go see her son must have known someone very high up the chain of command. And then he abruptly changes the subject, as he realizes this conversation is only leading to a place where she'll realize the reason she is being sped to her son is that the chances of her finding him alive are slim. "You want to know what the true 'axis of evil' is?" she asks. "Men keeping confidences with other men."

" 'Axis of evil,' " the godfather says, smiling. "David never liked that phrase. He preferred 'crescent of concern.' "

As the plane lands, she asks why they're finally having this conversation.

VALENTINE

Jason appears to be waiting for a commercial flight, but it is not a real commercial flight. The men and women who board it will not all land at its stated destination. Because these are not ordinary passengers; this is not an ordinary flight. There are no civilians on the flight, although there is no indication of that at the gate. Everything looks normal.

The commercial airliner has been arranged for use by the Teams in order to avoid being detected in foreign air space. The purpose of this particular mission is the insertion of a small NSW team in a foreign country. Team guys and other SOF personnel occupy this entire leg of the flight. Forty minutes after takeoff, the plane will change course. Jason and his Team will parachute out. Jason has done this before. It's not stressful. This will be the last thing he does here before heading home to train with a new Team, for a late spring mission. Because he focuses on one hour at a time, he is not thinking much about that yet. This insertion should be simple. He has done many like it before. He is hungry, so goes to find something to eat before boarding.

Near the gate there is a coffee shop. The girl who rings up his drink puts a little sparkly red sticker—a star—on Jason's cup and says, "Happy Valentine's Day. Don't break any hearts." There is a man there, at the sugar stand, and he holds his cup up; he has two stickers. "I think she prefers older men," he says. Jason had seen him before; he had been talking with some of the other guys earlier which meant he was on the flight. Like Jason, he's wearing ratty olive cargo pants, a polo shirt—and a beard. He asks Jason to sit with him, and he does. He asks Jason his last name, and Jason lies. He asks Jason what he does, and Jason lies again; he's not unsuspicious. Lying's a default setting in these circumstances, another skill. If the man presses, Jason has various levels of lies, as even the most persistent questioners tend to pull back after the third try. He guesses the man is former military. Maybe he's a contractor. He's old. Then the man mentions working in Saudi, for a Jeddah-based private aviation corporation. Then he mentions David and uses Jason's surname. And so they begin to talk.

The man knew David well. At least, he knows a lot about what David did—or claims to. Jason listens. His mother had never discussed these things with him, so he was always left to make them up. He would absorb bits and pieces here and there—something about the Kennedy administration, something about Laos and Vietnam, something about the Agency and a Project Phoenix, and something about the importance of data and statistics. He had always concluded that his father was a kind of private investigator: he followed dangerous people into dangerous places; he collated facts. He knew his father had had a role, ultimately, at a desk at CIA and that he hated it, and he knew that his father had later left for the Middle East—perhaps to make money, perhaps for love. There were always rumors. But his mother didn't seem to care about the details. She cared about the emotions. And in any event, they had only ever treated David as the one who abandoned them, the one who never said goodbye. Sara likely thought through all those years that his absence was too painful for Jason to discuss.

An unforced error, on her part, unforced errors being the essential occupational hazard of motherhood.

The man at the gate tells Jason about his father's work for Kennedy and clarifies—"technically, he was staffed under Ted Sorensen, writing. I'm sure you've read all those speeches."

"No, sir."

"You've never read JFK's speeches?"

"No, sir."

" '*Ask not what your country can do for you but—*' "

" '—What you can do for your country.' I know that one, sir."

" '*In the long history of the world, only a few generations have been granted the role of defending freedom in its hour of maximum danger. I do not shrink from this responsibility. I welcome it*'?"

"I never heard that one."

"Well, Kennedy had a lot of flaws, but he had superb command of the English language. He was *very* young—not too much older than you are now—well, close enough that were he alive and the age that he was when he assumed office you'd consider him a generational peer. And he was running a country at the height of its power and at the height of a cold war. He made some good decisions and some bad ones, but he made people believe—he made people believe that there was something worth fighting for. That's powerful. He was a hero, too. That helped."

"It's hard to imagine what a cold war is like."

"It is now, isn't it? Well, it was horrible."

"I know President Kennedy understood the importance of Special Operations Forces."

"He did. When you send a group of covert operatives to invade a country and they get slaughtered on the beach, it's a stark reminder that tanks and nukes serve to assist, but not replace, wise manpower."

"Tanks, nukes, and mercenaries."

"I met your father in Vietnam. I led a SOG team. You know about SOG? The Studies and Observations Group."

"Yes, sir."

"You could as well call today's Special Operations Forces our global Studies and Observations Group, given what we did and what these guys do today, in some respects. We did what you might call 'field studies.' Mopping up the messes after Arc Light strikes, that kind of thing. Some of the assets we had in Vietnam were Buddhists, did you know that? Your father found that very amusing. He was a bit of a Buddhist himself."

"Really?"

"He knew a lot about it. The Four Noble Truths. 'The path to the cessation of suffering.' You don't remember—he never talked about those things with you?"

"No, sir."

"Well, we never knew if he brought that knowledge with him or if he learned it on the job. Certainly helped. He knew how to talk to those people and understood that if we needed them, we would have to speak their language. They formed our informal intelligence network. Our HUMINT. Our RUMINT."

"He never talked about that time in his life. At least not—at least not that I remember. I was little when he left."

"All the SOG teams and our subsidiaries—you know, like the frogmen—had access to discretionary funds for recruitment, but the guys we found on the ground were mainly Buddhists. Buddhists for the foreign war effort; how about that?"

Jason has never heard the frogmen described as "a subsidiary of SOG," but it's best to be polite in these cases. This man may know a lot. This man may know absolutely nothing. Jason was trained not to trust, but he was also trained to behave. And he was curious. "I've seen some pictures."

"It was wild. Nobody had M-4s fresh off the production line. We had sawed-off Swedish-Ks, untraceable. And one guy"—he is laughing now—"one guy carried a kitchen cleaver."

"A kitchen cleaver?"

"Yeah. It scared the shit out of everyone. And he used it, too. It had a case. Its handle was carved into the shape of a monkey's head."

"It sounds interesting."

"What does that mean?"

"It sounds more . . . free."

"What's your definition of 'free'?"

Jason notices a gold chain around the man's neck, but he cannot see what's on the end of it. He's wearing bracelets, too, like a kid. The bracelets are made of woven, brightly colored plastic threads—pinks and reds and golds. He also has an orange ribbon tied around his wrist, with words written on it but the words have cracked and faded. Jason wonders what it was about him that this man recognized. He has no defining attributes, by contrast—and by design. His sleeves cover his ink.

"I gave your dad some *boots*," the man continued, emphasizing the last word, as if he were holding them in his hand now. "The DOD kitted them out for us with little footprints on the soles—so the impressions they left in the grass or mud looked like shoeless VCs, not Charlies, had been there. We had a great time. There was a VIP room at the officers' club at CCN HQ, in Nha Trang. David loved it there. You could tell when he was in residence because of his songs."

"Songs?"

"Yeah. You know"—and at this point he starts to sing softly—" 'He's got the whole world in his hands'?"

"Yes, I know that song, sir."

"Yeah. Yeah, well, David changed the lyrics and he sang, 'I've got a CAR-fifteen in my hands. I've got a CAR-fifteen in my hands. I've got a CAR-fifteen in my hands, I've got the whole world in my hands.' "

"And," Jason says, dispassionately. "Did he have a CAR-fifteen?"

"Your father became as invaluable a resource to them as they were to him; he was always slipping in to do little deals to make their lives better."

"Deals?"

"Deals. He brokered the sale of a used fire truck to a group of Montagnards. In exchange for their weapons."

"That's creative."

"Well, the guys wanted the weapons, and the Montagnards wanted that truck. Your daddy liked to think of himself as the diplomat, making peace all around."

"Sounds more like an arms dealer."

"But he didn't profit! He couldn't add. Have you ever seen a Montagnard? They rode that thing back and forth to work every day. I never saw that in a history book. That was David. He wanted to be accepted by the military guys. He wanted to be accepted by the intelligence guys. He wanted to be loved by the Vietnamese. He didn't want to be seen as an observer, as an Ivy League . . . dove."

"But he didn't want to fight."

"He lost his chance. He was better behind a desk."

"Too short for Spec Ops."

"Well, he liked to say he was seven feet tall when he stood on his brain."

"I guess he always knew what to say."

"And he knew what to believe. He—the guys at State used to say that your father saluted the flag with his soul."

The man tells Jason a story about the last time he saw David, twenty years ago, and how David had spoken proudly about his only son. Jason tells the man that "today," Valentine's Day, is his father's birthday. He says that his dad would call home on this day each year and always said he was calling because it was easier to remember than his son's birthday. Jason says that every single year when that call came, his mother would give the same speech about how lazy men are, and about the fact that David was Phi Beta Kappa *summa cum laude* at Yale, and had nominally worked in "intelligence," but he still could not remember his only child's birthday. Sara said "intelligence" was not the right word for it; that they should call it "boarding school"—because once you entered it, you got to do a lot of damage under the aegis of forces acting *in loco parentis*.

"Did your father ever talk about Skull and Bones?"

"No, sir."

"Skull and Bones is a secret society at Yale. And many of its members, at one time, were tapped to go into service for the government."

"Interesting," Jason says, not finding it interesting at all.

"Service like working for the OSS."

"Yes, I'm familiar with the OSS. But my father wasn't in that."

"No, it was over before his time. But he would have been aware of it. Its lure set a standard for the last bits of lure left, for those who were keen to do something in service to their government at the time when he graduated."

"Lure. Well, I've read a bit about their training."

"Fascinating stuff."

"Long marches on country club lawns. And a lot of psychological testing, right?"

"You never had any psychological testing?"

"I believe you're thinking of the Rangers," Jason says, smiling.

"You never had—"

"We're always offered post-deployment counseling, if that's what you're asking."

"Have you ever taken it?"

"No, sir."

"It would be—"

"Respectfully, to be assessed—and potentially benched—by someone who had not served in our shoes, if you know what I mean, is not really—"

"Not really *on*."

"Correct," says Jason. "I read something about the training and how it was all conducted in secret."

"Well, they didn't run their trials on public beaches."

Jason hated this kind of conversation. And he didn't know enough about this man to concede what he thought this man thought he knew. While he considered histories of earlier, even international, special operations forces fascinating, it all seemed very different from what his own experience has been throughout the Academy and his tours. Midshipmen don't spend too much time thinking about Yale. And operators don't spend too much time thinking about their own mythological prowess. If they considered themselves part of an elite, it was elite as defined very differently from the way it might have been defined by another generation. They were warriors. They didn't care for country clubs.

"DNA matters," the man said. Jason notices for the first time that he's holding a KSA passport.

"Pardon?"

"DNA matters. That's all I'm trying to say. There's a line that stretches straight from Omaha Beach to this gate. It's a genetic line, a line of guys who made a choice to do the right thing. A line of slaughter and service and failed missions and quiet triumphs, of wives waiting at home for husbands to arrive. You're not married, are you?"

"No."

"A girl?"

"My mother believes that good things come to those who wait."

"And does she believe in love?"

"She does."

And as Jason stands, the man grabs his sleeve, a gesture Jason automatically, physically recoils against; it's too much, too soon. Then he realizes that his own snapping back was disproportionate to what the old man perhaps simply meant affectionately, like a veteran who lashes out at his wife in the night when she's simply trying to hold him close. It's instinctual, an uncalculated response to what his body reads as the presence of a threat.

"I'm sorry," the man says. "I was only wondering: is your mother happy?"

Jason is too distracted to answer. He is distracted by the clock on the wall out of the corner of one eye, and by the appearance—and sound—of movement at the gate flashing by the corner of the other eye. And, formed faintly from yet a third peripheral blur, there is an additional distraction: the impression that the girl at the coffee shop is moving away from her post. *Observe, orient, decide, act.* These incomplete snapshots fit together elegantly, like a Rubik's cube. They form a virtual map in his mind, the map he calls What Is Happening Now Around Me. It is a map attended by a conversation about how to interpret and react to it, a conversation he can carry on skillfully with himself without seeming to. He can collate an impressive array of information while still listening to someone else with one ear. And the conclusion of this latest little intelligence report is this: last chance to send an e-mail before boarding the flight.

"Is she happy," the man says again, not looking at him this time.

"I guess that depends on your definition of happiness."

When Jason and his teammates are called to board the plane, the man shakes Jason's hand, hard, and walks away. Jason does not give too much more thought to the encounter, as he is focused on the task at hand. He makes a mental note to tell his mother that he met someone called—but the man never gave his full name. And he makes a mental note to look up the Arc Light strikes. He remembers learning a bit about them, remembers someone—was it a teacher? Could it have been his father?—talking about them as "bomb operas." He remembered that phrase. The planes, B-52 Stratofortresses, flew in concerts of three per cell, each equipped with up to thirty tons of weaponry. It was all about attrition then, and creating a consistent climate of fear. Unlike contemporary warfare, then we wanted the enemy to see us. We wanted them to hear us, too. We wanted them always aware of the threat, the copter blades always audible overhead, another Charlie company lying in wait just behind the next grove. All this to prop up one domino. Overwhelming force forgave the absence of precision in those days.

One year earlier Jason's platoon had been involved with a coded mission, one where people were "read into" planning, where all things surrounding planning and execution were classified around a code name. Now, on the plane when the guys guessed what the upcoming op would be called, someone referenced Churchill.

Churchill had a whole philosophy for naming missions. "The heroes of antiquity," as he'd put it in a memo to a general, "figures from Greek and Roman mythology, the constellations and stars, famous racehorses, names of British and American war heroes, could be used, provided they fall within the rules."

CASUS BELLI

NAVAL AIR STATION, SIGONELLA, ITALY

MAY 12, 2011

As the plane hits the runway, Sara thinks about how smooth the ride has been. She would have slept through Sigonella, but the stewardess woke her gently, encouraged her to step outside and "see sun," while they paused for a new crew. Sigonella, she knew, had been the place where an American president had told a team of shooters to wait as they surrounded a plane filled with hostages. Italian special operators surrounded them. Diplomacy dictated that the home team would lead the terrorists from the plane. So the Americans on the tarmac that day held their weapons down.

"Il Crisi di Sigonella" was what the Italians called their chapter in the *Achille Lauro* incident, and Sara knew about it because she was home with her baby that day when the story broke. CNN was new then; it was all anyone in Washington—especially those who were home during their days—watched. She remembered hearing about the "naval aviators" who guided that plane to land. She didn't really know then what a naval aviator was, but it certainly sounded impressive. The news didn't mention the fact that the Italian PM had changed his mind about those Americans on his tarmac, having originally authorized their presence. In changing his mind, he placed them in danger, he compromised the "mission." He would have done all this from safe, baronial remove in the Palazzo Chigi. All Sara remembered was what felt like yet another flare-up of something called terrorism, something that seemed to involve parts of the world irrelevant to her own. She wouldn't have connected the dots; she didn't know the dots existed. Hiroshima seemed closer. Hiroshima had just marked the fortieth anniversary of the bomb. *An anonymous bomb:* that was a threat that felt more real than men boarding a plane wearing masks.

When the pilot descends the stairs, Sara is standing there. The godfather had gone into the base, but she was afraid to move too far, as if they might leave without her. The sun is blinding, and she's shielding her eyes with her hand. She can see a mountain.

"Ma'am," he says.

"Sara," she says, and offers her hand. "Thank you."

"It was a pleasure," he says. "I know your next pilot. He's a good man. You'll have a smooth ride."

She doesn't know what to say. So she just says, "Yes."

"Etna," he says, pointing to the mountain. "She's active."

The new stewardess is walking toward them. She looks vaguely like Anita Ekberg. *Is she active, too?* Sara thinks, but instead she holds out her hands to the woman and says simply, *"Piacere."*

Sara has eaten breakfast (eggs Benedict, bacon; why not?) and lunch (tea sandwiches of cucumber and lime) by the time they touch down again; it is almost evening, Jeddah local time. She wonders whether what she is wearing—a black shift and flats—is appropriate. She thinks about how different her son might look now and wonders if she will even recognize him. She thinks about the neighbor's garden; she knows her son will ask about it, as he always has. "How is the garden?" has become their code for other things too hard to say over and over, like "Are you surviving? Did you see anyone die today?" As the plane slows on the runway, the godfather tells her they are not going to stay here, either; they are simply picking up another passenger. The final destination has changed. The plane lets down its ladder, and Sara sees a man come across the runway. It's David.

He is in his mid-seventies now, he has a beard, and he is thinner, but it is him. He is wearing a beautiful suit, his blue collar (always a blue collar) open at the neck just enough that she sees a glint of gold. A necklace. He always liked nice things, an air of disrepair shattered by the presence of a Rolex submariner or a double-stitched Charvet tie. Yet what strikes her first is the fact that with this thinner frame, he looks so much like Jason. He never used to resemble their son more than marginally, but now she sees it. It is the shape of his eyes, and it's the line of his stance. He has a pair of silver Oakley sunglasses pushed up on his head, giving him the effect of someone much younger, someone who doesn't take himself too seriously. His gray eyes are still the most beautiful she has ever seen. He hugs, and thanks, the godfather. The godfather says, "I serve at the pleasure of, you fucking bastard."

David holds on to her for a long time before saying anything.

"Where is he?" she asks, not letting go.

And David looks her right in the eye, and she sees that his eyes are wet. And he holds on to her shoulders and tells her that their son is a hero, and that he will be awarded the Medal of Honor.

"He's going to be fine," he says, letting go of her, stooping to look out the window.

"I want to see him," she says. "Look at me."

And he stands up and puts his hands on her face.

"Tell me again," she says. "Tell me again and take the glasses off."

David drops his head just enough that the glasses slip down his nose. "He is going to be fine."

"I want to go now," she says.

"Here we go," he says, and tips his head back, quickly, as if he's been pushed. The action slides the glasses back into place.

"Here we go where?" she says.

"Afghanistan," he says.

*

The stewardess offers them drinks as the plane moves swiftly down the runway; they could not have been on Saudi ground, she thinks, for more than ten minutes.

"Orange juice," David says. "*Shukran.*" And then, "Sara, breathe." He is sitting in front and across from her, leaning over the tiny tray table now newly set with fresh linens and small pots of nuts and jams.

"I want to know—" she starts.

"I am going to tell you everything. I promise." He looks out his window. "We'll veer west now, right?" he asks the stewardess. "The plane won't fly over Mecca with us infidels on board. Could I please have some ice with this?" Sara was not sure if he was showing off, but she recognized a gesture, the academic flirt. A dish of ice is placed on the table, and David stirs it into the juice with his fingers. She notices he's not wearing a ring. "You'll be able to see the sea."

They sit in silence for a few minutes. She considers being sick, or making herself sick; she can feel her body settling into the early stages of rebellion, the sticky pot of fish eggs stirring in her stomach. They were exceptionally salty. *Character is what a lady exhibits in a crisis,* she can hear her mother say. David takes the OJ like a shot, in one swill, then places the glass on the mirrored chips and wipes his mouth with the napkin. Something about the shock of seeing him is, physiologically, downgraded to an emotional place just below panic, still above apathy. There is something utterly unsurprising about it, perhaps because a part of her never believed he was gone; all the stories felt like simple stretches of other truths he'd stretched throughout the years. There had been rumors, periodically, that he was still alive, and the force of the denials that accompanied them had never quite felt true to her. It was easier, almost, to have him dead. Dead was a tragedy; abandonment was a shame.

Seemingly more to the air than to her in particular, he says, "Remember Yoni Netanyahu? Sara, you know the story. Yoni was the young Israeli Special Forces soldier—Sayeret Maktal. He oversaw the design of the Entebbe mission, the rescue of the hostages who were being harbored by Idi Amin, in Uganda? The mission was—is—critical to the history of special operations."

"David," the godfather starts.

"Na, na, na—I have a point."

"What is your point?" says Sara sternly. For a moment, she considers that this is the most vivid—and longest-lasting—nightmare she has ever had. This cannot be happening. None of this can be happening. And yet, throughout everything, she has never been able to hate him. Throughout everything, the only thing she ever felt when he appeared was better. He always made everything a little bit better. He seems quite comfortable on the plane. He knows how to adjust the seat. He doesn't bother with the belt.

"My point is that the mission was a success," he says, leaning back, crossing his legs. "Yoni died. But the mission was a success. It still stands as the great psychological and symbolic success for the State of Israel. And Yoni Netanyahu is a hero. He was thirty years old. He led that mission, and he was killed almost before it began."

"David—" Sara starts.

"It was night. Total darkness, excepting the lights on the runway, and they weren't even expecting those. And they'd landed at Entebbe and come out of the planes in a Benz—you know, so the local guards would think it was Amin. They'd even painted a few of the Israelis in blackface, initially, but then pitched that part of the plan, having decided that if they did run into Amin it would have been a shit-storm. But they came out of the planes, and almost immediately after Yoni left the car he was shot. And no one stopped to help him."

"Is this meant to make me feel better?"

"Why not?" asked the godfather, leaning in. "Why didn't anyone stop to help him?" He was playing along as he considered this monologue a strategic choice on David's part—a calculated strategy for keeping Sara from asking more questions before their arrival.

"Why not? Because Yoni's orders had been that no man down should be attended to until all of the hostages were put back on the plane. And the men followed those orders. And they recovered all of the hostages. All but one, one had been taken earlier to a local hospital. Amin's people murdered her later. But a nation could say after the fact that that mission was a perfect success, because its brightest mind was killed in action but the objective was still achieved. Peres delivered the eulogy."

"Peres was—" the godfather starts.

"Minister of defense," David says.

"What is your point, David?" Sara asked quietly.

"My point is that loss is . . ."

"Loss is?"

"My point is that . . . that our son was given a task in the service of his country and he rose to the task."

"He is not dead."

"I'm simply saying that loss is always part·of the equation."

"Equation of what?"

"Of war."

"*Is* this a war?"

The plane makes another sharp and fast ascent, and David leans back in his chair. As they hit the cloud line, he starts to talk about what he knows of the last ten days.

But Sara doesn't care for his history lessons—ancient, near-historical, or of the last week. She doesn't care about the mission. She doesn't care that a man that Americans went to kill has been killed, or if and to what extent there were other casualties. She doesn't care about the maps and the medals and the "framing" of the story for Fox News. She will not care, when she learns of it, that this mission has resulted in the recovery of an unprecedented cache of intelligence, intelligence that might save lives down the line or perhaps even bring about a nearer end to the current conflicts. She doesn't care when David tells her that the president of the United States is going to call her. "I want to see my son," she repeats softly while he carries on—just as he always did—with explanations and speculations. He was devout in his allegiance to fact and erudition: everything had a story, and everything could be explained. He did not seem shaken at all by the fact that a child had gone missing and was kept in God knows what conditions for almost ten days. He sees heroism. She sees mindless sacrifice. He has not seen a downside to the equation. Yet. It is at this point that she realized he is not there for her; he is there to welcome a great hero and to claim him as his own.

*

This is what Sara learns: her son had been flown, severely wounded, to a base hospital at Bagram. "That's Afghanistan," David adds when the godfather says the word, even though he's just named the country, their destination, an hour ago. His inimitable instinct to footnote everything for everyone is still intact, she thinks; his always operating on the assumption others knew less than he did undeterred by the possibility that in these last decades Sara might have grown a little bit, read some books. In this, he had not changed.

He goes on: Jason had gone missing off of a mission, a very high-level mission but one whose details had not yet been released to the press in the hope that first their son would be recovered.

While the story of a missing American had been leaked, Washington claimed to know no more than this, whetting the press's—and the people's—appetites; another day in the life of the wars was immediately elevated to a "story." Sara mentions the reporters at the end of her drive. She mentions that she had heard he had gone missing and that somewhere along the way he had been injured. She says she heard this not from the official channels but from another Team mother, who heard it from her son.

"He would have been leading the assault team," David says. "His rank, his experience, the nature of the mission. It's unclear where and when he was injured. And it's unfathomable that they would leave someone behind so—we can't speculate." And then he speculates. "He was probably injured in the house."

"What house?" asks Sara. And she immediately thinks, *Kill House.*

"They were clearing a house. Or several houses. They were clearing a large compound. They were looking for someone."

"Who?"

"We don't know. I don't know."

"Where?"

"I don't know that either."

"Could you speculate?" It's hard not be sharp with him.

"Sara."

"I want to know where he was. I want to picture it."

"Actually, you don't."

"I do."

"I've told you everything I know."

She could not tell if he was lying. He had pulled his sunglasses back down.

"I do not know where they were," he repeats, looking down at his hands, fingering his bracelets. He enunciates each word as if

English were a foreign language he had newly begun studying. "I swear to you. But I know that something went wrong, and when it did, the rest of his Team was unable to recover Jason in time. They had to extract the men they could. Jason either escaped or—or it's possible he was taken in by someone. Locally. It's possible someone took him in and cared for him. We do not know that yet either."

"And how did they find him?"

"The intel guys found him. Someone gave him access to a communication device, and he used it. That's all I know."

"A communication device?"

"A phone."

"That sounds alarmingly imprecise."

"At this time we know very little. But they *found* him, and he was *alive*, and they brought him to the hospital. And as soon as I knew any of this, I set about getting you to him. I worked very hard to try to get you to him before the story was released in any way to the media."

"How—how did you know all of this?"

David stays silent.

"How did you get me here? Why am I here?"

"I knew his condition was critical."

"His condition is critical?"

"He is going to be all right, Sara."

David explains that he had been following the progress of the mission and its aftermath thanks to an old friend in the Teams, now at JSOC. David had been among the very first to learn that Jason was the American who was missing. He had been the one to raise holy hell to be sure Sara was notified a.s.a.p., even before they had perfect information. They sit in silence for a while. Anita Ekberg brings plates of chocolates and bread. David asks for marmalade, and a jar of marmalade appears. Sara wonders whether, if she asks for her son, they could pull him from the wood-paneled cupboard, too.

"David?"

"Yes?"

"Where have you been?"

"Pardon me," he says. And he stands up. "Just give me a minute." And goes to talk to the captain.

When he returns, he has an apple in his hand, and a knife. He hands it to her. He knows she can peel it, that it will give her something to do with her hands. Like an infant, he prefers his fruit without the skins. And she dutifully complies, noting that the knife is sharper than any one she has at home. He starts over again, artfully eliding her question.

"I saw him."

"What?" she says, and looks up.

"Mind the knife," David says. "I saw him three months ago."

"Where?"

"Germany. His team was transitioning and I ran into him in the airport."

Sara puts down the apple. "You ran into him?"

"Yes. And Sara, he—he doesn't know it was me. I didn't tell him who I was. I thought it was too much."

"Well, that was an adult decision."

"But I talked to him. He's—God, he's great, Sara."

"I know my own son."

"Sara, he was ready. He was ready for this."

"How can you say that? Did he talk about himself, or did you just talk at him?"

"He talked a little bit. But I saw him with his guys. I know how to read that dynamic."

"What does that mean?"

"It means he was ready."

"He was ready to die?"

David swills the ice in his drink. He looks out the window. And without looking back at her he says, "Yes. He was ready to die for something he believed in."

"How would you know anything about that?" she wants to say. And then without saying anything, she can feel his disapproval shifting the space between them. How does he do it? How does he commit the crime, then make the victim feel like the criminal?

David takes his coat off. He rolls up his sleeves. He reaches across the table and takes Sara's hands in his. And he talks about Mecca. He tells Sara why he loves this part of the world. He has become spiritual, an effect that—maddeningly—makes him more attractive as, having lacked it before, he was always a bit too hyperconcerned with the now.

He tells Sara about falling in love with the way of life he found "here," and why he decided never to leave it. He tells her about lying in a Saudi hospital, having almost died. He says he began "for the first time in my life" to consider what "I really wanted." He explains how this was made possible through the generosity of a few local, well-connected friends. He tells her that the lies he had to tell those years ago felt "Augustinian."

"Pardon?" Sara says.

"You know, in the service of a higher purpose."

"Right. 'Make me chaste: but not yet,' " Sara says.

"*Exactly*," he says, as if she's just aced an oral exam he was administering.

He talks about falling in love with someone with whom he had shared the last decade, and how she left him abruptly ("a taste of my medicine"). He talks about how this experience made him think about the things he had left behind and made him miss his son.

"Miss your son," Sara says.

"Yes!" he says, as if he's divined the solution to a riddle, rather than stabbed at the center of her heart.

And he tells her how he got back in touch with the guys who subsequently gave him the tips that allowed him to happen to be at the airport in Germany that day, and about how the guys had told him how proud they were, already, of his son, the man his son had grown to be.

Sara is silent for a while until he says, "It's not breaking any law."

"Pardon me?" she says, firmly.

"It's not breaking any law to change your life, Sara. To start again."

But when he takes her hands and starts to talk about how faith will carry them through anything, Sara pulls them back, and shakes them in the air, like he's made her dirty. She stops listening. He keeps talking. And although she feels betrayed and in shock, something in her is still deeply comforted not to be alone in this moment. Now this man is her only family. And like all the moments in life that defy the dictates of reason, this one morphs from the shocking to the scenic in the space of an hour, like a soap opera plotline.

*

"Thus endeth the lesson?" she asks, finally, when he pauses for air. His eloquent riffs on mourning rituals and the Hajj are wasted on her; she knows him too well and can only experience his speeches as variations on a theme, his only theme, cool proselytizing. Yet even given this, she still experiences a familiar pull, a movement toward rather than away from him. She would go with him now if he asked her to.

David leans forward and lowers his voice so the godfather cannot hear him when he says, "You look exactly the same."

And she doesn't say anything, so he raises his voice and continues. And then he moves to sit with the godfather. She can hear them. "So. Their HC-130s flew low, so low, over Africa that night; they didn't want to be detected." He is making his hand into a plane, sliding it just an inch above the table, along the top of the mosaic. She sees now, sitting back, what it is: it's a map. "That was part of the reason the mission was so high risk; they were flying into an ostensibly friendly nation, but that nation was harboring terrorists. Amin was a liar. A narcissistic, psychopathic liar—the worst kind. Alas, not a rare breed. So the Israelis made the decision not to tell Amin their plans. But they were cleverer than even that. They kept Amin on the phone throughout the planning of the mission and leading right up to its launch. They kept him on the line with one of their great—retired—generals, someone he knew, someone he trusted. They kept him under the impression that this general was negotiating for their government, without ever saying so, of course. They let him think he was in the position of power. They let him think that if things went well, he would be seen as a hero. They coddled him. They delayed him. They prevented him from imagining that they were simultaneously planning one of the most dangerous and high-risk operations in the country's history."

"Amin—" says the godfather.

"Amin believed he was engaging in a sophisticated back channel. He believed that these late-night conversations with the general were assurance that he had the Israelis lying down. But they had him exactly where they wanted him. Like a fish on a line."

"And the team went in at night."

"And it wasn't until that general called him up—at his home—and woke him the morning after the raid that Amin knew something had happened."

"What did he say. The general. To Amin."

"He probably said, 'Congratulations.'"

"Congratulations."

"Yes, 'Congratulations.' And 'Thank you. Thank you, General Amin. We are so grateful to you for your help.'"

"And Amin had no idea what he was talking about."

"None."

"Impressive," says the godfather.

"Yes. The raid was carried out swiftly; they weren't on the ground much more than an hour, I don't think. Because once Amin had the sense something was happening, everything was over. A nation coupling power and psychosis is the thing we have most to fear."

"I would think so," Sara says. She has moved to stand over them.

"I know so," says David.

As the men keep talking, Sara realizes she has not felt this much emotion since the day Jason left on his first deployment. Before that, it was the day of his decision to join the Teams. And before that, the day of his acceptance to the Academy. And before that, 9/11. Further back than that, her mind will not go.

*

Her emotional history's high-water marks were almost exclusively losses. And the first shock of fresh loss, she now remembers, feels so much like fear. This is where the anxiety comes from. When he notices her breathing, David offers her a pill. She takes it without asking what it is. At a certain point, the godfather leaves them. He moves to the back where a screen descends from the ceiling and allows him to watch *Patriot Games* with the sound turned off.

"You know the weekend after his graduation from the Naval Academy there were—" Sara starts but then stops.

"There were what?" said David.

"There were, like, twenty weddings in the little chapel at Annapolis."

"That sounds like a lot."

"And he—he asked me, 'Mommy, do you wish I was getting married, too?' "

"And what did you say."

"I said . . ."

"You said?"

"I said commitment is not a substitute for meaning." She looks up at David. "I was angry."

"Are you still angry?"

She feels the plane dip. "Is everything all right?"

"We're descending. Sara, we're almost there."

"Dick Cheney delivered the commencement address. At graduation." And she laughs awkwardly.

"Sara, we're almost there."

"You should have been there, David."

"I'm sorry."

"Why weren't you there."

Just before landing, Sara checks herself in the bathroom again. Her white streak is oddly prominent in this light. *He found me*, she thinks. She used to fantasize about David finding her, running into him in Adams Morgan, on the street, or in the law library at school. And in the fantasies she was always impeccable, of course. And he would hold her, and beg her forgiveness, and promise never to leave again. And in those fantasies he didn't look half as good as he did now. That was the thing about fantasies: we think what we hate about them is that they exceed our reality, and then something reminds us that what we hate about them is that they don't even come close.

David gives her a shawl to pull over her hair. Apparently there was a stash of those onboard, too. It's black. As the door to the plane opens into a wall of bright heat, she sees an armored military SUV, presumably waiting to take them. There are three officers standing there, a fact that strikes her as a bit excessive. David helps her down the stairs; she's a bit shaky from all the time in the air.

En route, David sits in the front seat and talks politics with the young lieutenant driving them. The godfather has his arm around Sara, and as they pull in front of where they're going, he squeezes the back of her neck tightly, touching one point in particular with his index finger. He whispers in her ear, "I love him, too." She does not know if he is talking about David or Jason. When they get to the hospital, he stays in the foyer while she and David are walked down a white hall and met by a very young doctor.

"Where is he?" says David.

"Sir," the doctor starts.

And Sara can tell by the look on his face.

"Christ," she says.

And the doctor says something that sounds like "an hour ago" and something else that sounds like "tried" and then some things that sound like "fight" and "brave" and "battle." And then Sara loses consciousness. When she wakes up, she is lying on a bed, and David is holding her hand. "I want to see him," she says.

*

He is not wearing his uniform. He is wearing clothes clearly given to him by someone else. A white linen shirt and loose white linen pants. He never wore white, as she can remember. He looks cared for. He looks as if someone has cared for him and cleaned him. His face is immaculate, except for one long—and deep—cut running from his ear down to his chin; it looks more like a threat than a battle wound, but she catches her breath when she sees it. *Who did that to him.* He has a full beard, which surprises her. She wants—badly—to open his eyes so that she can see them but understands this is irrational. *I have so much left to tell you,* she thinks. And she can feel the sadness swelling and shifting into rage.

David leaves the room briefly and returns with scissors (marked PROPERTY, U.S. GOVERNMENT) so he can cut the locket off of his son's neck. Jason is wearing it attached by a piece of thin leather.

Sara takes the scissors, cuts if off, and slips it into her pocket. David then cuts off a piece of Jason's shirt and offers it to Sara.

"I don't want that," she says.

"You didn't dip him in the river," he says, folding the cloth into his hand and folding his hand into a fist. "But he is immortal now." He kisses the top of her head. Sara asks for a moment alone with her son.

She kneels down on the floor and presses her forehead into the side of the bed. The floor is ice cold. *Why didn't they get us here faster.* She holds on to her son's forearm, the same place she'd held so many times throughout his life—the "special place" that would calm him when he woke up in the night, or when something had upset him. She had not touched him there in a long time, the inviolable line where a mother no longer comforts her son once he's become a man having been crossed long ago.

She thinks about the physicists and their black holes. She remembers another professor from that same film, old and English and very Oxbridge, describing what it might feel like to fall into a black hole. He described how, before you lose last sight of the world, you are able to see things happening, lots of things happening, at a radically accelerated rate. These things would be flashing by your eyes so fast as to appear like "fireworks." *The fireworks of the future.* And the image last seen of you by others, he explained, is the image frozen at the exact moment when you cross the event horizon, or the edge of the hole. Cross, poof. The quality of your disappearance is lucky for the others; their last image of you has grace, and there is nothing graceful as you fall deeper into the hole and are ultimately destroyed. Had he said, "obliterated to bits"? He had said "It would be a very exciting way to end one's life." And then he said, smiling, "It would be the way I would chose, if I had the choice."

Had her son died in an "exciting" way? People might say that he had—not to her face, but they might say that. But there was nothing exciting about death. And she decides in that moment, in that room, in that country where so many have died for what seems like so little for so long—she decides that she will remember her son, frozen forever, before he slipped over the horizon, into the hole. She will remember him as he was when she last saw him—not as she is seeing him now. When she last saw him, in the fall, at home, taking the cake from the box. He had lifted the little flag from its center and licked the icing off before planting it, firmly, on top of her piece. "*Sic transit Gloria mundi*, Mommy," he had said. And now she hears him say that and she remembers: "*When we assumed the soldier we did not lay aside the citizen.*" Or the son, she thinks. Or my son.

END EX

"Rabbit, rabbit," Jason says, almost under his breath. It is just after midnight on the second of May, local time, still technically the first of May back home. They're flying with SOAR, the 160th Special Operations Aviation Regiment. One of their mottos is "Death waits in the dark," a motto more true for these wars, perhaps, than for others. Wasn't there a time when, like football games, wars had formal starts and finishes, more well-articulated time-outs and civilized stand-downs for meals? Now war was continuous and unrelenting. The definition was not the conquering of a place or a people or a patch of grass; no one "conquered" anyone anymore. The definition of success in wartime as Jason's generation knew it was the prevention of future bloodshed, the corralling of "terror."

The plan was to fast-rope out from the helo (a modified Blackhawk this time) if they could, onto the roof of a building. They knew the exact size and shape of the building and the dimensions of its interior spaces; they'd worked with a mockup for weeks. The mockup got the guys used to things as simple as how to turn around inside a particular hallway, and how to categorize exit options (in this case there were very few.)

Even though the stakes tonight were higher than they had

been on other nights, the squad's temperatures were not raised. They were doing exactly what they knew how to do, the thing at which they were, of all the special operators in the world, uniquely skilled. They would land, as planned; if an unforced error required another kind of landing, they would accommodate that fact. They would land as planned, and they would clear this house and find what they were there to find: an individual, and an item—a "document," someone said. They were well covered and well watched. It occurred to Jason that this is just the kind of mission his godfather might one day be invited to observe, live, from a secure location.

The weather mattered on all missions, of course, but particularly on missions where helicopters were part of the plan. In terms of complexity, insertion via helo ranked below combat swimmer or HAHO, but above foot patrol from an FOB or ground assault force movement with Humvees, or MRAPs. Even the most sophisticated piece of aviation technology is susceptible to strain. And the history of mechanical mishaps was well known among them. They were lucky: the weather this night was perfect. The moon complied. They had to fly low over the land, so low that Jason could see the shapes of individual trees through the window, and the lines where snow was starting to melt into water. The air was cool, but the forecast read even for the next twenty-four hours. This was auspicious, much more time than they would need. They were hoping to take an hour—or less—and then they would turn around, return home, and have one of the best night's sleeps they had had in a while.

He had been to this country before and, over the last weeks, had read as much as he could about its history. Certainly he'd look back on these days at another time in his life and be glad that he'd been there, right? This was the center of the world now, if not the cradle of her civilization. It was the place where bad things were bred, according to certain politicians who selectively blended their facts; it was the place through which the money coming from bad things flowed, according to others. One fact was uncontested: it was a place of rich traditions and history, of revolutionaries who had founded it on a belief in the idea of a free and independent state, just as Americans had done in another nation over two centuries ago. Jason knew an NCIS officer who'd been born there, a girl, and she'd told him many times how magical it was. She'd made him promise to go. For a nation of its size, it performed a remarkable trick of holding larger nations in the palm of its hand by virtue of wisely timed obstinance, and threats. And access to capital. "Just follow the money," his mother's friends in finance would say. "I can follow the money and predict your next six missions."

He had called his mother earlier that day but didn't reach her. So he had sent her a text asking how her day was, assuring her he would be home soon, wondering whether they could take a trip this summer, just the two of them, something they hadn't done since he was a kid. So many of his other leaves had been spent training; there was never an absence of opportunity for that, and so the guys always waited to purchase plane tickets before knowing the various "school schedules." That was all behind him now. The longest he'd been home these last years at any one time was a week. Now he wanted more downtime. He wanted to sleep late. He wanted to play golf, poorly, and run around the local reservoir. He wanted to make spaghetti with clams, and eat it while watching college ball. He wanted to do all the little things that people did.

He had sent an e-mail to Sam, reminding him of his promise to take care of Sara should anything happen. That was enough,

he knew, for Sam to know that something was up, a signal that
Jason was going somewhere perhaps particularly "hot"—the word
they would use as a catchall for trips civilians might call "dangerous" or "suicidal." He reminded Sam about the letter he wrote,
where it is, what is to be done with it. Jason knew that In Case Of,
Sam would say just the right thing to all the right people. Sam
wouldn't be intimidated by Sara's occasionally icy exterior. And
he wouldn't be intimidated by anyone who crowded around her,
from the wealthy country mothers to the Washington machers
whose pieces she edited. Sam had even read the CACO hand-
book, online, in his spare time, teasing Jason that he'd read it "just
for you, buddy," after they'd discussed Jason's choice to redeploy
one last time. "Can you believe they actually have a line item saying, 'Do use the word *dead*'?" he'd said.

His last night with the girl before going, he cracked. There was
nothing separating this goodbye from its predecessors, except he
cared more now. What he felt for her was the closest thing he had
ever felt to love, and he was not sure he liked it. What he felt was
that he didn't want to leave her, and he'd never felt that before for
anyone. He felt he didn't want to leave her not because it occurred
to him that he might not be back but because it occurred to him—
regularly now—that life is short, and time moves too quickly, and
when you find someone you want to be with, that's rare. The real-
ist in him tried to kill this train of thought, but the romantic,
newly skilled with evidence, fought back. And so lying in bed that
night, he'd cried. The release of emotion was a rare indulgence.

"Hey," she said, and sat up. "Hey."

"I'm good," he said, and laughed, as he knew how that must
sound given how he looked.

"You are good," she said, and she put her hands on his heart.
"You are good, and you are going to be fine."

"Roger that," he said.

"Take those rocks with you—just a few. A lucky charm."

"Will they heal me?"

"Yes."

She awoke before he did. She tied a bit of myrrh into a little pouch and slipped it into his pocket when he came toward her.

"Rocks," he said, and smiled.

"Yes, Achilles. You would have forgotten."

"Thank you."

He'd called his godfather. Something about the conversation made it clear to Jason that they each knew the other knew more than what was said about what lay ahead.

"I want it in writing that you're retiring after this," his godfather said.

"Sir?"

"I want it in writing."

"You know, I think I lost all my pens," said Jason.

"I want it in writing."

"Do I get a retirement gift?"

"Anything you want."

"Anything?"

"How about a car. You have a license, don't you?"

"And I have a car."

"Okay, how about a job?"

"How about a trip."

"A trip?"

"Yeah. A nice, long trip."

"Done. Rome? Vienna?"

"I'd like to go see the mountains."

"You've spent five years in the mountains, and you'd like to go see some mountains?"

"I'd like to see the Rocky Mountains."

"Really?"

"They're eight million years old."

"Really."

"Inhabited solely by skiers and wildlife."

"This is true. So you want some quiet."

"I want to learn how to snowboard."

"Great. Snowboarding lessons. That's my retirement gift. Lessons and plane tickets."

"Ah, I don't need lessons. Just a board."

"Jason, be safe."

"Yes, sir."

"Don't be a hero."

*

He is holding the myrrh per his orders, and he smiles at the strangeness of that. The guys would crucify him if they knew; sentimentality and metaphor were not generally part of the load-out. But why were those rocks any odder an emblem than everything else he had on him right now. Suddenly it all seemed strange—the guns, the ammo, his highly customized NVGs. He'd be terrified if he ran into himself in an alley. *This is just another mission*, he tells himself, one in many ways not unlike ones he's been through many times before. The intelligence is good; the team is small. The equipment is the most sophisticated ever designed in the history of warfare. No one has kitchen cleavers tonight. If successful, Jason's participation on this trip will lead to other, similar requests, and a potential change in his attitude about staying in the game. It is time, after all, for a promotion, the nature of naval promotions still having to do more with time served than variation of service. What would it feel like to sit in one place all day—for the rest of his life? It would never feel as good as this.

Yes, this is just another mission, even as they are all aware that it is not. The prize is the pride they take in their quiet accomplishments. "We're just a bunch of half-crazy drunks!" someone had shouted in a bar a few nights before they left, responding to a girl who had asked his mate if he was "in the Teams." Jason smiled, remembering that. He inhales and exhales and closes his eyes. When he leans his head back it thwacks against the window; he startles himself. "Sweet dreams," someone whispers to his left. He smiles. Without opening his eyes or responding, he realizes his girlfriend's brother is sitting right next to him.

Every night, every op, every house: death is always a possible outcome. Even taking into account the vast network of supports watching over them once they were at target—backup copters; ISR, including drones—nothing could save an operator from an unanticipated contingency or surprise. Tighter OODA loops won't save a soldier from a hostile adolescent holding an RPG. But death is not where his mind is now. His mind is entering the place it always enters in these moments: a carefully modulated yogic focus. They have about one hundred miles to go—then one hundred miles more before they are back at the base.

*

He thinks about the stories most commonly shared within this group about this group, a collection in which tonight might take its place, a collection of names that celebrate risk but sounded like they celebrated peace and protection: *Earnest Will. Praying Mantis. Desert Shield. Restore Hope. Active Endeavor.* Even guys who'd never cared for history knew the elements of these ops by heart: how in Grenada the operators had fast-roped from the bird with a chainsaw to cut down the trees that blocked the LZ (the helo had had to touch down because a CIA officer on board didn't know how to fast-rope). How in Mogadishu the Somalis lined both sides of the street and shot to the center. How in Iraq a uniquely skilled sniper used an overturned crib to mount his gun; it was the only piece of furniture in the room, and it was the perfect height.

These were the stories that wove together to become the legend. There were failures, but we learned from them. There were controversies, but they evaporated in the face of increased needs to meet new threats. And there were always detractors, those who generally thought wars were too time-consuming and costly, who felt the lives of young Americans were better put to use back home, in a factory or a pharmacy. Still, the military withstood the storms of opinion. After Panama, and apropos of the wisdom of mission names, General Powell pointed out that "even our severest critics would have to utter 'Just Cause' while denouncing us."

Jason thinks about the question his Academy English professor once raised: Athenians versus Spartans? Did we really know fewer Spartans by name because they were not as skilled in battle, or do we simply lack memory for their heroes because skill in battle is not the axis on which history turns? History turns on the stories handed down to us, and the Athenians had far finer storytellers. "Athens or Sparta?" When the professor posed that question, all hands had shot up for Sparta. If they were all polled now, having served, would they say the same thing?

He knows it is important to breathe. He starts trying to clear his mind of everything other than what is in front of him. Studies done on the brains of young operators have shown that they not only respond differently to fear than most of the civilian population; their minds actually adapt—through training—to a more mature processing of threats. It's psychological, but it's also chemical. Some of the most successful operators find that their blood pressure drops when they're working. Those same guys might see their pressure rise when they drive down a quiet suburban street. In combat, they are still. Everything is still.

Once, in the Pamirs, Jason carried ski poles on a jump, like James Bond. After David died, one of the people at that party in Georgetown, a former KSA ambassador, had said David "was the closest most of us would ever come to knowing 007." Now it sounds silly, but at the time it sounded about right. At the time, all Jason wanted to hear was that his father had been a great man, a man people loved. Jason wanted to believe that whatever was true of his father would become true for him, too. He knew just enough then to revere his father but not quite enough to resent him. The loss had not set in in a way that made it feel final. It didn't feel like a moment of mourning, not to a little boy.

Someone had repeated the Bond line to a journalist approaching a deadline; she had used it on the air later that night. And then it went viral—or what passed for viral in that time, which meant traveling the lengths of critical dinner tables before spilling over into the three papers that mattered. By the end of the week, six separate sources claimed the quote, then retracted it, then just let it drift. And then it stuck. Each succeeding account and obituary repeated it, and by the time Jason entered junior high, it had become part of the official story of David. And myths hold. While that night was the first time Jason had ever heard of MI6, he would become obsessed in the ensuing years, and Sara later lent him her collected Ian Flemings, hand-me-downs from

David. She was always careful to reinforce the fact for her son that "this is fiction, honey; it's fantasy. It's not real."

There is no room for a book in his assault pack this night, but if there had been, he would have brought one along. He always tried to carry something to read, something to force his focus on, perhaps something moreover to give an appearance to others of being calm. This way he could avoid talking. Which book would he have chosen? He thinks about his mother and remembers her reading to him about Jason and his Argonauts. He can see the cover of her worn D'Aulaires edition, its childlike illustrations and their palettes grounded in golds and greens. He liked the story at first because the boy—the hero—shared his name. What was so special about the Jason in the story; why was he the one chosen to recover the Golden Fleece? Now he cannot clearly remember. It had been so long since he last read it, and he cannot even recall the value of the fleece. He cannot recall what the hero wore or if he even carried any weapons. Did Neptune watch over him and his warriors on their ship as they traveled? When Jason pressed his mother to explain the difference between "myths" and "fictions," she had thought about it for a while, and then said, "A myth is a fiction that matters."

He remembers BUD/S, and all those times he swam the length of the pool without breathing. What was his secret to swimming underwater? What was his secret for holding his breath? "We tell ourselves stories in order to live," his mother used to say, quoting her favorite writer. Each time he would enter the water, he would start a new story, usually with "The year is X and we are in Y." His rule was that he was not allowed to breathe until the story was started; as training progressed, so did the complexity of his plotlines. He would later learn about meditation and realize that his stories were his way of meditating, of—almost accidentally—controlling his breathing. Like a *"fuck you"* for Christmas, his gift is a curse.

He remembers a phrase they learned in Qualification Training: *bunbu itchi.* A Samurai maxim, it means "pen and sword in accord." Operators, like authors, are trained to notice things. A sniper will see a window crack open from more than a half-mile away. And the finest shooters possess emotional intelligence, too—a gift that cannot be quantified on a test or through a drill. The finest operators possess emotional intelligence and emotional *celerity*, the abilities not only to understand instincts but also to act on them. Where were these skills learned? Were they—as the man in the airport, with the two hearts, had put it—"DNA"? Not every operator can dial his emotions like a desk clerk dials a rotary phone, controlling the speed at which they rise and fall—but the best ones can. *Click. Click. Click. Click. Click.*

He thinks about the sacrifices of the friends he has lost, what those friendships meant. *Greater love hath no man than this, that a man lay down his life for his friends.* John, the Bible. Kipling taught him that line, forever mock-shocked at the "godless" house Jason had been raised in. And Kipling taught him this, too: the total number of American war dead, from all wars, was one million, three hundred forty-three thousand, eight hundred twelve—and counting. That was almost exactly the total population of San Diego, the city where both boys had lived during the happiest just-less-than-two years of their lives. The city felt a lot smaller than that then, just as this war felt a lot smaller than what he'd imagined it might feel like when he first deployed. They were all aware of its scope now, but on a daily basis their more immediate concerns were the blocks, homes, or stretches of beach where they were stationed. He must have run over a thousand miles in sand since he joined the Teams.

"No losses," the young guys say, to a man. "Zero casualties." They say this when asked what their goals are before going out the first time. They say this because this is what they're told is the goal. Sometimes Jason wanted to say to his senior officers, "If the goal is no casualties, why are we going on a *combat* mission?" But he never did. Conflating loss with failure wasn't right, but making them distinct was risky. *One million, three hundred forty-three thousand, eight hundred twelve*: a number almost equal to the populations of Oklahoma City and Austin combined. Higher than Indianapolis plus Long Beach; lower than D.C. plus Jacksonville; almost equal to Detroit, Olathe, Salt Lake, and Aurora combined. If you added up the total populations of Grand Island, Rogers, Union City, and Shreveport—and then added in those of Green Forest and Angwin and Willits and Southern Pines—you would arrive at a different number. Olathe, Aurora, Angwin, Southern Pines, Austin, Willits: these were all cities that sent sons to serve and lost them. "A helicopter is a dangerous vehicle to go to war in. When you step into a helicopter, you're taking a risk," said the judge who'd presided over the Sikorsky case, the one who came to squire Sara after Jason moved back east. No successful mission makes the losses matter less. And yet while preserving the memory of lives lost was critical, an ability to avenge them slipped like sand through a jeep's grill. *After the peak there comes the challenge of how to ride down the other side.*

"Here we go," someone says. They are losing altitude.

*

He remembers being asked to help design this mission and how carefully he planned each choice and contingency. Actions at the objective were particularly challenging in this case given the known presence of myriad women and children throughout the house. He called on all he had learned to date. In the briefing at the base, one of the guys had leaned over and whispered, "Pray." But he wasn't one for calling on God in these times. Most of the prayers he knew were prayers he had learned since leaving Coronado, ones guys kept posted above their bunks on the bases, ones they knew by heart. The Special Forces Prayer wasn't bad: *Go with us as we seek to defend the defenseless and to free the enslaved. Grant us wisdom from Thy mind, courage from Thine heart, strength from Thine arm, and protection by Thine hand. It is for Thee that we do battle, and to Thee belongs the victor's crown. For Thine is the kingdom, and the power and the glory, forever. Amen.* Did the other side pray when they heard us knock on their door?

He remembers the Vietnam-era documents he found online after meeting the man in the airport, in Frankfurt. The docs dictated questions raised by another era's SOPs: *"Camouflage: what lies will we tell the neighboring people, so that they do not know about our intelligence mission? If the enemy should capture our informant just as he leaves the house, what lies will he tell to explain why he was visiting the house? What secret sign will be used to tell our informants that it is safe to enter the house?"* The Teams in that time were different, but the ethos was the same. Those Teams set the ethos. They set the mythos, too. Everyone today knows what they did then: navigating in a jungle with no GPS, no one waiting in wireless war rooms telling you what might lie around the corner. Were they scared? He wouldn't place a bet against them for anything.

He thinks about the videos Sam showed him that day at the beach, the last free day before they'd been called up to go out on what would prove to be a particularly bloody deployment, rich with upset and casualty. He and Sam shared an obsession over old Cold War–era government videos, especially ones instructing children about necessary preparations in the event of a nuclear strike. The "duck and cover" joke of their generation was the notion that a school desk could protect you from anything, let alone radioactivity. Sam had pulled up clips of "daisy cutter" bombs exploding, the same bombs we would use in Tora Bora. In Southeast Asia they were used to clear jungles. They were effective not only for creating flat, wide spaces in the place of brush, for opening up landing zones, but also for psychological intimidation. They were the same bombs not so slyly referenced in President Johnson's controversial "Peace, Little Girl" campaign ad, another obsession of Sam's. In the ad, a pretty little girl counts the petals on a daisy until, at "nine," a ground control operator's voice overtakes hers. He is counting down to zero—*Nine! Eight! Seven! Six!* And as the countdown ends, the camera closes in on the child's eye, and her iris fades into an image of a mushroom cloud. Johnson's voice then announces, "We must either love each other, or we must die," a line cribbed from a British poet. The little girl in the ad was only four years old. He thinks about carrying Sam on his back down the stairs in that house, how bloodied his hands were when he laid his friend down and how he waited until late that night to wash them clean.

*

He thinks about the Creed. It was written only recently, during his last year at the Academy. "Brave men have fought and died building the proud tradition and feared reputation that I am bound to uphold. In the worst of conditions, the legacy of my teammates steadies my resolve and silently guides my every deed. I will not fail." This is his prayer, in fact. Its seriousness and simplicity tie it to a history of creeds and pledges, ritualistic totems that helped a culture hold. Creeds kept the edges of a culture sharp. Of course, they were meaningless if the truth did not support the things they preached. *All ambiguous behavior is interpreted negatively.*

As he feels the bird turning and hears the guys click their belts free, he goes over in his mind the first things he will do when they land. There is no water here, only sand and rock and dry grass and trash. The level of trash accumulated by the house's occupants had been one clue to their number. The volume of traffic in and out had been another. Knowing he won't taste water for a while, he remembers to take some. If all goes well, this will be fast—one hour, or less. If.

And then someone else, almost inaudibly this time, says, "Hail Mary, full of grace."

*

When his feet hit the ground he will think only of what is in front of him: his task, and the need to accomplish this mission with alacrity, care, and minimal collateral damage. His skills at close quarters combat will serve him well. When the helo stops outside the house, he will enter it, and it will seem eerily familiar, as if he has been there many times. Like pool to ocean, or dirt dive to sky: you train for the work, and he had been trained to within an inch of his capabilities for this. *Proper preparation prevents poor performance.* If this was his last mission, he thinks, it was a fitting culmination of everything he had learned. The guys will enter the target structure. And with the confidence of athletes—or gods?—they will maneuver its elements to ensure that any inno-cents are secured. Their jobs are "elimination" and "collection": eliminate the threats; collect the evidence. Like Confederates pressing up against Union flank lines at Gettysburg, they act on orders. "Pray," Jason repeats to himself under his breath. And the prayer he chooses is simply "Get us all home."

The total time of preparation for this moment—not the years of training but the split-second assessment following an actual accounting of the space, the threats, the presence of unknowns—was an instant: less than the time it takes to dress a child for school, or to make a round of pancakes, or to walk a bride down the aisle to her groom. This timeline would enter the annals of history and be debated and disputed, before being codified into accepted truths. The anonymous participants on both sides that night would take their places in the classic warfare texts, standing somewhere after poppies sprouting in English trenches and before the presence of relative peace in an era where unmanned birds rained missiles down from skies a world away from their pilots. Did this mission matter. Would it change the course of history. It would alter the politics. And it would shatter the economy of lives, in particular those left behind by men KIA. "Courage is not the absence of fear," the cliché goes. Correct: courage is the ability to control fear. Courage kicks in instinctually when you throw a door.

Jason directs the assault train, the others guys in line behind him. As they spread throughout the house, they'll maintain lines of sight to the extent that they can; buddy systems become burdensome when things get busy. On entering, they need to make sure that anyone unarmed is not wounded. And they need to neutralize threats. In the first room, a room larger than its counterpart in the mockup, Jason finds several elderly men, three women, two young boys, a very young girl. There are also eight military-age males in the center of the room. One of those men raises his hand. He's holding a weapon. That gesture sets things in motion.

When Jason opens fire, he can almost count the rounds, as

if a guardian angel is sitting on his shoulder and whispering the numbers in his ear as they pop. An operator will shoot hundreds of thousands of rounds over the course of a career; you quickly get used to the feeling of recoil. There are thirty rounds in his primary weapon, only a little over a third of which he'll use to dispatch the eight MAMs before performing a tac reload, a reload performed while moving. It's easier said than done. But it's easier done, in certain cases, than switching from one gun to another; you don't want to have to change your primary for your secondary when it's raining bullets. Within what feels like more but is less than a minute, they've cleared the first room, one guy staying behind with the women and children. Later, they'll be moved to a marshaling area and interrogated. The original room in which they were found will be noted.

Everything is going as planned. Now with only one guy right behind him, Jason moves through three more rooms, all empty. Then at the end of the long, wide central hall, a door opens. Three men emerge, and one of them is the man they have come for, the High Value Individual. They've studied his face, the way he walks. He is standing in the center—almost, it seems, physically supported by the ones on either side of him. It's clear that all three are armed. Jason fires, not caring to spare rounds this time. The hall gets crowded. "Take a picture," someone says. And then they hear shots coming from another room.

Turning to address the noise, one of the guys makes a mistake. He fails to seat the magazine of his gun. If you fail to seat your mag during a reload, the weapon jams, and that eight pounds of trigger pressure suddenly becomes stuck. In what would in any other circumstance be an insignificant delay, things change. Rather than switch to his secondary, after the last bullet remaining in his chamber fires, the operator elects to reseat his mag, and this action results in a distraction. Mapped onto that distraction is another, larger one: something rolls into the hall, from one of the rooms. It's a stun grenade—a nine-banger grenade that will set off a series of small explosions designed to disorient rather than harm.

After the noise, when he opens his eyes, Jason hears a baby crying. There is no more shooting now. He makes it clear to the other guys that he will check it out so, stepping into the room, a room they've already cleared, he goes toward the sound; it's coming from a closet. He remembers another baby in another room, and this time he knows what to do.

Yet when the guys go back to find him, no one is there. Everyone else was accounted for, dead and alive. (Intelligence hadn't tracked the fact that a child had been born in the last few weeks.) The mission was accomplished. The order came down to exfiltrate immediately, and though there was argument, orders trump arguments. The guys were told they had to get the helo out before the light changed.

And for those next nearly nine days, we have no idea where Jason was. What's clear is that someone fed him and cleaned him and clothed him. Someone kept him alive until his teammates could return, which they did. And when they did, as the papers faithfully reported, "there were no prisoners taken" during the recovery mission. The guys wouldn't stop this time for interrogations or checking closets. Once stabilized, they laid Jason in the chopper.

Someone had beaten him, badly, but whether for torture or simply for show was unclear. At some point someone had threatened him, their version of a threat being to carve a knife-line down one side of his face. A spinal cord snapped high enough ensured that he'd never have walked again, that snap's coup de grâce the resulting damage to his brain—and so to his will. When he arrived at the hospital he was breathing, but he was entirely without affect. He couldn't say his name. The neurologists at Bagram had done their best. When David called the godfather on the jet by a secure line in Jeddah, he simply said, "He's almost gone. I will tell her. Let me tell her. Let me decide when to tell her."

*

Later, the baby's mother would identify herself and be reinterrogated. She would claim to have put her child in the closet to protect him. (She wouldn't say if anyone else had been in the closet. Or if the closet was connected to an exit, one not on the maps the men had seen in training.) She would be keen to describe how carefully a "soldier" had wrapped the infant, covering his head. She was touched by that. She would say that her power to keep that soldier alive accrued from her husband; her husband had been killed in the house. In that little town the story, re-told ad infinitum, would always start with the fact that the American had been holding "guns and myrrh."

ARMISTICE

That letter still sits on the desk off the office upstairs at the little farmhouse. Sara will read it eventually, but only months after she's back from Bagram, after Arlington, after the heat breaks. Before opening it, she will hold it in her hand sometimes, before placing it back in its drawer, unread. She is waiting for a moment that feels right, a moment when she feels strong. Something in her still cannot believe that this is all real.

David evaporated into the desert just as he had appeared, instantly, without remorse or emotion. Or explanation. He had always provided a task, a deadline, as explanation for his exits, and then he provided a lesson, a recap of what had been learned during their time together; this was his tic. Or his trick. He had walked down the jet's stairs backward, slowly, glasses off, looking at her. He was saying something, but she didn't listen too closely; she knew they both knew the point of this visit had been Jason, and that now there was no more point. There was no promise he would see her soon or ever. There was no promise to check in. When she said goodbye, in the doorway in Jeddah, she'd handed him the letters she'd printed.

"Soldier, scholar," he'd said.

"Soldier, scholar, son," she'd said.

As he turned around and walked across the tarmac to the waiting car, she realized he had drifted, at last, to that higher plane he'd long desired to live on, where nothing could hold him to gravity's laws. He would float above feelings. He always had. But what was her task now? What was her lesson?

The godfather had returned to the Hill, to fight the good fight and, soon enough, to take his place in the cast of characters inevitably immortalized once that one night's story—the mission, the mother, the loss, the legacy—emerged. The story inspired several books, several documentaries, and at least one film with movie stars. The story reinforced the ideas of some and challenged the ideas of others. The story was never discussed by its central participants, though, further underlining the irony of storytelling, at least when it comes to certain topics. The story as experienced by its protagonists, as English professors would call them, was not a "story" at all; it was their lives. Yet they were all changed by it—the godfather, in particular. He would work to end the wars sooner, and to elect a president who pledged to do so, even as the public seemed more anxious for peace than most of the politicians who gauged its viability.

Sam had returned to his life, too, but he called every day. Like clockwork, her phone would ring around seven p.m.—what she had come to consider her "witching hour," the hour after which the phone almost never rang, the hour in which she would begin to prepare a meal for one, the hour in which the stretch of time between it and the hour of bedtime seemed a river she couldn't bear to cross again. Every time the phone would ring. And every time she'd smile. Sam would always open with something like "What's for supper?" And she would talk about what she was making, and he'd give gentle, critical tips ("Remember to use the wide pan with the high sides for shirred eggs"). He would become like a son to Sara, and she would spend holidays with his family out west, in the mountains.

A steady stream of Team guys, wives and mothers, would reach out to her in those months, too, and she would have the very clear sense that she would never be alone in the world in quite the same way again, that some new chapter of her story was opening and that part of it would be, ironically, a deeper connection to the military than she had ever felt—or wanted. Her son had been her shot at legacy, but this was his: he had left her embedded in the community he had come to love, and that had loved him. She would make a place there for herself, and that place would insure her survival. And her sanity. One of the men who came to see her had been on the helicopter that night; his sister knew Jason well, too. He told her something she never forgot: that patients need less medication after surgery if the pain pills are placed at their bedside. If they know the pills are there, they don't have the anxiety of not knowing when or if help will arrive. Having the pills there allows them to go longer without taking them. "Are you the pill?" she'd asked, half-laughing, half-crying. "Yes, ma'am," he'd said. "I guess I am."

*

She reads the letter with Sam sitting by her side. He shows up one Sunday, and she realizes it's time. She takes it from its drawer and hands it to Sam. She asks him to read it. It is emblematic in its simplicity, so much her son in its tone:

Dear M.,

I want you to know something: I have found what I was looking for. I know now why I chose this path all those years ago; I chose it because I was looking for something. And I found it.

Remember Leander, who swam the Hellespont each night to reach Hero? I know Dad used to tell people he swam the Hellespont to reach you. I understand now the difference between fictions and myths; I understand what a hero is. I was looking for a hero; I was looking for someone to show me who I am.

And I found her. It's you. You gave me the courage to do what I have done. Please do this for me now: please try to understand it when I say that I am exactly where I am meant to be.

I was ready.

I love you.

Virginia Beach

April 2011

Enclosed with it is a page from the plays Sara sent during BUD/S, from the one she always referred to thereafter as "The Coronado *Hamlet*." These lines had been circled in bright blue pen:

If it be now, 'tis not to come;
If it be not to come, it will be now.
If it be not now, yet it will come:
The readiness is all.

And taped to the page is Jason's Trident. He had always told his mother that he had lost his "first" Trident, after having been forced to "give it back" after assignment to a Team, sometime during his initial eighteen-month predeployment training following SQT. He'd never explained to his mother that this "giving back" was part of a ritual, but he had told his godfather, who had mocked the tradition as typically military and "a bit Princeton." The thinking behind it is that in giving back what you have just received, you are reminded: the earning is not over. *You were not born with this.* Traditions surrounding the Tridents were myriad, and Sara only knew of some of them. But Jason had not lost his first Trident; like most guys, he had hidden it and purchased proxies for other use. They all did.

Sam had told Sara about another custom. He said that the one place you can "lose" your first Trident is when you pound it into the lid of a fallen teammate's coffin. Sam had done that once. He'd explained to Sara that this ritual was the most important one of all—or at least the one through performance of which he had felt most connected to the Teams. Smashing the Trident into a coffin reinforced the thing "we all know—you, me, Buddha," Sam had said. "Nothing lasts forever." Sara will turn her son's Trident in her hand. She knows what she must do with it.

*

"Angel flights" is an apt description. The military transport planes that bring home the dead land at Dover, and Sara has been there before. She'd written speeches one summer for a Delaware legislator who was working to repeal the state's Rockefeller-era drug laws, the mandatory minimum sentencing policies that kept U.S. prisons packed. The legislator, a newly minted assemblyman, an army brat who had settled in Delaware only after losing his father in another war, was a brilliant idealist, already recognized by the national press as a possible future presidential candidate. His thing was criminal justice reform, and his argument was that the laws, while assisting good officers sent out to police the streets and keep crime down, were creating a permanent underclass. He saw the laws as flawed. He saw them as, almost accidentally, perpetuating a portion of the population who would rotate between sentences without being given the time and chance to psychologically process their crimes, and without being offered the chance to reform. And he understood that putting a good man in a place with bad men was not a recipe for redemption; it was a recipe for repeated criminal activity. The legislator believed in forgiveness; he was Catholic. He saw the "man-mins," as they were known, as unnecessarily punitive, and as failing on the counts of both cost benefit and social welfare. Said another way, *fucking bad incentive alignment.* Sara had spent some time with him visiting those prisons and talking to those prisoners.

She had come to believe in the cause, and so when the legislator made his case before the Delaware State Senate, in Dover, she'd gone, too. Jason was away on deployment at the time. She'd stopped by the air base afterward, because it was close but also because—missing her son—she'd wanted to see the planes come in. By chance, on that day, an angel flight was landing, and she'd watched as the coffins were carried down to and across the tarmac as the families lined up on the runway to receive handshakes and hugs from what appeared to be several very young officers. One woman there that day had a priest on either side of her, white-collared and robed. She had started to faint when the officers approached her, and the priests had caught her and carried her inside—one holding her under her arms and the other under her legs. Sara had rushed over, offered to help, and had brought the woman a paper cup of water.

It had never once crossed her mind that she might one day be there herself, in that same situation, with those same emotions. This is the power of the mind to protect us: imagining herself in that woman's place would have been the most obvious thought to have at the time, but Sara's well-trained brain would not allow her to have it. She had driven home that day thinking not of priests and caskets but of cops: the officers who had lined the walls of the state senate that morning, staring down in protest at the legislator while he spoke the words Sara had written for him. Afterward one of them had given her his card. "Know thine enemy," he'd said, as he pressed it into her hand.

She smiled, remembering it now. It was the first time she'd smiled all day.

*

That same cop, astonishingly, had picked her up at the train when she'd returned home from Bagram, a not uncommon coincidence of living in a small town. He was quiet and deferential, and because she didn't know what to say, she was quiet and deferential, too. They drove in silence. This was the prettiest time of year in this part of the world; fall and winter were beautiful, too, but the spring just shouted out "life." Daffodils, a flower she didn't otherwise care for, bloomed so suddenly and in such vast numbers now that for their few first weeks they defined the main streets; to hate them would be like hating the home team. She could see kids scrimmaging on the school fields that ran along the edge of the highway, the start of summer camp for fall field hockey. *Teamwork*, she thought. As the car turned onto the road that would lead to her street, she prepared for the worst. She smoothed the lines of her skirt. She put the window up. The cop switched his lights on. "Do you mind?" he asked. "No," she said. She was grateful he didn't switch the siren on, too.

But when they get to her driveway the reporters are gone. Had some Samaritan cleared them away—or had they lost interest? They are gone, yet the last stretch of street leading to the pretty white gate now installed isn't empty; it's lined with people. On either side they are gathered at least three or four deep, and in most places parents have pushed the children to the front. Some of them hold cameras, some hold signs. She can see that one of them reads "We Love You, Sara." As the squad car turns onto the driveway, she can also see that the entire length of it leading to the house has been lined with flowers. Lilies and roses and broad bunches of peonies are laid carefully in rows, or tied to the fence.

The cop offers to stay but she resists. There are six officers stationed at the end of the drive, and two squad cars.

"Someone covered the bill, ma'am," he says.

"Thank you," she says.

"These guys will be here as long as you need."

"That's—very kind of you," Sara says, but her voice feels disconnected from her body. Her ability to call on language feels limited. Because she does not know what else to do, she shakes his hand. She lets him carry her things inside, and she waits and watches as he moves his car around with a precise, three-cornered turn. Then she closes the door behind her and locks it. She is entirely alone for the first time in eleven days.

*

The house is clean, and when she looks into the icebox, someone has been to the market; it's full. The strawberries were almost the size of small limes; that's what happened at this time of year. "If you don't mind your garden, you'll have melons as big as missiles," the neighbor told her when they first moved in, eyeing her unused hoe. And that was true. It took years for her to learn that lesson well enough to gain the patience, and discipline, required for proper vegetable tending. But the rewards made the price a small one to pay: everything that came up in this season was the symbol of summer, and health, and blessing. Everything was delicious. She felt like she had been gone a lifetime.

Before she lies down and closes her eyes, she lays out clothes on the bed for her next trip, on Sunday, to Washington. She will drive herself to the train downtown, and Sam has promised to pick her up at Union. She'd briefly considered a burial at Strawberry Hill, at the Naval Academy, an admiral having offered his own plot, but opted for Arlington for various reasons, primary among them the thought that she would visit more often. She might even move to D.C., to be closer by. Sam is there. The godfather is there. She should reach out to people; she should reach out and tell her story—her version of her son's story. She can start again. She is still young. This is what people are saying now constantly: "You are still so young, Sara."

Her last trip to Arlington had been bitter cold, but what she most vividly remembers now is how slowly she moved then. She wanted to walk carefully, in order not to slip, in order to protect the little life growing inside of her. She simply wanted to get to the top of that hill, and then see just enough to allow her to ace her class paper. She hadn't known how struck she would be by the cemetery's beauty and by an urge to wander its grounds. She couldn't believe that this place had been, it seemed, hidden from her, kept secret, erased off of classic must-see cultural maps that always included places like the Met or the Getty or Monticello—the places that defined America. *This is the first place people should come if they want to understand us*, she had thought at the time, proud of her uninvited surge of patriotism.

In the abstract, all those years ago, the graves seemed so noble in their anonymity. She possessed no connection to them—no parent or grandparent, as far as she knew, was buried there. In fact, no one she knew then was in service or had ever served, though she knew people who knew people who had. Everything then that crossed her mind concerning wars was political or theoretical. It was inconceivable to her that one day she would return to this place to bury her child, a war hero. It was inconceivable to her that one day she would be presented with the flag, folded neatly, stars on top. Everything before now was inconceivable.

But all those years ago she had left Arlington with one clear thought: that it would be good to return, perhaps on a day when the weather was not quite so biting, and when she was in a physical condition that allowed her to walk more, and faster. Then, it had snowed so much over the previous weeks that the trees were bowed with white weight, the headstones all capped in thick hats of ice. She knows when she goes back this time it will be green, like a garden. Jason would like that. He preferred spring.

On that day all the gods looked down from heaven at the ship, and those men of courage half divine, who then were sailing o'er the sea, a picked crew; and upon the tops of peaks stood the Pelian nymphs, marveling to see the work of Itonian Athene, and the heroes too, wielding their oars in their hands. Yea, and from a mountain-top came another night unto the sea, Chiron, son of Philyra, and he wetted his feet where the gray waves break, and with his right hand he waved them on full oft, chanting the while as they went a returning free from sorrow.

—Apollonius Rhodius, "The Argonautica"

Acknowledgments

I'm not sure how to acknowledge a group of people who by nature prefer to go unacknowledged: the many active, reserve, and retired Team guys who met with me. My instinct is simply to mention "the many who met with me" and hope that doesn't fall short of the mark. In his 1995 book, *Spec Ops: Case Studies in Special Operations Warfare: Theory and Practice*, Admiral William H. McRaven wrote:

> The view of special operations personnel as unruly and cavalier, with a disdain for the brass, was not borne out in this study. The officers and enlisted whom I interviewed were professionals who fully appreciated the value of proper planning and preparations, of good order and discipline, and of working with higher authorities. They were also exceptionally modest men who felt that there was nothing heroic in their actions and often sought to downplay their public image.

Exceptionally modest is an understatement. Even the officer who spoke so eloquently on Leonidas, and let me use his words, preferred to go unnamed here, as did the guy who knows more about Plato and Pynchon than many English—or philosophy—professors I've met. The three men who made time to review an early draft of this book when they had far more important things to do, thank you. And the officers who explained free surface effect, and waterfall charts, and didn't mind my making them into metaphors: thank you two, in particular.

A certain classmate and friend of LCDR Erik S. Kristensen, and Sam Kristensen: for flight paths, and lessons on loss.

Discretion, valor: no operational details, classified tactics, techniques, or information pertaining to real world missions were disclosed to me at any time by anyone affiliated with the Naval Special Warfare community. Errors are my own.

Ed Victor, who started it all. Adrienne Brodeur. Chris Heinz. Lex Sant. Ken Wilson. Ambassador Frank Wisner. At Knopf, Sonny Mehta, especially Shelley Wanger, and Peter Mendel-sund. Beau Biden, Judge Louis Freeh, Judge Eugene Sullivan. My mother, Carroll Carpenter; my husband, Cliff Brokaw. And finally, my little ones, Vail and Alexis. Everything is for you.

Edmund N. Carpenter II: soldier, scholar, father.

Glossary

AOIC	Assistant Officer in Charge
AQAP	Al Qaeda in the Arabian Peninsula
CACO	Casualty Assistance Calls Officer
CBI	China, Burma, India
CCN	Command and Control North; one of three detachments under the Military Assistance Command, Vietnam—Studies and Observations Group
CO	Commanding Officer
DAM NECK	An area, part of Naval Air Station, Oceana, Virginia; home to twelve tenant commands including the Naval Special Warfare Development Group
DEVGRU	Naval Special Warfare Development Group
DOR	Drop on Request
FOB	Forward Operating Base
HAHO	High Altitude High Opening
HUMINT	Human Intelligence
ISR	Intelligence, Surveillance, and Reconnaissance
JAG	Judge Advocate General
JG	Lieutenant, Junior Grade (LTJG)
JSOC	Joint Special Operations Command
KIA	Killed in Action
KSA	Kingdom of Saudi Arabia
LAR	Lung-activated Rebreather

MAC-V	Military Assistance Command, Vietnam
MAM	Military Aged Male
MBITR	Multiband Inter/Intra Team Radio
MRAP	Mine Resistant Ambush Protected (vehicle)
NCIS	Naval Criminal Investigative Service
NSW	Naval Special Warfare
NVG	Night Vision Goggles
OODA	Observe, Orient, Decide, Act; a strategic concept developed by John Boyd and usually referenced as "an OODA loop"
OSS	Office of Strategic Services
PRODEV	Professional Development
QRF	Quick Reaction Force
SEAL	Sea, Air, Land
SECDEF	United States Secretary of Defense
SERE	Survival, Evasion, Resistance, Escape Training
SOCOM	United States Special Operations Command
SOG	Studies and Observations Group (MAC-V-SOG)
SOP	Standard Operating Procedure
SQT	SEAL Qualification Training
UDT	Underwater Demolition Team
ULT	Unit Level Training
UBL	Usama bin Laden
XE	Xe Services, LLC. A private security contracting corporation, formerly known as Blackwater USA, currently known as Academi

Bibliography

These works informed my understanding of war and of special operations forces, Naval Special Warfare in particular. This list is not complete. Yet it was never meant to be complete. The four articles were ones that stayed on my desk long after I'd read them. The *Congressional Record* contains references to the JAG memos that Jason cites in his letters.

At the end of *The Iliad*, Priam visits Achilles to beg for the body of his son, Hector. (Achilles killed Hector to avenge the death of his friend Patroclus.) Enemies, Priam and Achilles bond over loss. And so Achilles agrees to give the body back, and to stand down his armies for the time required for a proper burial: eleven days.

Admiral McRaven oversaw Operation Neptune Spear, the raid in Abbottabad, Pakistan on May 2, 2011, that killed Osama bin Laden. According to public record, eleven other raids were conducted that night. This story is inspired in part by that coincidence. We don't know about those other raids and likely never will.

BOOKS

Bahmanyar, Mir, and Chris Osman. *SEALs: The U.S. Navy's Elite Fighting Force.* Oxford, 2008.

Bowden, Mark. *Black Hawk Down.* New York, 1999.

Chalker, Dennis, with Kevin Dockery. *One Perfect Op: An Insider's Account of the Navy SEALs Special Warfare Teams.* New York, 2003

Colby, William. *Honorable Men: My Life in the CIA*. New York, 1978.

Couch, Dick. *The Warrior Elite: The Forging of SEAL Class 228*. New York, 2001.

——. *The Finishing School: Earning the Navy SEAL Trident*. New York, 2004.

——. *Down Range: Navy SEALs in the War on Terrorism*. New York, 2005.

——. *Chosen Soldier: The Making of a Special Forces Warrior*. New York, 2007.

Counterinsurgency Field Manual. Chicago, 2007.

Cunningham, Chet. *The Frogmen of World War II: An Oral History of the U.S. Navy's Underwater Demolition Units*. New York, 2005.

Dockery, Kevin. *Navy SEALs: The Complete History*. New York, 2004.

Durant, Michael, and Steven Hartov. *The Nightstalkers: Top Secret Missions of the U.S. Army's Special Operations Aviation Regiment*. New York, 2006.

Eversmann, Matt, and Dan Schilling. *The Battle of Mogadishu: Firsthand Accounts from the Men of Task Force Ranger*. New York, 2004.

Filkins, Dexter. *The Forever War*. New York, 2009.

Finkel, David. *The Good Soldiers*. New York, 2009.

Fussell, Paul. *The Great War and Modern Memory*. New York, 1975.

Gormly, Robert A. *Combat Swimmer: Memoirs of a Navy SEAL*. New York, 1999.

Greitens, Eric. *The Heart and the Fist: The Education of a Humanitarian, the Making of a Navy SEAL*. New York, 2011.

Grossman, Dave. *On Killing: The Psychological Cost of Learning to Kill in War and Society*. New York, 1995.

Hedges, Chris. *War Is a Force that Gives Us Meaning*. New York, 2003.

Herr, Michael. *Dispatches*. New York, 2009.

Janowitz, Morris. *The Professional Soldier*. New York, 1960.

Junger, Sebastian. *WAR*. New York, 2010.

Kelly, Orr. *Brave Men, Dark Waters: The Untold Story of the Navy SEALs*. New York, 1992.

Kerry, Bob. *When I Was a Young Man*. New York, 2002.

Krakauer, Jon. *Where Men Win Glory*. New York, 2010.

Kyle, Chris. *American Sniper: the Autobiography of the Most Lethal Sniper in U.S. Military History.* New York, 2012.

Luttrell, Marcus. *Lone Survivor: The Eyewitness Account of Operation Redwing and the Lost Heroes of SEAL Team 10.* New York, 2007.

MacPherson, Malcolm. *Robert's Ridge: A Story of Courage and Sacrifice on Takur Ghar Mountain, Afghanistan.* New York, 2005.

Marlantes, Karl. *What It Is Like to Go to War.* New York, 2011.

McRaven, William H. *SPEC OPS: Case Studies in Special Operations Warfare: Theory and Practice.* New York, 1996.

Mitchell, Stephen, trans. *The Iliad.* New York, 2011.

Netanyahu, Iddo. *Yoni's Last Battle.* Jerusalem, 2002.

———. *Entebbe: A Defining Moment in the War on Terrorism: The Jonathan Netanyahu Story.* Tel Aviv, 2003.

OSS Assessment Staff. *Assessment of Men: Selection of Personnel for the Office of Strategic Services.* Scranton, Pa., 1948.

Pfarrer, Chuck. *Warrior Soul: The Memoir of a Navy SEAL.* New York, 2004.

Plaster, John L. *SOG: The Secret Wars of American Commandos in Vietnam.* New York, 1997.

———. *SOG: A Photo History of the Secret Wars.* Boulder, Colo., 2000.

Reske, Charles F. *MAC-V-SOG Command History Annexes A, N, and M (1964–1966): First Secrets of the Vietnam War.* Ohio, 1992.

Rottman, Gordon L. *US MACV-SOG Reconnaissance Team in Vietnam.* Oxford, 2011.

Russ, Martin. *The Last Parallel.* New York, 1957.

SEAL Sniper Training Program. Boulder, 1992.

Sebald, W. G. *On the Natural History of Destruction.* New York, 2004.

Shephard, Ben. *A War of Nerves: Soldiers and Psychiatrists in the Twentieth Century.* London, 2000.

Stanton, Doug. *Horse Soldiers.* New York, 2010.

Stevenson, William. *90 Minutes at Entebbe.* New York, 1976.

Stouffer, Samuel et al. *The American Soldier: Adjustment During Army Life.* Princeton, N.J., 1949.

Tucker, David, and Christopher J. Lamb. *United States Special Operations Forces.* New York, 2007.

U.S. Department of Defense. *The Armed Forces Officer.* Washington, D.C., 2007.

Wasdin, Howard, and Stephen Templin. *SEAL Team Six: The Memoirs of an Elite Navy SEAL Sniper.* New York, 2011.

Weiner, Tim. *Legacy of Ashes: The History of the CIA.* New York, 2007.

Williams, Gary. *SEAL of Honor: Operation Red Wings and the Life of Michael P. Murphy, USN.* Annapolis, Md., 2010.

Von Clausewitz, Carl. *On War.* London, 1968.

ARTICLES

Holbrooke, Richard C. "The Smartest Man in the Room." *Harper's,* June 1975.

Kaplan, Robert. "The Humanist in the Foxhole." *The New York Times,* June 14, 2011.

"Osama bin Laden." *The Economist,* May 5, 2011.

Schmidle, Nicholas. "Getting Bin Laden." *The New Yorker,* August 8, 2011.

GOVERNMENT DOCUMENTS

Congressional Record—Senate, July 25, 2005, S8772.

FILMS

The physicists referenced in the story appeared in Errol Morris's documentary, *A Brief History of Time.*

SITES

Text of Churchill's note to General "Pug" Ismay, First Baron Ismay, on naming missions, can be found at http://www.winstonchurchill.org.

ETC.

The concept that "all ambiguous behavior is interpreted negatively" was developed by Harvard Business School professor Thomas J. DeLong.

A Note About the Author

Lea Carpenter lives in New York with her husband and their two sons.

TWO
ROADS

stories . . . voices . . . places . . . lives

Two Roads is the home of great storytelling and reader enjoyment. We publish stories from the heart, told in strong voices about lives lived. Two Roads books come from everywhere and take you into other worlds.

We hope you enjoyed *Eleven Days*. If you'd like to know more about this book or any other title on our list, please go to www.tworoadsbooks.com or scan this code with your smartphone to go straight to our site:

For news on forthcoming Two Roads titles, please sign up for our newsletter.

We'd love to hear from you

enquiries@tworoadsbooks.com

Twitter (@tworoadsbooks)
facebook.com/TwoRoadsBooks
pinterest.com/tworoadsbooks